ORPHANS OF EMPIRE

ORPHANS OF EMPIRE

A NOVEL

GRANT BUDAY

BRINDLE
AND GLASS

Brindle & Glass
An imprint of TouchWood Editions
touchwoodeditions.com

Edited by Claire Philipson
Copy edited by Meg Yamamoto
Cover design by Tree Abraham
Interior design by Sydney Barnes

Front cover imagery from the following sources:
[Top] The Seven Sisters, Stanley Park [postcard; date unknown] RBSC-ARC-1596-1-03-14.
[Middle] Postcard of man standing on trail. [postcard; 191]. BC_1456_33_012.
[Bottom] Roadway, Stanley Park, Vancouver, B.C. [postcard; 1930]. UL_1628_0045.
   All reprinted with permission of the University of British Columbia Library, Rare Books and Special Collections.
[Top right; inset] American Black Bear. Lincoln Park Zoo mammal. 1900. Illinois Urban Landscapes Project. Courtesy, Field Museum. Z84222.
[Middle left; inset] Exterior of the New Brighton Hotel [Photograph; 1886]. Photograph shows George Black beside, and G.B. Corbould on, the horse. City of Vancouver Archives. AM54-S4-: Dist P13. Public domain.

CATALOGUING DATA AVAILABLE FROM LIBRARY AND ARCHIVES CANADA

ISBN 9781927366899 (softcover)
ISBN 9781927366905 (electronic)

TouchWood Editions gratefully acknowledges that the land on which we live and work is within the traditional territories of the Lkwungen (Esquimalt and Songhees), Malahat, Pacheedaht, Scia'new, T'Sou-ke and W̱SÁNEĆ (Pauquachin, Tsartlip, Tsawout, Tseycum) peoples.

We acknowledge the financial support of the Government of Canada through the Canada Book Fund and the Canada Council for the Arts, and of the Province of British Columbia through the British Columbia Arts Council and the Book Publishing Tax Credit.

This book was produced using FSC®-certified, acid-free papers, processed chlorine free, and printed with soya-based inks.

Printed in Canada at Friesens
24 23 22 21 20   1 2 3 4 5

Facts are but the Play-things of lawyers,—
Tops and Hoops, forever a-spin . . . Alas, the
Historian may indulge no such idle Rotating.
—The Reverend Wicks Cherrycoke

MOODY – 1858

THE *ASIA* WAS SCARCELY OUT OF LIVERPOOL upon the Irish Sea when Moody's daughters turned a pale green and began opening and closing their mouths like cod on a dock. Whimpering, they clung to their mother who did not look much better. Moody's son, John, climbed a bollard and vomited over the rail. Patting the eight-year-old's back, he said, "There, there, John. There, there. Be strong." This was a disorienting experience, for he heard himself speaking in his own father's voice, felt his face assume the expression his own father wore during rare moments of sympathy. Moody took care to blow his cigar smoke away so that the lad did not endure its fumes.

Now Mary and the girls staggered to the railing. The girls stood high on their toes but could not reach so knelt side by side and were sick through a scupper.

The tars ran to set more sail. There were whistles and shouts and cursing so visceral, so briny, so strangely imaginative—much of it to do with whores and toads—that in spite of the chill late October wind Moody's ears did in fact burn. Men ran up the shrouds and along the booms with the agility of apes. Great spreads of canvas were slammed wide by the breeze. What an engine was a ship, what an orchestra. Moody was exalted. The ship heeled hard, and he clung to a rope as fowl flapped and squawked in their cages. The wind came coursing in off the canvas and the sea rushed past the hull like a river through a narrows as the bow surged and then sank and then surged once more.

To port was Holyhead and to starboard Ireland, not that the Green Isle was visible in the mist. The grey sea rose and rolled while the *Asia* strained and twisted, her ropes aching and sail edges humming as the men continued to shout. A long voyage lay ahead of them, but at least they were not condemned to go around the Horn. They would train across the Isthmus of Panama and then proceed north once again by sea and, God willing, spend Christmas of 1858 at Victoria. A journey of two months. It had taken Moody that long to reach the Falklands in '41.

Moody stood five foot seven, slight of build, with narrow shoulders. His predominant features were his dense dark wavy hair, parted on the right, and his equally dense dark beard, which reached the top of his sternum. His cheeks were florid and his right eye slightly lidded as though warily gauging everyone he met for loyalty or deceit. Now he positioned one hand on each of his daughters as though his touch bore some power to soothe. He looked at John draped like an empty sack over a lifeboat. He went to Mary who gripped the rail and stared at the horizon—the one stable thing in view—and he put his arm around her shoulders. "Deep breaths," he murmured, "deep breaths."

She nodded bravely. "The ginger is helping," she lied, assuring him, assuring herself. The wind tugged long wisps of her sandy-brown hair from her black bonnet. She tried to smile and almost accomplished it. She was small, like Moody, a figurine of a woman, sharp chinned, smooth browed, her hazel eyes ever focused, refined and yet defiant.

"It will pass," he said.

Nodding quickly, she said, "Don't talk," and renewed her grip on the rail.

Moody tried to take heart in the fact that she did not seem so bad as on the crossing to Malta two years ago. He was about to remind her of that but thought better of talking when she'd asked him not to.

Clive Gosset appeared, ruddy faced and square shouldered, sideburns and hair as thick as pelts. His missing left eyebrow gave him a severely judging appearance.

"Moody," he said.

"Gosset."

"Family appears a bit off."

"It will pass," said Moody.

"And you? Stomach sound?"

"Perfect." He drew deeply on his cigar, then tossed it overboard. He'd always been good at sea.

"The roll is light yet," said Gosset, as if the best were yet before them. He began packing his pipe, tamping the tobacco with his forefinger on which he wore a sizable ring with a square ruby. Turning away from the wind, he struck a pair of lucifers and stoked a good blaze in the bowl. He smoked dryly.

Moody restrained himself from remarking upon his own not inconsiderable maritime experiences, having been to both the South Atlantic and Mediterranean, for Gosset would only smile in amusement.

Over the proceeding days of the voyage, Gosset's morning cal-isthenics became a ritual. He did them loudly, for all to see, counting each repetition, breathing in, breathing out, apparently believing that should he sound like a locomotive, he would achieve the power of a locomotive. Squats, lifts, prone presses, abdominal compressions, dumbbells, the Indian club, shadowboxing, even kicking.

"I learned kicking from a Japanese. Kimoto-san. Join me, Moody. Strike with the heel like so. On the exhalation. Ha!"

Moody lit his morning cigar.

"Bad for the wind," said Gosset.

"The wind will be fine, I am sure," said Moody, gazing at the sails vibrating under the breeze, and not reminding Gosset that he smoked a pipe.

"You don't want a repeat of Malta," cautioned Gosset.

Stung, Moody said, "Malta was food poisoning."

"Diet is paramount." Gosset executed lunges, right foot, left foot, thrusting an imaginary bayonet. "Too much fat is bad."

"It is said that the elephant lives to seventy-five," said Moody.

"And the tortoise to a hundred. But the last I looked, sir, I was neither an elephant nor a tortoise."

Tars gathered to watch Gosset's antics, some smiling, some frowning, many exchanging glances and most smoking clay pipes.

"Be there any pugilists among you?" called Gosset, shaking out his fists and dancing on his toes. "I have an American silver dollar for any man who can tag me."

By now the foredeck was crowded with sailors as diverse as a barrel of last year's apples, scarred, scabbed, shrunken. Mary ap-peared with the girls and John, who had all gained their sea legs. John had his wooden sword in his belt.

"A silver dollar," called Gosset.

Moody felt his son looking at him and feigned an easy indifference to the challenge. Eventually a man stepped forward. He was a head taller than Gosset and twice as broad across the shoulders.

"Do take off your hat," Gosset advised. "You wouldn't want it damaged."

The man merely smiled a slow smug grin and set it more firmly upon his head. His biography could be read in his face: nose canted to one side, lumpy brow, one eyelid half-closed, torn ear, an absence of certain teeth.

"What is your name, fellow?"

"Dub."

"Well met, Dub. Are you fit?"

Dub allowed his gaze to roll across the assembled audience of sailors and said he reckoned he was fit enough, earning himself a chorus of snorts and cackles.

"Is that a Manchester accent?"

"Ancoats."

"Most excellent." Gosset was enjoying himself immensely. He slipped the ruby ring from his finger and threaded it onto the lanyard around his neck beside the Saint George, shook out his arms one last time, and set his fists at eleven and three.

The two men circled each other. Dub's fists were bricks in size and shape and colour. The sailors cheered and wagered and elbowed each other.

"I see by your earrings that you've crossed the line, Dub."

Dub swung.

Gosset sidestepped and jabbed, striking Dub's chin, driving his head back. More shocked than hurt, Dub blinked and grimaced and then bore down, hunching his shoulders higher. He feinted; Gosset rolled away; he feinted again; Gosset smiled.

"You've a tell, Dub. Each time you're about to swing you squint your right eye. Not much, but enough." This opened a crack of hesitation just wide enough for Gosset to fill with his fist. Dub's nose bloomed red and a moustache of blood soon covered his upper lip.

Moody heard Mary escorting the children away with John protesting that he wanted to watch. Moody remained, rooting silently for Dub each time the man threw a punch, flinching each time he took a Gosset blow. And he took many Gosset blows. The fight did not last long. All too soon a right hook to the jaw dropped Dub to his knees, where, arms limp, eyes wallowing, he toppled slowly forward. Gosset caught him under the armpits and lowered him gently to the deck, then patted his back as if wishing him sweet dreams.

"Anyone else?" asked Gosset affably.

Moody felt something at his side and saw that John had escaped his mother and returned to the fight. The boy looked inquiringly at his father who led him away, cautioning him about avoiding the antics of the lower orders. Down in their cabin John held up his fists and pummelled an imaginary opponent. His mother and sisters pointedly ignored him while his father broodingly drummed his fingers on the arms of his chair. The following morning John went missing and was found on deck taking boxing lessons from Gosset. Moody corralled his son.

"But it is a valuable skill," said Gosset, grinning widely.

"I will educate him," said Moody, smiling thinly.

"You're an adept in the art?" There was challenge and surprise and bemusement in Gosset's tone.

If Moody's face burned, later that day his thigh froze when, sparring with John, the boy heel kicked him square in the quadriceps, leaving Moody limping for the remainder of their Atlantic crossing.

As they sailed into the Caribbean and past the islands it was inevitable that Moody recall Barbados where he'd grown up. Not so much St. Ann's Garrison but Bridgetown, and the Negroes and Mulattoes who moved like loud shadows that would suddenly pause and turn and regard him. He remembered the smell of a bloom called white-flower, which was like warm sugared milk. Even aboard the *Asia*, a mile from shore, the occasional scent of earth and foliage reached them. He remembered the smell of rain on hot sand, low tide in the heat, the must of his father's felt coat.

―――――――

Dear Father,

What an excellent callisthenic is a sea voyage! It was touch and go at the start for Mary and the children but they are bending well to the life. I am sorry to hear that your gout persists. But if you have taught me nothing else it is that perseverance is all. Perseverance and direction. These qualities—thanks to you—got me through eight years on the Falklands and my year on Malta. Now, God willing, I am ready to meet the challenge to which my life so far has tended: building the new Colony of British Columbia.

My best to Mother, and I hope that she is not too overcome by melancholy due to the sunny skies.

*I will write again tomorrow and hope to dispatch the letters
when we reach Aspinwall.*

In the meantime I remain,
Your son,
RC Moody

That Moody's father had been dead for sixteen years, and his mother for seven, did not deter him from writing two, sometimes three letters per month.

One evening Moody found himself alone after dinner with Gosset. The portholes were wide open and yet the room smelled of shag and coffee and vinegar and the unwashed bodies of men.

"Great things," said Gosset.

"Excuse me?"

"Great things are expected of you. Roads. Squares. Boulevards. Will you cause boulevards to be constructed in the wilderness?" The very shape of the word *boulevard* seemed to please him.

"Derby will begin as a small but functional city," said Moody. "A base of operations from which to defend the colony. A hub."

"A hub?"

"As in a wheel."

"You have a vision, sir."

"I hope so."

"And what about McGowan? Will the wheel of this vision roll over him?"

"I will deal with Ned McGowan."

Gosset widened his eyes, mock impressed. "He's an agent provocateur who has a force of thousands."

"First of all I will gather intelligence."

"Just so. The lay of the land," said Gosset, his smile revealing teeth that were very long and very grey. He had shed his black felt coat and unbuttoned his collar and rolled his cuffs, revealing formidable forearms. "But you'll need more than intelligence."

Moody felt no need to explain or rationalize his methods to Gosset. At the same time the man unnerved him. He still did not know exactly why he was on board. "It's late. I'll retire."

"But you are scarcely begun your great endeavour of creating a capital and defending the colony against the Americans!"

Moody allowed a flicker of a smile as he indulged Gosset's wit. "Then all the more reason to be rested."

"Yes," said Gosset dismissively. "Go to bed."

Moody halted and faced him. "Just what's your business in the colony?"

Gosset sat forward and set his hand on the table as though to display his fighter's knuckles and ruby ring. "It's a formidable land. Wild animals. Wild men. Trees wide enough to drive a team of horses through."

"We will go around those," said Moody, rather pleased with himself, quick wit never having been his long suit.

Gosset sat back. He did not care to be taken lightly. "And behind every tree one of Ned McGowan's Yankee spies." He trapped a roach under his palm, then held it between his thumb and forefinger. Moody feared that Gosset would dismember it or, worse, eat it. There had been a man in his corps on the Falklands by the name of Yardley who had gone mad and taken to eating insects. Gosset tossed the roach aside.

"Direct force against a numerically superior enemy is foolish," said Moody as if quoting a manual.

"Spoken like an administrator, sir."

"And you are being evasive about your role in British Columbia, Gosset."

Gosset smiled his smile and sucked his teeth. "Information. Observation. Evaluation. And much else. Reporting directly to Governor Douglas."

Moody muttered good night and departed with Gosset's last statement lodged like a pimple in his ear.

The Americans called it Aspinwall and the Spanish called it Colón. By either name the port city on the Caribbean side of the Isthmus of Panama was oppressive. The air was mud and brine, the inhabitants stunned and ragged, and most of its buildings teetered on stilts. The dogs under the houses panted and the chickens blinked and the air was grey with mosquitoes and smoke. A short carriage ride along a gravelled road led to a station where everyone sweated and a locomotive pumped steam into the low overcast. The inescapable Gosset appeared at Moody's side displaying a saurian smile and pointing to a row of barrels. "Pickled corpses," he said with the satisfaction a wine merchant might show for a cargo of vintage port. "Shipped to the medical schools of Europe and America. Wogs doing their bit for medical science."

Children corralled in her arms, Mary turned away from Gosset as though from a stench. John, however, escaped her embrace and asked Gosset, "Are you going to box some more?"

"Ah, young sir." He winked and grinned and sent a slow left hook through the sultry air to which John responded with his own left hook. To the boy's profound embarrassment, his mother called him and he reluctantly joined her, leaving Moody and Gosset watching the preparations for departure. Porters humped bags and bales and a gang of navvies squatted by a stack of ties. Beyond the steam and the sheds stood jungle, a dense barrier of nameless weed wood that appeared to watch and wait. Moody envisioned a decisive shove from the train sending Gosset into that jungle, which might chew him up.

A shrill high whistle.

Moody ushered his family to the first-class carriage and was relieved that it was no worse than many another he'd ridden in England, though there was the not insignificant issue of a sizable snake curled on one of the seats. Moody backed Mary and the kids out of the compartment and called for the porter.

"Víbora," said the man.

"Fer-de-lance," said Gosset.

"Is it poisonous?" asked John hopefully.

"Among the worst," said Gosset admiringly.

The porter, sweating richly in his blue and silver uniform, threw his cap at it. When the snake struck the cap, the porter cut the reptile in two with his machete, then shovelled the halves out the window, causing a commotion among the trackside vendors. Another whistle blew, the train lurched, Moody reached to steady Mary, and the carriage began to move and the vine-strangled trees to slide past. Amanda and Abigail sat, their feet not quite reaching the floor, and kicked their heels against the hardwood of the seat-facing whose crimson grain suggested the ripples on a pool of stirred blood. Moody placed his hands on his son's shoulders—how slim and frail they felt—and gently drew him away from the window. John looked more like his mother than his father and this endeared him all the more to Moody. "Keep your head in, lad."

"Will we see Clive again?" asked John. "He's coming, isn't he? All the way to Victoria?"

Moody and his wife looked at each other and then at their son.

"Yes," said Moody, "Mr Gosset is en route to Victoria as well."

Satisfied, John took recourse in his stack of penny dreadfuls with their corsairs and gunfighters.

"But he will be quite busy," cautioned Moody.

John looked up hopefully. "Killing Indians? Boxing Yankees on their ears? Running them through with his sword?"

"I rather doubt anything so dramatic," said Moody.

"Why does he have only one eyebrow?" asked Abigail and Amanda simultaneously. "He looks queer."

"Does not," said John.

"Does."

"I should like to have only one eyebrow," said John.

Moody demanded to know why; his son responded that it was manly and the twins tittered.

Soon the train was rolling so loudly that at first Moody did not realize he was also hearing a cuckoo clock calling the hour. He looked to Mary who was equally bemused. He stepped into the corridor and looked both ways, and as the mechanical bird continued to call he went along the aisle past Gosset's compartment to one in which a pale woman sat in stately solitude in a black lace mantilla and veil, her head turned to watch the jungle, her hands folded on her lap, silver rings on all her fingers, while on the seat opposite sat the cuckoo clock, the door slapping open one final time and the bird emerging on a scissor mechanism—*cuckoo!*— then clattering back in. They had departed exactly at noon.

Birds fled screeching from the train and Moody believed that he saw faces peering from the jungle, faces staring, frowning, judging, and he felt obscurely indignant even as he felt obscurely aware of some wrong that had been committed, a wrong that he chose not to examine too closely. They passed a man on a horse leading a string of horses laden with sacks and in one case a naked corpse. He shut the canvas blinds and sat back and closed his eyes and tried to rest.

His mother had spent most of her days in shuttered rooms, oppressed by the invasive glare of the Caribbean sun. She had been reclusive and melancholic and perpetually exhausted, lost in the fogs of her own remote gloom, while his father, stalwart, vigorous, rode every day and addressed young Richard as "sir" and expected the same. Moody, hurt by his son's attachment to Gosset, reminded himself that he had learned boxing and fencing not from his own father but from a Corporal Braddock whom, now, he could scarcely remember.

His father had overseen fortifications and roads and drainage in Bridgetown. When he returned home each afternoon he'd hand young Richard his pith helmet to wipe with a cloth dampened with lemon water and then hang on its peg. The boy would smell the odour of sweat and fabric and hair oil. This small ritual was precious, for his father's helmet was important; it bore the cross of Saint George, patron saint of England, the greatest country on earth. In the evenings the Moodys sat on the lawn of scrubby grass, careful never to place their chairs beneath the coconut palms. Whenever one of the five-pound nuts dropped, Moody's father would raise his eyebrows and nod forebodingly as if to say: Let that be a lesson to you on the lurking dangers of the tropics.

The one time he saw his father and mother jolly was at Brighton Beach, in the year 1829. Richard had been four years at school, and his parents had come to England and collected him. They stayed in Brighton's Queen Anne Hotel and there, in August, his father, in a blue and white striped bathing costume, had pretended to trip and fall into the waves while Moody's mother, usually averse to heat and sun and display, had slapped her thighs and laughed while sixteen-year-old Richard had run into the water and frolicked with his father, each taking turns at pratfalls and plunges in the glittering green sea. Later, they'd eaten mutton curry and remarked with approval on how red the sun had burnt them, something that never happened in Barbados where they avoided exposure at all costs. Thus Brighton earned a special place in Moody's heart.

Their arrival at Colón on the east coast had felt like a closing in, whereas the vista of the Pacific on the west was an opening out. The train descended the western slope and passed the port, and Moody set John the task of categorizing the ships: twenty-two of them lighters and tugs, ten sailing vessels, four sternwheelers, and one half-sunk galleon. Moody gave the boy a ha'penny, which, to his father's bemusement, he tested between his teeth.

That evening the Moodys dined with the acting vice-consul, Charles Toll. The children were delighted by a parrot that recited the alphabet in English and Spanish, as well as by one of the balcony posts that hummed because it was infested by a certain beetle. Toll had held positions in Valparaíso and Lima, and though at forty he was five years younger than Moody, he looked ten years older, suffering a palsy of the right cheek and eye, hair loss, a waxy complexion, wens on his neck, and an array of other tics. They ate strips of braised alligator and drank red wine with lemon juice. Toll spoke slowly and listened with great concentration. He talked of an article he had read on the subject of mould by a Mr Darwin and claimed that Panama City was a glorious location for the stuff, which was everywhere, even in his shoes. The evening ended when Toll fell out of his chair and began to shake uncontrollably and froth at the mouth, much to the fascination of the children.

Two mornings later they boarded a ship north. As the hurricane season was over, the weather was fine with clear skies and a steady warm wind from the southwest. They were all feeling like hardened travellers, and no one was seasick in spite of the different roll of the vessel. San Francisco, in contrast, was heavily fogged and rainy. They boarded a paddle steamer for the final leg to Victoria and were joined by no less than two hundred and thirty gold seekers who filled every inch of deck with their kits, singing, shouting, swearing, brawling, spitting, and performing other bodily functions. Off the coast of Oregon the seas grew rough and many were violently ill. Like a visitor to a prison, Gosset entertained himself by strolling amid the rabble. "Of course," he remarked to Moody with easy confidence and evident satisfaction, "half will be dead within the year, making our jobs easier."

FRISADIE - 1865

New Westminster, Colony of British Columbia

A HAND SNAKED OUT AND PINCHED FRISADIE'S backside, causing her to slop the tea. Laughter erupted around the table until Mrs Frame appeared in the dining room entry drying her red-knuckled hands on a rag. She glared the men into silence and reminded them that she possessed a goodly stock of Hawke's Rodent Remedy.

"You see," she said, with a rare display of satisfaction, "the sugar hides the bitterness of the strychnine while the opium sends the rat off to a sleep from which it don't never return. So you lot keep your filthy mitts to yourselves."

The lodgers cleared their throats and wiped their faces and scraped back their chairs—or tried not to scrape them for fear of scarring the floor and incurring more of their landlady's wrath— and fled the table, plucking hats and coats from pegs and heading off to work, most being clerks in the river trade.

When they were gone Frisadie cleared the table and dumped the remaining oatmeal into the pot where it would be added to the evening's pudding. Then she scrubbed and stacked the dishes and lugged the tub outside and sluiced the front steps. Lingering on the porch she watched two boys not much younger than her pass with fishing poles. They were in rolled pants and shirt sleeves and heading for the river. Across the street the cooper was hammering barrel staves with a mallet. It had rained in the night but now the sun shone and the first flush of April mosquitoes whined in her ears.

"Frisdadie! See to the beds."

Armed with broom, pan, and rag, she entered the dormitory and slid up the window for the air smelled of armpit, hair oil, and shag, then gave everything a going-over. She gathered the pages of *The British Columbian*. As usual the lodgers had scrawled all over the business section. There were listings with one, two, or three stars by them. The words BUY!!! or SELL!!! or BOLLOCKS!!! frequently adorned the margins.

"Frisdadie! I'll have that paper!"

"Right away, Mrs Frame."

It was slated for fire starter and the thunderbox. Folding it neat, Frisadie went to Mrs Frame's office, an alcove separated from the kitchen by a weighted sheet hung by tacks from the ceiling.

"Put it there," she said, tapping the corner of the trestle table that served as her desk, and continued to page through her ledger. Her handwriting was surprisingly stately, even if her hand itself was as cracked and dry as her shoe. Her hair was thin and her teeth yellow, though her chin bore a stylish curve, like the scrollwork on a fancy table leg. There was no evidence of any Mr Frame, no photo or portrait, no ring on Mrs Frame's finger, and the lodgers never dared ask. If she had children they had fled or died and Frisadie did not inquire. A copy of *The Illustrated Police News* lay on the desk. On the cover a constable was in the process of apprehending a dusky-hued thief picking the pocket of a gentleman.

Frisadie returned to the lodgers' room, which smelled better now, and shut the window. It faced north so the light was muted, the plank floor dull and scuffed. She wiped the sconces, then collected the candle stubs that supplemented the gas lighting and added them to a pot for remelting.

"Now take care with them rugs," called Mrs Frame. "Don't beat them through. I've no intention of buying new ones."

"Yes, Mrs Frame." She dragged the rugs onto the back landing and draped them over the rail and gave them a measured thrashing with the paddle. To the left was the outhouse and to the right the riverbank where boys fished and shoved and shouted and boats and barges drifted. The sky was a deep blue with clumps of white cloud, so she left the rugs to air and went inside and got busy sweeping the rat droppings from the corridor. Scarcely a decade old, Mrs Frame's house already seemed ancient, sagging in on itself like a rain-battered mushroom. The stairs complained under the weight of every footstep, the lath and plaster was swollen, the slats in the wainscot so loose the roaches travelled in and out at will. Along with the smell of river mud there was the smell of fried fat, and something else that Frisadie could never quite name; perhaps it was the odour of the colour grey. At eleven by the cuckoo Mrs Frame invited her to a cup of the Queen's Blend in the dining room.

"Now about these rats, Frisdadie. Are you laying out the Hawke's?"

"Yes, ma'am."

"I had a Frenchman here who said in many corners of the world rat is rated a delicacy. Did you eat rat in Hawai'i?"

Masking her indignation, all too used to such notions of island life, she said no, she had not. "Fish and pork and chicken. Though there were many rats on the *Cowlitz*. Forty-six times I saw a rat. I counted."

Mrs Frame was alarmed. "The same rat forty-six times?"

"I don't know. Different rats, I think. It was always dawn or dusk so hard to say, and they were very quick to avoid the ship's cats."

"You have led a wide life, Frisdadie."

"Yes, Mrs Frame." In fact her life felt as tight as small shoes though she didn't contradict, just as she never corrected the mispronunciation of her name.

"Now bring those rugs in. I don't trust this April weather. It's topsy-turvy."

Mrs Frame was right; the sky was closing over and the air cooling.

"You'd best get to the market toot sweet if you want to miss the deluge." She handed her a list.

This was the best part of the day, for she loved exploring the streets and shops of New Westminster. She arranged her shawl of red and black checks and took two gunny sacks and went along Front Street past the wharves and up to Columbia. New Westminster felt different from Victoria, where she'd lived nearly nine years. Victoria was all sea and rock and glare, while New Westminster was all forest and river and mosquitoes, though both were a hodgepodge of people, mostly white, or off-white—it was often impossible to tell due to the filth—as well as many Natives and Chinese, speaking every sort of lingo.

As usual, Frisadie took note of which businesses were lively and which idle. Cran & Sons Barber Shop, smelling of pomade and cologne, did a steady trade, though she wondered at a day spent staring into heads of hair, especially those of men largely indifferent to hygiene. Gleason the cobbler bent goblin-like over his last. Frisadie liked the sweetish scent of leather and paused to look in his window, admiring the strength of his hands as he worked even as she shivered at the thought of being touched by such trollish fingers. He was never short of trade, though. Boots and shoes of all styles and in every state of wear lined his racks. She passed the Grelley brothers' Colonial Hotel. Their ad ran regularly in *The British Columbian*: rooms by day, week, or month, a dining parlour welcoming parties and families, a billiard salon, a taproom featuring a full stock of ales and wines and whiskeys, as well as cigars and sundries. The door opened and two men rolled out.

"Hello, my darlin'!"

Frisadie looked away and hurried on.

"No need to run, my brown beauty!"

She took refuge in a chemist's that smelled of chalk and vinegar and found herself studying the skin whiteners. There was Malablanche's Emollient, Venetian Cerise, Fair Lady Maiden Soap, Pink Whisper, and Victoria's Lightener, which provided visual proof of its guaranteed efficacy in the form of cartoons showing the transformation of a distinctly dusky lady—dense cross-hatching indicating her skin tone—into a woman as white as the Queen herself. She touched one jar and then another with no intention of purchasing because in truth she rated her colouring far more attractive than the frog-belly white of the man behind the counter giving her the hard eye lest she pinch something. She was sixteen years old. At five foot eight and eleven stone, she stood out. Her eyes were black, as was her long and wavy hair, the dimples in her cheeks were deep enough to hold pennies, her chin strong, and her teeth would be called perfect but for a gap between the two front candidates. Peering out the chemist's window, she saw that her pursuers were gone.

"Good day, sir!" she called to the clerk and sailed out. At the market she bought potatoes, squeezing them to find the least spongy, for Mrs Frame did not approve of a spongy spud. On the walk back there was thunder, a burst of rain, and shouts from men in a doorway inviting her with lewd gestures to come hither. One began to follow her and she ran. Fortunately he was drunk and fell in the mud, much to the entertainment of his fellows. Stumbling into the kitchen out of breath, she took a moment to recover, then draped her shawl over the drying rack.

Mrs Frame was sharp eyed and no fool. Seeing the girl's agitation, she divined the cause. "You've got big 'uns, Frisdadie. I've told you, bind them tight. And keep your gaze down and be brisk about your business. If louts give you stick send them to me and I'll put the boot to their arse." She poured her a cup of tea strong enough to take paint from a hull and they sat by the stove, which had not been fed since breakfast so the tea was all but cold.

"Finish that tea," she said after a few minutes' repose. "Now, there's good dry fir branches up back of the Customs House. I saw them the other day. Fetch them. They'll be snapped up if we don't hop to it."

Shawl still damp, hatchet rolled in the lumber sling, Frisadie headed off. The rain had stopped and the brick walls steamed in the sun. She found the branches and, down on one knee, hacked them into lengths, working with her face averted and one eye shut against chips and splinters. When she had a good stack she hoisted the sling over her shoulder. The wood wasn't as dry as Mrs Frame thought but it would burn and best of all it was free. On the way back some boys shouted, "Hey, brown Betty, will you hot my pot?" and made queer gestures.

Mrs Frame had the woodbox open and waiting. When it was filled she said, "Now go for your break, Frisdadie. There's a good 'un." She said this with the air of a great and noble soul bestowing blessings upon the needy.

Her room was long and narrow with a slanted ceiling. She pulled the window up and leaned out and smelled brick and tree sap and outhouse, as well as the mud of the riverbank where boys threw their arms up in triumph as if at the endless possibilities before them. Truly it was a man's world. She shut the window and lay on her pallet and pulled the quilt up to her chin and fought back tears. On a shelf sat the carved wooden pineapple that she'd sawn from the newel post in Mrs Mace's house. Sitting up, she cradled it in her arms. Before coming to New Westminster she'd lived from the ages of seven to fifteen with Mrs Mace in Victoria. Mrs Mace had tutored Frisadie in drawing and needlework with indifferent results. She'd yawned over poetry, played the piano clumsily, danced with leaden feet, and was incontrovertible proof that not all Polynesians could sing.

"This is not a bad thing," announced the indomitable Mrs Mace one afternoon when the girl had failed to distinguish a C-flat from a C-sharp. Mrs Mace was lean and old, with white hair, bright blue eyes, powdered cheeks, and boundless optimism. "Our aim is not to make you what you are not, but to find out what you are. What are you, Frisadie?"

"I don't know, ma'am."

"Then we must search. Close your eyes and look within. Like so." She raised her chin and shut her eyes and breathed deeply. "Are you looking within, Frisadie?"

"I'm trying."

"And what do you see?"

"Nothing."

"Look deeper. Look with all your eyes."

How exalted that sounded, as if choirs of angels awaited inside of her. She tried but saw only dark.

"This is a practice perfected by the sages of Hindustan, Frisadie. Be diligent. Practise every day, morning and evening, and you shall thrive."

She did as she was directed, yet her mind wandered and she found herself counting, forward or backward, adding or subtracting, multiplying or dividing, anything to do with numbers.

"Have you found yourself, Frisadie?"

"I think so, Mrs Mace."

"What are you?"

"A zero."

"You mean to say that you are nothing?"

"I don't know; I'm afraid I just don't seem to add up."

Mrs Mace had adopted Frisadie and her mother when they'd arrived from Honolulu. They were destitute, her father having sickened and died on the voyage, and his money, admittedly not much, having strangely, inexplicably, vanished. He'd been offered a position with the Hudson's Bay Company in Fort Victoria, what with the plans to close the post in Honolulu, and saw it as an opportunity, even if it did mean leaving Hawai'i over his wife's objections. She had no interest in the Crown Colony of Vancouver Island and was highly skeptical of *haole*, whom she rated loud, malodorous, and deceitful. All these years later Frisadie could still hear her voice, adamant and pleading: *You can't trust them!* Frisadie and her mother had not been three days with Mrs Mace when a boy from the company sought them out. He wore a ragged frock coat and top hat with cards and feathers in the band and presented Frisadie's mother with a letter informing her that she owed the fantastic sum of fifty-two dollars—twenty per adult and twelve for the child—for their fare from Honolulu to Victoria, which her husband had contracted to work off via his employment. Frisadie's mother went all but catatonic. In spite of Mrs Mace's best efforts to placate her, Frisadie's mother became a ghost, withdrawing into herself and vanishing into the shadows of the house, rarely speaking or eating, drifting along corridors and through rooms, lingering at windows, pausing to touch the wooden pineapple carved atop the newel post at the foot of the stairs. Eventually Mrs Mace's solicitor negotiated a settlement with the venerable company of twenty-six dollars, which Mrs Mace paid with no thought to compensation. Seven years old, Frisadie was shattered by the loss of her father, stunned and confused at the state of her mother, and terrified by the spectacle of the strange new city of Victoria with its wild gabble of people, all too many of them *haole*. Seeking something familiar, she was drawn to that pineapple newel post.

Now, eight years later, lying on her mattress in Mrs Frame's New Westminster boarding house, cradling that very same carved wooden pineapple, which she'd taken with her, it seemed to Frisadie that two paths lay before her. One led to matrimony and motherhood; the other led to money and independence. In short, she had to find a husband or a business. She knew nothing of men, and if the ones she met in the street and in Mrs Frame's establishment were anything to go by she didn't much like what she saw, for they were loud and hairy and brutish, and some even piddled the beds.

Yet if not marriage then what business? She had no skills other than washing clothes and swabbing floors. The only natural inclination she seemed to possess was a facility with numbers, taking pleasure in equations and the beauty of a balanced ledger. She knew that Mrs Frame's lodgers would be happy to pay more per week if her coffee was stronger and her stews contained more meat, that the increase in revenue would far outpace the costs of supplies. An investment in better-quality linen and tableware would also have paid off. Frisadie did not offer her opinion, however, having no desire to begin a war with Mrs Frame, the one person in the world who, since the deaths of her mother and Mrs Mace, looked out for her.

Lying there cradling her wooden pineapple, she stared at the water stains on the ceiling slats and breathed deeply in and out, recalling old Mrs Mace's advice that it soothed the spirit, which it did, somewhat.

"Frisdadie!"

In the kitchen, Mrs Frame gave her the hard eye and remarked that she was very pleased that she deigned to join her. When Frisadie apologized and said that she'd dozed off, Mrs Frame observed that she was a great one for sleeping. "Now, here's the evening's menu."

Frisadie held the page written out in Mrs Frame's surprisingly elegant penmanship:

Fish head soup
Pork stew
Roast potatoes
Beet salad in sweet pickle juice
Pease pudding with raisins
Tea or coffee

"They should be grateful." She returned the menu with both hands as though it was a rare document.

A slight narrowing of the older woman's eyes betrayed her suspicions that Frisadie might be having her on, but the girl met her gaze with wide eyes and innocence. "Gratitude?" she said. "From that bunch?" She dug a lump of lard from a pail and dashed it into a skillet and clanged it onto the stove while Frisadie got busy with the spuds. Soon enough they heard their lordships stumping up the front steps and come clamouring in all afroth over the newspaper, for it seemed there had been some event of note.

"Mr Lincoln has been assassinated!" cried one. It might have been Daniels or it might have been Wadge; Frisadie could never distinguish one from another behind their beards.

"The American president?" said Mrs Frame, emerging from the kitchen.

"Yesterday! At a play. In Washington."

"And what's it got to do with you lot?" demanded Mrs Frame, fists on her hips.

They stared in bewilderment.

"Look at youse," she said. "Like a row of owls."

They fell to chattering again. If they had proven themselves great financial experts marking up the newspaper, they now adapted their wisdom to political analysis, and all through supper and into the evening their voices rose in excitement and then dropped as they leaned their heads together and conferred profoundly. Frisadie went to sleep to the sound of their voices echoing up the stairs. Assassination. Revolution. Anarchy. She had of course read many articles in the newspaper about Lincoln. A great man, his gaunt face etched by the many strains of life and office. Mrs Frame had been more cautious, rating the emancipation of the American slaves a complex affair that would unleash an untold fury, while Frisadie, all too aware of her own status, kept her counsel and tried not to make waves.

The next day when she went out to do the marketing, all New Westminster was talking. The president of the United States— murdered! But one gent was unimpressed, and standing outside the Colonial Hotel he made his opinion loudly known for all to hear.

"Old De Quincey had it right: the venerable art of assassination is degraded; it has lost its way. Where is the imagination, the craft? A good murder is as savoury as well-cured bacon, as satisfying as a demitasse of French roast." Aligning his cuffs, he squared his shoulders. He was of middle years, tall and straight and vigorous, stylishly dressed, with a straw boater, granite beard, and imperious air, gripping an ivory-knobbed cane more as a weapon than as support.

"The bugger had spark," said his companion, a much younger man, thickset, eyes gleaming with amusement.

"You can have all the spark you please, plus piss and vinegar, and gunpowder up your nose, but give me a decent murder, a strangulation, a smothering, a poisoning. *Guns* . . ." Scornful, he looked up and down Columbia Street as if to ask, Was there no one to give him a good poisoning? "No, Maxie, guns are not sporting. By God, should a murder of the first rank brighten my courtroom, I'd be hard pressed not to let the artist off with a decoration."

"Judge, have you ever tried a pig?"

"For what?"

"Why, murder of course. I read of a case in France."

For a moment it looked as if the judge was irate. Then he laughed hugely, head back, a great baying guffaw. "They might be difficult to hang. They have no neck to speak of."

Maxie entered into the dilemma. He frowned and tapped his chin. "A firing squad. Or the guillotine."

"Just so," murmured the judge, "just so," as though taking note for future reference.

This scene took place while Frisadie had been pretending to peruse the buns and loaves in the window of a nearby bakery, but she could no longer contain her laughter. The two gentlemen discovered her and touched their hat brims, the judge apologizing for speaking overloud and Maxie acknowledging that the topic was not for the feminine ear.

"Au contraire," said the judge. "The female is by far the more earthy creature. I assure you that at hangings none bray louder to see the condemned dance." He shook Maxie's hand, nodded gravely to Frisadie, and, brandishing his stick, walked on.

Maxie observed the departing judge with fondness, then turned to Frisadie. "But it is balmy." He swept an arm back as if introducing her to the spring air, which was indeed pillowy. He was not as imposing as the judge; in fact Frisadie was taller than he was. "Maxie," he said, introducing himself with a bow and then, consulting his pocket watch, he remarked that it was noon and offered her tea.

Before she had to respond to such an unheard-of offer, the door to the Colonial banged open and a man bellied forth as if driven by a breeze. The hitching rail caught him and he jackknifed over it and hung there, his bowler dropping off into the gutter, rocking and then lying still. Frisadie didn't know whether to laugh or go to his aid. The man began to groan and grope for his hat but it proved evasive.

Maxie turned from the fellow to Frisadie and renewed his invitation of a cup of Darjeeling.

"Thank you, but I suspect that tea isn't the beverage featured here."

He was aghast and cried that he did not mean the saloon but the restaurant. *Ress-toe-rahn.* "Scones and cream and a cuppa."

The sounds of Columbia Street receded and passersby became vague shapes. Tea? A gentleman was inviting her to tea? This was more than she could take on board. Stammering her thanks, she apologized and then fled.

———————

That evening there was botheration at the boarding house. Mrs Frame's toad-in-the-hole was under attack, consisting of too much hole and too little toad. The lodgers knew better than to tell her, of course, preferring the safety of their room for speaking their minds, and Frisadie did not blame them in the least, Mrs Frame viewing anything less than wholehearted approval as an assault and a betrayal. Prudently, they kept their voices low. The complaint wasn't new, only another example of what they endured week in, week out, and there was talk—as there often was—of moving to other boarding houses: McBraine's, Coughlin's, the Salt and Pepper. Once again Frisadie thought that if Mrs Frame improved the quality of her fare she could raise her rates and thereby her profits.

The following morning after she had cleaned the dormitory, an ad in *The British Columbian* caught her attention: "For Sale: Bostwick's Boarding House. Terms negotiable." On the way back from the market that afternoon she took a turn past Bostwick's. It stood higher up the slope with an unimpeded view of the river and the land southwest. The building itself was well kept, with a lawn, a walk, and flower boxes brilliant with daffodils. The day after, she walked past again. It was a fine afternoon and a few men sat smoking in wicker chairs on the porch. The third day, she returned wearing her best shawl, its saffron stripes complementing her hair. She had left Mrs Frame's in her regular shawl of red and black check for fear of arousing suspicion, and then swapped, folding the one into her handbag, a modest but decent article, into which she also stowed the gunny she used for marketing. Relieved that the porch was empty and she did not have to run the gauntlet, she knocked. A voice called, "Come!" and she entered. The foyer was airy, with a black lacquered table to the left, and on the right a tall white vase decorated with blue Chinese pagodas. Directly ahead was an office and behind the desk sat a man and next to him stood a woman. It was a case of speak or topple from fear.

"Mr Bostwick?"

"The same."

"I've come about—"

"We've no need of help. We're trying to sell."

"Exactly so, sir. I—"

"Try Billings. Or Wentworth."

"I want to buy," she said, compelled to shout.

The man and woman looked at each other, then at Frisadie. "Buy?" The woman's tone dripped disdain. "You?"

Mr Bostwick smiled slowly and then sat back and raised his arms in a large and leisurely fashion while clasping his hands behind his head. He was clean-shaven and small-eared, his bald head an almost perfect sphere. Eyes round in amusement he laughed cagily, as if seeing through the ruse.

"It's Beets, isn't it."

"Excuse me?"

"Beets. He put you up to this. Where is he?" Bostwick leaned left then right to peer past her.

"I assure you I don't know any Mr Beets. I've come about the boarding house."

Mr Bostwick's eyes hardened in disappointment at being robbed of a good prank. "And I've told you we are not hiring."

"You persist in misconstruing—"

"I persist in my business, young lady. Now, you found your way in, pray find your way out. There's a good girl."

Enraged and frustrated, Frisadie took a long route back to Mrs Frame's. Three men delivering stove wood catcalled her and then congratulated each other on being great wits, but she scarcely noticed for she was thinking of old Mrs Mace who'd left her a legacy upon her death. Frisadie had never known what to do with it. Now she did. If she could persuade someone to take her seriously, she'd buy a boarding house. She had no doubt that Mrs Mace would have approved.

She was a great champion of the underdog, Mrs Mace. As a young woman she had been a member of the Female Society for Birmingham and had worked alongside such crusaders as Sophia Sturge, Lucy Townsend, and Elizabeth Heyrick. Because her family fortune had come upon the back of the slave trade, she had determined to devote her life to the cause of emancipation. She met a naval officer, David Mace, who was beguiled by her independence and strength, her erect posture, the set of her chin, and the far-seeing attitude in her eyes. It was a prolonged courtship, with him absent for months at a stretch, but she eventually joined him on a voyage to the Pacific aboard the HBC schooner *Cadborough*, his first command, touching at Valparaíso, Honolulu, and Victoria, where they built a small but dignified house where Mrs Mace, still faithful to the cause, continued the good work.

Mrs Mace outlived her husband by twenty years and died at the age of eighty-eight. She'd been feeling punk for some time when one morning she said to Frisadie, "I am not yet at death's door, Frisadie, but I am certainly approaching its veranda. Soon enough I will be gone. You must consider your independence. Nothing makes a woman independent as does money. How much money do you have?"

"Two dollars and four cents."

"Then you are not independent."

Shortly after this chat Mrs Mace not only went up the steps to death's veranda but crossed it and passed through death's door as well. The next day a letter from her solicitor said that Frisadie had to leave Mace House, for everything was to be sold and the money divided among charities that included animal shelters and a school for the left-handed. As for Frisadie, she was to receive a lump sum of five hundred dollars. She'd reread the letter three times before believing it. Fifty would have been a boon. But five hundred . . . Before leaving she sawed the wooden pineapple from the newel post and put it in her bag. She thought of returning to Hawai'i, but she had been warned by Mrs Mace that for all its nostalgic lure and its unquestionable virtues, of which she had no doubt there were many, it was nonetheless a bastion of antediluvian ignorance, pagan superstition, cannibals, disease, prejudice, wickedness, licentiousness, degradation, filth, and repression, so she took her five hundred and two dollars and four cents—minus the seventy-five-cent fare—and boarded the boat for New Westminster where she was determined to make a fresh start: a new city for a new Frisadie. At fifteen years of age she found a position at Mrs Frame's and kept mum about the state of her financials, counting it no one's business but her own.

FANNIN – 1881

LONDON

WHEN HENRY FANNIN WAS FIVE YEARS OLD he collected beetles and kept them in jars. This practice troubled his father who would squint at them and then at his son, as if he were not his son at all but an imposter who merited a drubbing. Butterflies and honeybees aside, bugs were vermin and vermin was filth and filth should be killed, not collected. Still, Bob Fannin recognized the boy's spirit of inquiry, a smart lad, a boy with an interest in the world, and therefore did not criticize him. Further, he defended him against any insult, for to mock his son was to mock him, and no lout dare steal or stomp Fannin junior's bugs for fear of Fannin senior beating him.

Fannin senior had accomplished precious little in his life, but no one could deny that he had raised beating to an art. His beatings exhibited distinctive features. Usually they opened with a shout—Oi!—and if that failed then a short punch to the forehead. Or no shout at all, merely the heel of his hand thrust upward into the underside of the offender's jaw. Then again it might commence with a hammer-like fist brought down on top of the skull, as if it were the head not of a man but of a spike to be driven into a plank.

All were equally effective entrances. Certainly they captured attention. Once the offender was down, Bob Fannin brought his feet into play and the proceedings took a decidedly musical turn, his footwork echoing the drums of a military march accompanied by the woodwind groanings and pleadings of the man on the ground. There was admirable rhythm to his blows, two punches followed by two kicks and then a quickening of the tempo, a series of left, right, lefts, the fists and feet dancing a jig, after which he would slow the pace with more bass work of the boots. Bob Fannin was not a big man, five foot five and ten stone, but he was fierce and he was thorough, dotting his i's and crossing his t's as it were, even if he was illiterate. It all culminated with him hurling himself straight up into the air, arms aloft, crying out his triumph—this avatar of correction, this reclaimer of the errant to the straight and narrow—and driving his knees down upon the spine of the offender, who was very unlikely to ever offend again.

In contrast, young Henry took after his mother who had been carried off by a fever. He had reddish hair, his father, black hair, and a slender nose whereas his father's was flat due to various meetings with a variety of fists. Henry was retiring though industrious, curious about all things great and small, while his father feared the great and dismissed the small.

From the age of one to three Henry was minded by an old woman called Mrs Plate. When she died, Henry's father, wishing to save money, took the boy along with him to work at the dock where he pounded oakum into the hulls of ships. He tied the boy to a leash two fathoms long so as to give him a measure of freedom but keep him in sight. This was how young Henry discovered the world of insects, studying them with an innate sense of system of which Linnaeus would have approved, noting means of locomotion, leg count, wing position, length of antennae, and whether they did or did not sting or stink. When he outgrew the leash he was allowed to wander under his own recognizance, exploring the Thames with its gulls and rats, its dogs, cats, and weasels, its gangs, gropers and perverts, dossers, opportunists, molls, thugs, and flim-flammers. On the muddy riverbank he saw corpses bloated and corpses dismembered, clothed and naked, shaved bald where they had ought not to be. It was a rich if erratic upbringing. He saw his first monkey on a ship returned from Guinea, beheld a python from India and a sloth from Brazil, as well as stacks of bull hides from California and beaver pelts from Canada. Bulls and beavers were creatures his father could appreciate. Not the insects his son collected. He demanded to know what good they were. The boy loved his old dad, for he knew things, such as how to tie a double carrick bend and how to make rum, so how could he ask such a question? "For studying."

"I'll get you a dog. You can study it." A few days later his father pulled a pup from his coat. It was black and white and, though blind in one eye, was of an engaging personality. "Take care of it." Henry did his best, but it was a runt and sickly and died. He put the corpse in rum, for he'd overheard men on the docks talk of bodies carried home all the way from Australia preserved in rum, and envisioned men and women floating inside casks like plums in syrup, sad but welcome gifts to their waiting families. So he put the dog in his father's rum bucket where it floated peacefully in the amber liquid.

But it was not peaceful when Henry's father found the corpse, though it wasn't the death of the dog as much as the waste of good drink that enraged him. He raised his hand to strike his son but held off, for he never struck his son; he had promised the boy's mother on her deathbed and besides could not bear to see him cry. Bob Fannin had principles. He never broke his word and he rarely missed a day's work, no matter how hungover. The slime-slick scaffolding at St Saviour's dockyard was treacherous in spite of the sand flung down for grit, and the wrights fell regularly and fell hard with the result that Bob Fannin's spine was as rigid as a rusted chain. At home he spent most of his time on the floor of their one room with his deceased wife's shawl folded under his head, drinking his rum and demanding young Henry read to him from *The Illustrated London News*. He was captivated by the ongoing search for survivors of the Franklin expedition. When the American army lieutenant Frederick Schwatka led a team into the Arctic and recovered relics and a skeleton and interviewed Esquimaux who had seen the men alive, Fannin wept, the tears seeping down the sides of his head and pooling in his ears. Both father and son would go silent in contemplation of those men lost in that frozen realm of snow and ice. Equally moving were the stories of intrepid French balloonists. While Franklin went north, they went up, and while up they defended Paris against the Prussians or crossed the Channel or traversed the Alps, inaugurating an era of aeronautics.

"Flight . . ." whispered Bob Fannin as if in the presence of gods.

Henry read him *Five Weeks in a Balloon* and *A Journey to the Centre of the Earth*, to which his father had responded with a stunned silence, shaking his head slowly side to side as if unable to catch his breath, as if such accounts were as real as the blood blisters on his hands. Never were father and son closer. "And so we are the children not of God but of monkeys?" he asked after Henry read out an article upon the death of Charles Darwin.

Reading these stories prevented Henry's literacy from stagnating, for after a brief career in a school called Mrs William's Academy of the Mind, his dad had withdrawn him and set him to work rolling oakum on St Saviour's Dock at tuppence a boll. His young fingers were well fitted to the work even if his brain was not, for he was bored. While his hands twisted the oakum his imagination tumbled like the crows and daws over the riverine mud, but ever and again his mind returned to one thing: Bell & Sons Embalmers & Taxidermists, which they passed each morning and evening on their walk to and from work. Above the door hung a set of antlers—eleven points, five on one side and six on the other. In the display window stood examples of their fine and ancient art: a hawk, a bear's head, a stoat, and a spaniel posed to evoke the innate nobility of the canine.

His father cursed the Bells for sick bastards, and placing his hand on Henry's shoulder he'd guide him on past toward the basket of oakum that was awaiting. "Fiddling with corpses." Bob Fannin shuddered as if he'd gulped vinegar.

But each time they passed Bell & Sons Henry stared, and all day sitting cross-legged on the plank floor of the warehouse rolling the oakum with which the men would caulk the hulls, his thoughts returned to the stuffed creatures in the window, and more particularly to the creatures not in the window—the human beings he knew must be displayed in some inner sanctum, the holy of holies of Bell & Sons. He wanted to see these embalmed people. He knew the word balm from the Bible. There was the "balm of Gilead." Balm was fragrant, like frankincense and myrrh. His dad had described summer evenings as balmy. To embalm then was good, not bad. He wished they had embalmed his mother so that she could be here with them and he could touch her hand and gaze upon her face. He had no memories of her, though he did dream of her, and so believed that somewhere inside him recollections lay like sediment in the bottom of a jug of beer. He asked his dad if the dead dreamed.

Lying on his back on the floor to ease his spine, his father had glared, not so much in anger as in confusion, for the boy was forever asking awkward questions. "The dead?" He frowned furiously as he mulled the problem.

"Do you think Mum dreams . . . of me sometimes? Because I dream of her."

Bob Fannin had a clamshell full of tobacco on his chest and his pipe in his hand. The hopefulness in his son's voice was crushing him. He began filling his pipe to cover a sob. "Every night."

"You think?"

"Sure, lad, sure." He lit up and puffed loudly, hoping the boy would move on to another topic. Sighing smoke, he resettled his head on the folded shawl.

Whenever he could Henry held the shawl, knowing she'd worn it, and inhaled its scent though after all these years it smelled like his dad, all smoke and sweat. There were things of his mother's in a box. Sometimes his dad opened it and held various objects, turning them in his hands. Henry would have liked to look but his dad kept it locked and Henry didn't dare ask what was inside. The box was wood with a scene carved into the lid of a lady in a bonnet on a bench under a tree. Sometimes Henry picked the box up and gently shook it and it rattled and he wondered if her teeth were inside. Many men down on the docks were missing teeth, as were most of the women he saw in the street.

Only in the worst of the winter did work halt on the ships and the men get sent home. On one of those frozen mornings, feeling punk, back seized, eyes dry, throat raw, ears ringing, unable to eat, Bob sent Henry around to the Hungarian for a bottle of Browne's Chlorodyne, croaking as his son went out the door for him to be quick about it. Henry ran, taking the shortest route past the Scalings Gasworks, where he was briefly pursued by dogs though he shook them in the Shoreditch Market, and was cursed for upsetting a crate of nails. As he opened the glass-plated door Henry was met by a smell both bitter and dusty, and he could well believe that witches shopped here for their supplies. There was a bat suspended on lines with its wings outstretched, there were snakeskins draped like garlands, a bottle that held a fetus that looked like a tiny mermaid. The Hungarian had a long chin and a soft mouth and the dark, swollen, drooping eyes of a man who was a stranger to either sunlight or joy. Henry pointed to the bottles on the top shelf. The Hungarian set the Browne's Chlorodyne on the counter and made change for a florin, and did not shoo Henry out but with a mournful disinterest, a monumental apathy, an exhalation that bespoke a weariness that went back centuries, allowed the boy to linger and gape at the pithed toads and dried beetles. There were antlers, spines, teeth, a jar of eyes like baby onions. The eyes varied in shape and size and colour, though all stared at Henry, who could not but think that, like the dreaming dead, the eyes still saw and were reaching conclusions.

It was there that he discovered magnets. An entire shelf of them, horseshoe-shaped magnets, square magnets, bar magnets, even chunks of rock called lodestone. He had read about magnetism. The earth itself was a magnet. A man's body was a magnet. He touched one, cold and hard, and then picked it up and weighed it in his hand. Holding it near another one, he discovered that they jumped and attached themselves to each other. Henry parted them easily enough and then let them click back together, fascinated by the invisible attraction, and wondered if it was a form of love or brotherhood, like with like. He looked up, breathless, and the Hungarian actually smiled a little. With the change from the Browne's Chlorodyne, Henry bought a halfpenny magnet, the smallest there was, and as he walked home he touched it to nailheads and doorknobs and grates and railings.

But he was not so entranced with his new toy to forget to detour past Bell & Sons where he saw two men stagger out with the mounted head of a moose. They struggled to manoeuvre it onto a waiting wagon. As Henry approached he saw that the door to Bell & Sons was open; without a thought he stepped on in and went down a corridor through a second set of doors, inset with panes of green and gold glass depicting angels. The ceiling was low and painted a pale blue. Gas lamps hissed an odour of coal and ammonia that blended with the smell of crushed flowers and something low and faintly nauseating but nonetheless intriguing. He was met by a gentleman in a full-length leather apron, a white shirt, and indigo surgical sleeves. The man held a keg-sized metal canister from which dangled a length of dripping hose. He inquired after the boy's business.

Henry did not answer for he was looking at a corpse in a dark suit, paint-black hair parted in the middle and equally black moustache waxed to a gloss, lying on a table holding a porcelain lily between folded hands.

"Take a good squint, lad. Fill yer boots."

Henry approached but off in a corner was another body, that of an old man, posed upright on a carved and padded chair with scroll arms and a spired back. This one did not look as good as the one on the display table. It was yellow and dry and shrunken, an inferior example of Bell & Sons' art. The corpse was clad in a frock coat, with a top hat positioned on its thighs between two gnarled and waxy hands. The booted feet were posed side by side and there was an odour of mothballs. Holding the bottle of Browne's in one hand and his magnet in the other, Henry peered into the corpse's face. The dry lips were slightly parted, revealing grey and carious teeth. The ears were large and looked moulded from paraffin. The nose looked like one of the corks with which his father bunged his rum. The thing seemed more suited to Madame Tussaud's.

"Wot're ye gawping at?" it demanded.

Henry staggered and nearly dropped his bottle of Browne's as well as his magnet. The corpse belched a gin-sweet vapour and reached into its coat pocket and pulled out a leather-covered flask very much like one Henry's father owned, unscrewed the hinged cap, and swigged. The men who had been moving the moose head returned and Henry found himself an object of scrutiny. Questions came at him from all sides. Was he after embalming? Was he in need of taxidermic services? Was he aware that Bell & Sons was a place of business and not a public thoroughfare? He stammered out explanations though the fear in his young face softened the interrogators to the point they offered him tea.

"He thought Dad was dead."

"Well, he looks all but."

"Oi!"

"You'll see a hundred, Dad," said the one in the surgical sleeves. Then he asked young Henry if he liked what he saw, that is, did he wish to join the fraternity?

Henry gazed from face to face. The resemblance was bold: narrow skulls, lengthy noses, ears that could catch a breeze, extravagant sideburns. He nodded that he did indeed wish to join.

"Family only," said one.

"We'd have to adopt you," said another.

"List your skills," said a third.

"I can read the gazettes," said Henry.

"Do you read the obits?"

"My dad says they're bad luck."

"Luck's got nothing to do with it. What about the natural sciences?"

Henry did not know the natural sciences. "I've a magnet," he said, holding it up.

They passed it around and tried it on their belt buckles.

"Come back in a year."

He came back in three months, on a morning when work on the ships was suspended due to torrential rain and wind and he was free to splash about the streets. Bell senior was in his chair and Henry went to pay his respects. The old man looked different, with a coppery cast to his skin while his eyes seemed to be made of buffed kid. When Henry said good afternoon he was told that he was wasting his breath for the old bloke was dead and they'd electroplated him last week. It was the son in the leather apron. "Very fashionable with the high-noses," he said. "Cover him in wax, sluice him in a solution of salts that will carry a charge, wrap him in copper wire, then crank the turbine. Some favour silver but I am partial to copper for it imparts a more natural hue as I think you'll agree."

Henry asked what had happened to the old man's head and Bell junior admitted that it had indeed suffered a bit of blistering up top. There was no need to inquire whether the old man had wanted his remains to be so treated, for it was a form of glory and immortality and beyond question or reproach.

As Henry walked home he scarcely noticed the odours of mud and sewage, nor did he observe that the wind and rain had eased and the grey puddles reflected the cloud-cobbled sky. Instead he looked at the people, the young as well as the old, the male and the female, the hunched and the straight, the ragged and the dandies, seeing them as they would be if embalmed, electroplated, resplendent on plinths or under domes of glass, or sitting at the supper table, perfectly preserved for their families who would never lose them, and he understood the direction his life must take: he would become an embalmer. He felt chosen; he felt light and radiant, like a boy soaring in a balloon, and for the moment forgot all about his dad's opinion of embalming.

When he got home he found his father on the floor, which was nothing unusual, except that he looked different, as though made of plaster. Henry said hello but received no response.

"Dad . . ."

Nothing. He knelt beside his father and stared. He gave him a gentle prod on the shoulder. Again nothing. He did not smell gin or rum or beer or see a bottle nearby, but then his dad could sleep anywhere at any time, as if he could pull a pin and down dropped a shutter and off he went to the Land of Nod. Still, he listened for his father's breathing and then put his hand on his brow—cold. He sat back on his heels, breathing fast, feeling sick, his thumping heart trying to flee his chest. Putting his hands over his face Henry curled forward trying to escape inside himself to a room, a small room, some safe corner where it was simple and he could sleep, but he couldn't sleep. He gave his dad another prod.

He walked about the room, which had been his world as far back as he could remember, with its sagging ceiling, its cabinet, the stacked bowls, the jug and ewer, the oil lamp on the table, the three ladderback chairs, the bench, the breadbox with an owl painted on—what an owl had to do with bread he did not know, nor had his father.

He thought maybe if he went outside and walked around and then came back everything would be different. He thought maybe if he ran to the Hungarian's shop and got a bottle of Browne's everything would be okay, for it had restored him to health the last time. He thought maybe if he shouted very loudly in his dad's ear he'd wake up, that his departing soul would hear and return. Or throw water on his face. He went to the jug; there wasn't much but he took it and poured it on his dad's forehead. Nothing, not a curse nor a blink. He set the jug down, then put his hands on his hips and tried to be manly, thinking that if he stood like his dad he could address the problem like his dad; above all he fought not to whimper, for his dad wouldn't approve of whimpering. He felt panic but his mind was clear and he saw that there were two things he could do. The first was that he could join his dad, run and catch up, but that would mean killing himself and he didn't think he could do that, indeed he didn't know how to even go about it, except maybe to climb into a cannon and get blown out, something his dad had said they did in the army to shirkers. The second thing was that he might contact Bell & Sons and have the body embalmed and in that way they could remain together.

Searching his father's pockets he came up with a half guinea's worth of coins. The rent was coming due because his dad had said as much, and yet half a guinea was not enough for both rent and embalming; he knew because he'd seen the price list at Bell's. He devised a plan: he would embalm him himself, or so he thought until he began to consider what exactly this involved. At Bell & Sons they gutted the corpses and stuffed them with rags, a thought too terrifying to consider, and as for the business of electroplating he had no notion how to even begin. Rum! He could pickle him in rum, the way he'd tried preserving the dog, except that there was scarcely any rum in the bucket. With the coins from his dad's pocket, Henry went to the shop and looked at the rum—Gunpowder, Old Monk, Admiral Rodney Extra Old—and saw that he didn't have enough to pay for the amount necessary, for he'd need half a barrel at the least. In the end it didn't matter because the next day some men from the dockyard came round to see how their mate Bob Fannin was faring and found him dead and stiff and young Henry stunned mute and empty eyed, and that very same afternoon the boy was escorted across London to a newly established Barnardo Home for the Lost, Wayward, and Indigent.

Aside from his clothes the only things he brought with him were his collection of magnets and the box that his dad used to study when drunk, and which Henry discovered contained only a few teeth, a ring, a brooch, and a glass eye. Had the glass eye belonged to his mother? He'd never know, though why else would his dad have kept it?

For the next five years Henry lived in a dormitory with thirty other boys and it wasn't as bad as the rumours he'd heard. He was beaten regularly though lightly, often mocked, occasionally coddled, but generally ignored, fed something vaguely resembling food, and made to memorize stretches of the Bible: "Behold, Micah, she also has borne children to your brother Nahor: Uz his firstborn and Buz his brother and Kemuel the father of Aram and Chesed and Hazo and Pildash and Jidlaph and Bethuel . . ."

He was taught shoemaking. When Henry explained that it was embalming and not shoemaking that he wished to learn, there was mirth. What a singular fellow young Henry Fannin was proving himself to be! It was explained that they did not have the facilities to teach embalming.

Henry informed them that the Bells were waiting for him. "The bells? What bells? Are you hearing bells, then? We must check your ears?"

"No." Henry tried to explain but they only said that that was outside what they termed their *curriculum as set by the Royal Pedagogical Board.*

Henry became familiar with the smell and texture of various sorts of leather—kid, pig, ox, horse—the care and handling of knives and scissors and punches, tanning procedures, the last and the hammer, brads, catgut, needle and thread. His world became focused upon feet, while his hands became permanently stained brown. While it wasn't as bad as he'd feared, it wasn't good either, and he missed his father. He wasn't allowed out except on supervised excursions, and he made few friends, for the other boys were forever busy fighting or weeping or masturbating or cutting themselves.

One summer a plague of polio spread swift and sinister through the orphanage and three boys woke one otherwise fine morning with headaches, unable to move their legs. Henry was one of them, paralyzed, his breathing difficult, neck sore, skull throbbing, and for the next year he was bedridden. For the last three months of that year he spent most of each day and night strapped to a board in an attempt to straighten a curvature of his spine that threatened to turn him into a hunchback. The other boys treated him alternately with deference or disdain, bringing him mugs of tea, dribbling water down his forehead to watch him squirm, poking stalks of grass into his ears, or else skirting wide past his bed and holding their breath for fear of being contaminated. Hunchback Henry, he was called. They chanted:

> *Hunchback Jack,*
> *Sleeps on his back,*
> *Pooper pointing down,*
> *Pecker pointing up,*
> *If he don't straighten out*
> *He's never going to tup!*

Tupping was not uppermost in Henry's mind, even if he did spend much of his time fantasizing romantic scenarios in which he was victorious against daunting odds, standing tall upon heaps of Saracen corpses with his broadsword or succumbing in glorious defeat against insurmountable odds to the piteous weeping of maidens who put flowers on his grave, vowing to know no other man . . .

During the interminable afternoons in the airless dormitory, while the other boys were off practising their shoemaking and tinsmithing, he recalled as much as he could of his parents, which in the case of his mother was nothing. Certainly his father had never said anything about her having a glass eye. Lying on his plank, shoulders squared and spine flat, Henry would hold the glass eye up and try to see his mother through it, convinced that she'd left it for him as a means by which he might contact her. He would hold the eye in his right hand and, when it grew numb, shift it to his left, or sometimes hold it in both hands, or he would position it on his chest overtop of his heart and raise his head as high as possible so as to see it, but that was not easy. When these efforts yielded no visions of the woman who had given him life, he'd lie back and simply grip the glass eye in his palm, thinking he might feel some vibration.

Inevitably the other boys discovered the glass eye. Some wanted to hold it and Henry obliged until one put it in his mouth and Henry had to grab him around the throat to prevent him from swallowing it, for the boy, Miggs or Maggs, swallowed everything from buttons to pebbles to coins. After that Henry didn't let anyone see the eye, much less hold it, yet this didn't prevent it from being stolen. One night a gang pressed a rag into his mouth and held his arms as they rifled his pockets and made off with the eye, which he never saw again.

With time bed rest was succeeded by exercise. A bible was placed atop his head to encourage him to hold himself straight, and a rod strapped across his shoulder blades to force him to stand squarely. In spite of his trembling legs and wobbly balance, he felt proud with his chin so high, as if he had grown taller, though when the book and rod were removed and he was allowed to return to bed he all but collapsed.

But he wasn't idle. He read *Robinson Crusoe*, *Masterman Ready*, and *The Settlers at Home*, as well as pamphlets donated from the Religious Tract Society: *True Tales about India* and *Thirty Years amongst the American Savages* by Miss Beatrice Bantom, and of course the Bible. But the library of the Barnardo Home was limited; there was no room on the shelves for political tracts or literature that was deemed racy, which made the presence of *The Mind and the Magnet* all the more odd. In it he read not only that magnets could cure rheumatism, fatigue, gout, and men's difficulties, of which he had only the vaguest notions, but also that they improved the eyesight, honed the teeth, sharpened hearing, and quickened the mind. "In short," wrote the author, "everything lives and perishes through magnetism." Henry had suspected this. Gravity kept man's feet on the ground and the moon in its orbit; therefore how could magnetism not but influence the heart and mind, that is to say the spirit and brain, of every man and woman, indeed every creature on the planet, from the ant to the whale?

Lying with *The Mind and the Magnet* open upon his chest one solitary afternoon, magnets in his pockets as well as a string of them around his neck for their fortifying influence, he heard church bells begin ringing at an unaccustomed hour, and it occurred to him that there must be a funeral and, half-adrift in the heat, he wondered what would happen if they put a magnet in a corpse—would it not attract the life force? This thought shivered through him like a galvanic charge. Better yet, put two magnets, or lodestones, in the body, one at the heart and one in the skull, between the eyebrows which corresponded to the Vedic third eye of spiritual insight. This would draw life force and wisdom, for, as the book's author pointed out, the mind itself, through the power of concentration, could also function as a magnet.

The Mind and the Magnet became Henry's bible, and he studied with devotion. He took it with him when he left the Barnardo Home at the age of fifteen. He stood a slim five foot eight—five foot six when he was feeling fatigued and not minding his posture— his complexion pale but not pallid, his hair having darkened to auburn, six shillings in his freshly darned pocket, along with a letter signed by three staff members attesting to his competence as a shoemaker. He knew exactly the course his life must take. He was wearing gleaming black brogans that he'd cobbled himself, had slicked his hair with orange-scented pomade to flatten its curls, possessed all his teeth but one, the gap not visible unless he smiled too widely, and most important of all he had purpose. After shaking the various hands extended to him he went out the gate, stepped across the sewage runnel in the middle of the road, and turned and waved once more. Carrying himself as tall as possible in spite of the curve of his upper spine, a free young lad on a fine spring day, he went left at the Dog & Wolf, still shuttered at this early hour, and, picking up his pace, hiked halfway across London directly to Bell & Sons.

Over the intervening years he'd often thought of the Bells. He'd have liked to visit but his routine at the Barnardo had been regimented. He passed the docks where he'd worked with his dad. Then he saw the sign, the antlers above the door, and soon recognized the various animals in the window. To his joy and relief, when he stepped inside he was remembered immediately and welcomed heartily. Brother John, he of the apron and surgical sleeves, appeared particularly pleased, claiming to have often wondered what had become of him. This was gratifying. Looking around, Henry was happy to see the old gentleman on his chair in the corner, exactly as before. How reassuring and reliable was embalming; such enduring consistency pleased him, for here was Man approaching immortality. He went to Bell senior who, upon closer inspection, was not quite as fresh as he recalled; the blistering up top had turned to scabs, the facial flesh had sagged, one eyelid was half-closed, and he was coated in a layer of dust. Still, Henry affected not to notice and, convinced that the old fellow could hear him even if he was dead in body, said, "Hello, sir," in a cheery voice.

A snort of derision came from behind. Henry turned to see a boy of about twelve in an apron and sleeves like those of John

Bell, next to whom he stood, looking up eager for approval of his mockery.

John Bell ignored the boy and addressed Henry. "Had you come around last year we'd have had a place for you." He cleared his throat and his voice deepened, suggesting a man accepting a less than ideal reality. "But as you can see we've taken on an apprentice. My cousin Ewan's son, Ewan junior."

Ewan junior smirked horribly and Henry departed following some polite chat with John Bell and his advice to keep a stout heart in his chest and a smile on his face.

MOODY - 1858

THEY ANCHORED IN VICTORIA JUST AFTER DAWN, Christmas Day, the sky a hard dry blue, the air frozen, the ship's ropes white with frost, the decks slick as iced ponds. Alongside Moody on the deck, John played with his frosty breath, pretending to smoke a pipe like Clive Gosset while Amanda and Abigail huddled under their mother's arms. The ship vibrated with the excitement of passengers preparing to disembark. The harbourmaster came aboard with an invitation for the Moodys to have Christmas dinner with Governor Douglas; that the invitation did not include Gosset was, in Moody's view, auspicious. They were taken off by lighter as the gold seekers crowded the rail looking on in envy and scorn. Moody couldn't resist scanning the faces for Gosset but failed to spot him, for of course the man would never give him such satisfaction and was likely lurking back amid the crowd, feigning supreme indifference.

At the wharf Douglas's carriage conveyed them to their temporary quarters in the garrison, the sprung buggy wobbling over the corrugations of the frozen mud. En route they passed every manner of dwelling, from tents to sheds to lean-tos, and even men sheltering under overturned boats. Their clothing was equally diverse: furs, skins, canvas; one man seemed to be wearing feathers, while another man sat atop a barrel hugging a dog under each arm. Desperate for heat, men had dragged driftwood up from the beach while others chopped at stumps splitting away pieces for their fires, which smoked and ran horizontal before gusts of icy wind. Along with bestially bearded white men, there were Chinese and Negroes and Kanakas, though, as far as Moody could see, few women. And there were trees on a scale he had never seen. He'd been warned that they rotted even as they grew, and they grew wide and they grew tall, perhaps unnecessarily tall. He also saw a Native family, girls and boys, women, and one elderly man standing a little apart, watching, frowning, silent, as Moody and his family passed in the carriage. Moody averted his gaze.

The governor's house glowed with lamplight. Coloured glass windows flanked the vast door, which was opened by a tall man with long white hair and silver-blue eyes who bowed them into a candlelit foyer. He wore a blue velvet tailcoat with gold buttons and braided cord, knee breeches also of blue velvet, red garters, and white stockings. Taking their coats and hats, he handed them to a young woman who curtsied, then he stepped to a pair of panelled doors that he opened as if throwing wide a set of curtains.

"Colonel Richard Clement Moody and family." The man had a stiff-jawed accent. *Der Kullnl Urchurd Klimnt Muddy und famil.* With a sweep of his arm he invited them to pass. As they did so, Moody caught the scent of lemon balm.

A stoutish woman of middle years glided forward to meet them. She wore black lace and a beige shawl and her silver-streaked hair was braided and wound about her head, accentuating the length of her black eyes and giving them a slightly exotic appearance. Gold earrings in the form of sunflowers caught the light and held it.

"Colonel Moody," she said in a voice rich with joy, and an accent that, if Moody hadn't been able see Amelia Douglas's Métis features, would have been difficult to identify. She offered her hand. He wondered for a moment if he was supposed to kiss it, but it was presented thumb up and so he grasped it, warm and dry and firm.

"Lady Douglas," he said. "An honour. May I present my wife, Mary."

Mrs Douglas caught both of Mary's hands in her own and held them against her heart as though taking strength. Lady Douglas had high wide cheekbones and dull copper skin. She was smiling and at the same time wary and appraising. Moody watched this scene, breath held in apprehension, even though his wife had met many people of many stations and had always won them over. She stood face to face with Amelia Douglas, whose smile suddenly widened as if pleased with what she'd found. Releasing Mary's hands she discovered the children.

"But how will I tell you apart?" she asked Amanda and Abigail.

"I have no teeth here," announced Amanda, opening her mouth wide to display the gap where two baby teeth had come out.

"Others will soon grow in," Amelia assured her. She next addressed John. "And who is this fine young man?"

"Are you an Indian?"

The floor tilted beneath Moody's feet while Mary, in a tone of terrified if jovial reprimand, said, "John."

Amelia benignly remarked that she was half-Indian. When asked which half, she said that that was rather more difficult to say, but she was smiling as she turned, chin raised, and called, "Ingemar!"

The sliding doors opened and the butler reappeared. "Ma'am?"

"Inform Mr Douglas that our guests are arrived. And fetch Martha and Jane."

Ingemar bowed.

"Please, sit."

Moody settled himself in a wing chair of buttoned black leather. The room swayed in a glow of candle flames and oil lamps and was dominated by a Christmas tree that stood ten feet high and almost as many feet in diameter, filling the air with its clean coniferous spice. It was decorated with twists of silver and gold paper, holly berries, and dozens of candles in tin cups reflecting their trembling flames. The children stood in awe at this giant. Above it the plastered ceiling was painted a pale blue, the four corners thick with roiling clouds and cherubs blowing golden trumpets, while the walls were panelled in oiled wood; on one hung a full-length portrait of James Douglas looking every inch the monarch. In a corner a bulldog panted in a wicker basket.

The doors opened again and two girls entered. Jane was John's age, Martha the same age as the twins, and she carried a volume of Tennyson. Perching herself on a chair, she opened the book with deep and solemn ceremony. Amanda and Abigail joined her, one at each side, as Martha read aloud with grave delivery:

> *It little profits that an idle king,*
> *By this still hearth, among these barren crags,*
> *Matched with an aged wife, I mete and dole*
> *Unequal laws unto a savage race,*
> *That hoard, and sleep, and feed, and know not me.*

I cannot rest from travel: I will drink
Life to the lees . . .
Far on the ringing plains of windy Troy . . .

While her sister thus intoned, Jane was taking the measure of John and announcing that she herself was taller. John, aghast at this undeniable truth, drew himself up as high as he could manage and stated, "I have a snake skull."

"Show."

He pulled it from his coat pocket and displayed it upon his palm.

"Wherever did you get that?" demanded Moody.

"Clive. It's a cobra."

"A fine specimen indeed, sir." Governor Douglas, huge and grey and as silently ominous as a storm cloud, had joined them. He stood with his hands clasped behind his back, tilted slightly forward at the waist to take a polite interest in the boy's prize.

"Sir." Moody stood.

"Colonel."

Moody introduced Mary. Douglas did not offer his hand but rather a deep bow. He towered over her as he did over everyone and everything but the tree.

"Governor. Thank you ever so much for the invitation."

"Not at all. You are newly arrived and it is Christmas. The voyage was not too wearing?"

"An adventure," said Mary, smiling. She had a small mouth and her even white teeth complemented her complexion, which was yet golden from their Caribbean crossing. Moody found himself proud of her smile and, as ever, impressed at her diligence in brushing her teeth each night with powdered chalk and mint oil.

"The new route," said Moody.

"Not like the old slog around the Horn." Vast in height and width and as monumental as a lion, Douglas regarded Moody with the eyes of a man who had faced down every danger and was perhaps a little amused by what stood before him now. Sensing that he was being measured, Moody found himself impersonating his father's square-shouldered stance. Perhaps reminded of the elder Moody, Douglas said that he'd met Moody's father in Jamaica and recalled that he was a fine horseman, then asked after his health. Moody stiffened as if at a sharp pain in the spine and said that he had passed; Douglas offered his condolences.

Ingemar entered bearing a tray on which sat a peach-coloured punch bowl, around the rim of which matching cups dangled by hooked handles. The scent of rum, raisins, and cinnamon mingled with the scent of the tree and beeswax. Ingemar set the tray on a table and then took three steps back as Douglas did the honours, ladling out the hot drink, first to Mary and Amelia, then to Moody, then to Amanda and Abigail and Martha and Jane, and lastly to John.

"Did you see whales, sir?" Douglas asked the boy.

"Humpbacks!"

Douglas widened his eyes and nodded as if much impressed. "Come spring they will be here in force. You can stand on the shore and watch them. Yet another resource the Americans would have for themselves," he said, turning to Moody who, appropriately appalled, responded that unchecked they would manifest their self-serving destiny to the ends of the globe.

"There is an expectation of civil war," continued Douglas. He smiled grimly and added that that might not be such a bad thing. "Many of them will go home. Though the cowards and shirkers will stay while an equal number of their ilk flood north."

"Cowards are controllable because they are cowards," said Moody.

"Cowards are sneaks," warned Douglas.

In his father's voice—an octave deeper, a grade more stentorian—Moody assured him that his sappers would be prepared. How fortifying it felt to be his father, like donning a suit of armour. Douglas began to ask if he'd read Machiavelli and was interrupted by Martha pitching her voice as she reached the resounding finale of "Ulysses," saving Moody from the embarrassment of admitting that it had been thirty years since he had read *The Prince*.

> *. . . that which we are, we are;*
> *One equal temper of heroic hearts,*
> *Made weak by time and fate, but strong in will*
> *To strive, to seek, to find, and not to yield.*

All saluted the verse's sentiment as though it came from the King James Bible.

Moody observed that there had been much in the news of late on the excavations of Troy, which caused Douglas to frown as he acknowledged the dubious allure of antiquity. "The copper light of the Mediterranean wields an appeal. But you and I, sir, we are in the business of building the future, not resurrecting the past. We will leave that to the Frank Calverts of the world."

Moody nodded his assent, though in other company he might have observed that the two were not so mutually exclusive. He might also have mentioned that he had met Calvert in Malta and been much impressed by his passion for Homer's city. Instead he sipped his punch, which was not as bracing as he could have wished.

John and Jane were competing to see who could hold their finger in a candle flame the longest. Amanda and Abigail and Martha were studying the illustrations in the Tennyson. Mary and Amelia were on the couch, heads tilted toward each other, voices lowered.

"I have written my own poem," announced Martha, closing the book with a thump.

Where to begin o where to begin, lamented the toad.
Why, begin at the end and then turn around, said the frog.

The mothers applauded. Abigail and Amanda cheered. Jane and John frowned and stared.

"Very fine, Martha, very fine," said her father. "You have mastered the half rhyme and are indeed your mother's child." He then turned back to Moody and conceded that there was of course much to be gleaned from the past. "But dwell overlong on things unearthed and one risks becoming Sir Thomas Browne." He smiled the rigid smile of a man who did not often joke.

Moody was swift to chortle approvingly, highly relieved that the governor was in such good spirits.

"What's the dog's name?" asked John, shaking the burn of the candle flame from his finger.

"Gwendollyn," said Jane, holding her scorched finger behind her back and trying not to wince.

Ingemar announced supper. Douglas offered his arm to Mary while Moody offered his to Amelia. She was buxom in contrast to Mary, who was lissome. Moody had no wide experience with women. A brothel in Kingston and one on Cape Verde—beyond that he'd always been awkward with the finer sex, and so when his hip brushed Amelia's he tried not to flinch at this indiscretion. But if Amelia Douglas noticed at all she hid it well. As always when anxious, Moody's mind bounded about like a grasshopper and landed in places that left him breathless with embarrassment. To mask this he now raised his chin and proceeded with slow dignity as they crossed the hallway and entered the dining room where a long table was set. He held Lady Douglas's chair; Governor Douglas held Amelia's chair; then the gentlemen took their seats. The adults were at one end and the children at the other. John, hungry, gripped his fork in one fist and his knife in the other like some famished trencherman of yore. They dined on goose, venison, mutton, oysters, fish tarts, and jellied eels, a welcome feast after two months of salt beef, stony biscuits, and sauerkraut. Ingemar served, and when he did not serve he stood by the door as still as a post but for his eyes, which darted about following the progress of the meal. Afterward, Moody and Douglas left the women and children and returned to the parlour. Douglas stood with one fist pressed into his lower spine, back arched, frowning at the cherubs on the ceiling as though at an infestation.

He said, "They will look back upon you and me someday."

Moody understood this as a reference not to the cherubs, but to the men of the future. He found himself trembling with pride and terror.

"They will read our reports and dispatches and letters and journals and reach all manner of inevitably erroneous conclusions," said Douglas. "The poets will perhaps come closest. Tennyson has a suitable gravitas. Let us hope there are more Tennysons yet to be born." He inhaled long and exhaled longer and pursed his lips and glared in disapproval at the painted ceiling. "Lady

Douglas's whim," he said. "I don't generally indulge whims, but she has earned a few."

Moody found a suitable expression for his face, a pained agreement at the simultaneous trial and salvation that was a good wife. The thought of life without Mary was unbearable.

Douglas poured them each a glass of port. The governor was not a great drinker, had scarcely touched his punch, had taken but a half glass of wine at supper, and the glass he now handed Moody was hardly bigger than a thimble. Before the Falklands Moody had not been a great drinker either, but soon enough a glass of stout at breakfast, a half bottle of Argentine Rio Tinto at lunch, followed by a medicinal tonic with gin in the afternoon, whiskey before supper, a bottle of claret with supper, brandy to follow, and mulled wine at bedtime were standard fare.

"To Derby," said Douglas.

"Derby," echoed Moody.

They clinked and sipped, Douglas merely wetting his lips but seeming to take a disproportionate satisfaction.

"You will lay the groundwork for the capital of what may well become Britain's richest colony. More lucrative even than India."

Moody felt his chest inflate. Glorious was his endeavour. He could not wait to write his father. "It is an honour."

"It is a monumental undertaking."

"Indeed, sir."

They sipped again.

"I will cross the strait and make a preliminary survey immediately," Moody assured him.

"You will not see it at its best," said Douglas, meaning the winter season. "But that is an advantage. You will be under no illusions as to the work before you."

"Worst first, best last."

"Just so."

All evening Moody had been aware of Douglas guiding the conversation to gauge Moody's views. They agreed that the Second Opium War was a regrettable necessity; they agreed that it behoved them to monitor China closely; agreed that the Spanish Empire was teetering though its collapse could take another half century. The French were, as ever, troublingly proud, tenacious, inconstant, and altogether too Mediterranean. The Dutch were playing far beyond their game, and the Germans, as fatally flawed as the French, were anxious and aggressive and insecure, lodged as they were between Russia and Austria-Hungary.

Moody now ventured an opinion. "I have been struck by the small countries that have exercised such enormous influence. The Portuguese, the Dutch, and of course none more so than the English. An inverse ratio, as it were, bespeaking undeniable genius."

Douglas considered this in his frowning fashion, a horseshoe shape visible in the set of his brow, and Moody chastised himself for such a banality. He'd been trying to impress the governor and come off like a junior cadet.

"Perhaps a worthy topic for a monograph," allowed Douglas. "In the meantime you will prepare a site well served by roads. This will facilitate settlement and commerce, which will encourage wealth to stay here where it belongs. Too much is being carried off south over the border. We are being stripped. This must cease. There are twenty thousand Yankees here in British territory, a dangerous disproportion. If spurred they could take the colony for themselves just like that." He snapped his fingers as if in demonstration.

"The border is now set," said Moody.

"The border." Douglas smiled thinly. "The border is symbolic and means nothing if they decide to ignore it. We are too far away and your sappers a token force at best. Here is a hard truth: the Crown is at odds with itself over British North America. They are still smarting over the American War of Independence. They lost thousands of men and millions of pounds. Hence they will be reluctant to commit men and money to defend this territory should the Americans decide to take it for themselves. Therefore it is up to the likes of you and me, sir. Are you capable?" Before Moody could respond, Douglas continued. "I have had letters from Premier Macdonald. He has a vision of Canada spanning from the Atlantic to the Pacific. It is a vision I endorse." Douglas downed his port, though the weight of the gesture was undermined by the lightness of the glass. "A capital will be a bastion of defence. It will be a tangible fact. A place for settlers to congregate. Loyalist settlers."

When Moody assured him again that he was eager to start, Douglas became even more grave. He tucked his chin and exhaled long and once more pressed his fist into his lower spine as though suffering spasms. He said, "Derby and his government actuaries expect the colonies to be financially independent as soon as possible. Indeed they desire revenues to cease flowing east to west and begin flowing west to east. And in very short order. The question is: Are you up to the task, sir?"

Moody could well believe that he'd been transported back to age twelve on the morning of his departure for England and school. On that day he'd been terrified and morose and had battled to control the tremor in his voice and twitching of his face. He'd not wanted to leave Barbados and yet he dared not disappoint his father by a show of emotion. His mother had moaned in the next room, though whether due to his imminent departure or one of her headaches he'd never know. He'd assured his father then, as he assured Douglas now, that he was indeed up to the task.

"Come."

Moody followed Douglas out of the parlour and onto the porch. The starlit sky was an explosion of glass arrested mid-blast. Scattered conversation and heartfelt hymns were audible through the trees and along the shore from various camps.

"I have given my life to the Company and to the Crown and to this place." There was pride and defiance and perhaps even wonder in Douglas's tone.

Moody was moved and uncomfortable and sought some suitable remark. "We are at the beginning."

"Apart from the Natives who have been here ten thousand years," said Douglas.

Moody felt chastised.

"But peoples rise and fall and are lost to time and dust," added Douglas. "Another terrible truth, but a truth nonetheless."

Moody observed a suitable sobriety and parsed the statement: people plus time equals dust. And yet from dust and sweat and initiative rise empires. Unless, he thought, empires were follies.

"I assume that you were informed of the other matter," said Douglas.

"McGowan."

"It would seem that this man has not merely set himself up as a de facto leader of a swarming mass of gold hunters, but that he has taken on the status of an oracle before whom these knaves bend the knee. You must deal with him—deal with him immediately. Go up the river and settle his hash, as the Yanks are wont to say."

Moody had hoped that the matter of Ned McGowan would have sorted itself by the time he'd arrived. "And if he remains unreasonable?"

Douglas exhaled hard and said that that was where Gosset came in. Moody felt the air go out of him and admitted that he'd met the man.

"Use him."

"I still don't know what he does. Or can do. Other than box."

"Exactly," said Douglas. "He's a weapon." He then reiterated that Moody's larger project was to secure the border, for without a secure border there was no secure Derby, and without a secure and efficient Derby the Colony of British Columbia would fail, be pillaged at the least and end up in American hands at the worst. "The two tasks are combined," he said. "The Americans must not be provoked into storming the border. Go upriver. Meet McGowan. Rein him in." He paused and then added, "By whichever means necessary." He gazed weightily at Moody, then turned and considered the stars. "It is said that he lives in a cave."

In bed that night Moody observed that the evening had not been wholly unsuccessful. He was lying alongside Mary and watching the trembling candlelight roll and flicker around the badly chinked room in the barracks. "Yes," he said, having gone over every gesture and glance, every silence and laugh, gauging each tone and pause for hidden meaning. "Yes, I think it went well enough. The governor and I see eye to eye on most things, even if he does stand a head taller."

"He's a big 'un," agreed Mary. "But there is big and there is big."

Moody waited for her to go on, and when she didn't he prompted her. "Meaning?"

Not at all displeased to be solicited for her views, she said she detected that his first loyalty was to himself. "Therefore his outlook cannot be vast," she said, "not truly vast, not profoundly, no matter how high his head or broad his chest. He may well be a great man, but not a *Great Man*. As for you, Mr Moody, you have earned the confidence of the Queen, of the prime minister, and of Bulwer-Lytton, and therefore you have no reason to doubt yourself. Remember that you too have governed." She turned to him and pressed his arm as though testing the power of his bicep.

It was Mary who had advised him to learn all there was to know about Governor James Douglas. Together they'd studied gazettes and reports, sifted reputation and rumour and hearsay, finding them often contradictory. Douglas was interested in astronomy; Douglas drank; Douglas was a teetotaller; he ate raw seal livers for breakfast; he felt bitter and undervalued by the Hudson's Bay Company and by the Queen and her prime minister; he rewarded loyalty but disdained grovelling; he'd never read a book; he wrote poetry in secret; he spoke fluent Cree; he was fond of hummingbirds; he would strike any man, high or low, who disparaged his wife.

Mary said, "Amelia says that the governor is quite off his oats about McGowan."

"You spoke of McGowan?"

"At length." Her tone suggested that this should have been obvious. "And much else."

Moody watched the candlelight swing about the walls like sea wash about a ship's hull. "Apparently he lives in a cave."

Mary rolled onto her right shoulder so that she and her husband were now facing each other. "You will take care." There was fear in her voice. "McGowan is the Minotaur," she said.

"Making me Theseus."

"And I will be your Ariadne," she assured him.

They interlocked their fingers; hers were warm. What a shrewd and observant creature she was. Enduring another pang of terror at the thought of life without her, he embraced her tightly and she sighed against him. She was the daughter of a schoolmaster. Her two brothers had died young, plunging their mother into irrecoverable grief, so that by the age of twelve Mary was taking care of her parents, directing their one servant, and even keeping the family accounts while her father drifted ever farther off into the calm cold remote realm of numbers. In the early days of their courtship, Moody and Mary had often walked on the downs and he remarked upon the silence that contrasted the Falklands, where you could never escape the cannonading of the surf that rumbled through the stony ground, vibrated the floorboards, agitated the window glass, and thumped in his very skull, while the endlessly shrieking winds were the eternal pain of a soul exiled. Her hand, gloved in silk, would reach as though through fog to draw him into the sun. She was thirty, he was thirty-five, both of them late bloomers in the season of love. Moody knew that his aura of a man returned from the edge of the world drew Mary and he'd taken care not to overdo it even as he'd revelled in her attention. Eight years on the Falklands: wind and rain, rain and wind, skies in perpetual tempest, the sea ever at war with itself, home thousands of miles distant. The men drank and fought with each other while Moody, in charge, drank and fought with himself. Within six months of his return to Britain he and Mary had met at a dinner in Liverpool.

"You are Robinson Crusoe," she'd said.

"I had eight years; he had three, and better weather."

"Did you discover God?"

"It was my understanding that He had already been discovered."

She'd laughed. She was pleased and said, "I have heard that late in life Mr Selkirk expressed the desire to return to his island."

Moody said, "I have no such desires." He added, looking into her eyes, "Certainly not this evening."

Such boldness had gripped her heart. She held his gaze, thinking that if he was merely passing time she would suss him out, and yet she saw by his eyes and manner and tone that he was in earnest, dauntingly earnest, and that a door to a future, to an entire life, was opening before her.

Lying in bed in the Victoria barracks, Moody held his wife and kissed her. He had never seen his father touch, much less kiss, his mother. The only time he ever saw his father express love was toward his mare, Peg. As a young boy Moody would step into the yard in the morning to watch his father mount her. The groom, Lukas, would bring Peg around and hand the reins to the captain, whose entire demeanour would soften as he stroked the animal's side, combed his fingers through her mane, all the while murmuring endearments, and always giving her a treat, a carrot, an apple. Then he'd swing up into the saddle, though before starting off he'd lean forward alongside Peg's neck, his cheek nestled against hers, and scratch her ears long and lovingly. His father and the horse would both close their eyes and young Richard would feel obliged to look away.

But he was intrigued. He began to study the horse. Every chance he got he slipped into the garrison stable and found Peg's stall. She was a grey, with a long mane and a tail that twitched ceaselessly shooing flies in the hot, humid, Caribbean afternoon. When she gicked, the dung dropped *thup, thup, thup* to the straw-strewn dirt, but this did not smell bad so much as rich and earthy. She'd swing her great head to look at Richard and, unimpressed, return to the business of eating. What was it that his father loved? Her calm, her enormous dark eyes, her way of exhaling gusts of air, that peculiar chortling noise that came from deep in her throat? Or was it her habit of lifting a hoof, then stamping it down like a petulant girl?

Moody practised these things. He nickered, stamped, exhaled, and adopted Peg's calm and sleepy-eyed demeanour. He then began exhibiting these new qualities after supper, when his father, in mufti, drank his gin on the deep porch with Richard's mother. His mother did not notice anything at first because as usual she had her head tipped back and a damp cloth across her eyes against her perpetual headache. Eventually one evening his father had had enough, folded his gazette, glared at the boy, and demanded to know what the devil he was doing. Richard chortled, Peg-style, stamped his foot, and swung his head slowly side to side.

His father said to his mother, "What's wrong with him? What's he up to?"

With great effort she raised her hand and drew the cloth from her eyes. "Are you ill, Richard?"

Richard nickered and stamped.

"Apparently he is a horse," she said.

For a moment his father said nothing. Then he said, "When I was a boy, Joe Ramps thought he was a dog. Two years he never spoke a word, only barked."

"Joe Ramps?"

"Died in Spain." Then his father raised his gazette and resumed reading while his mother closed her eyes and tilted her head back and replaced the cloth.

He ceased being a horse. But he did not cease thinking about Peg, nor did he cease slipping into the stable and staring at her. He was eight and due to begin riding lessons. How proud his father would be if he already knew how to ride, if he showed a natural aptitude, an aptitude inherited from him, so one Sunday afternoon he opened Peg's stall. Except he did not have the saddle or the blanket ready, or even know how to put them on, and Peg stepped past him and headed for the door. Richard grabbed at her tail but that was no use. He managed to cut her off by the gate but stumbled and the horse stepped on his foot, lightly, briefly, but down he went, wailing. Lukas came running. Richard's father arrived demanding explanations. He knelt by the boy and saw the state of his broken foot and called him a fool. He then told Lukas to carry him to the infirmary while he himself stayed with the mare to be sure that she was all right.

FRISADIE – 1865

FRISADIE HIKED UP THE HILL TO MOODY PARK for the Victoria Day celebration, her skirt and blouse freshly boiled and ironed, cuffs trimmed, straw hat aired and dangling a gold ribbon. She was still smarting from her treatment at the hands of Mr Bostwick and his woman—smarting but not thwarted, for there were other boarding houses, and in the meantime she was determined to be diverted by the festivities, having been given an extra hour by Mrs Frame, and allowing herself one dollar for whatever took her eye.

Moody Park spun. The trees were draped in flags and bunting and full of boys shaking the branches and yowling like monkeys. There were officers, soldiers, sailors in uniform, officials with their wives and children, people of every race and shape and age and station, all the way down to beggars and opportunists, and men so bristly, so lumbering, so rustic, so crusted with dirt that they seemed to have stepped that very morning from the forest primeval. She strolled around these groups with her hands clasped behind her back, her two half dollars wrapped in a handkerchief tucked in her sleeve, very much her own person. There was a crowd of young girls under the maypole and Frisadie noted young couples in the glory of courtship, young families aglow in the prospects of fine lives ahead, and while she was envious the day was sunny and everyone smiling and she refused, thank you very much, to crawl into the cellar hole deep in her heart and become gloomy as had been the habit of her mother. She chanted her anthem. One, two, three, you are free; four, five, six, beware of tricks; seven, eight, nine, this life is mine. Her father had taught it to her. A band struck up a march, earning shouts and applause. The scents of popped corn and grilling meat were everywhere. A volley of shots was followed by a squalling of bagpipes and more cheers as girls danced around the pole and the sun burned as bright as a new coin.

"But where is your harp?"

She turned to find herself looking down into the bearded face of a man. "Harp?"

"Do not angels play the harp?"

It was the audacious little fellow from last week. Maxie.

He plucked his hat from his head and pressed it to his heart. His hat was straw with a band of braided red cord. "I have been worrying about you."

The very idea that he, or anyone for that matter, had been thinking, much less worrying, about her was more than a little alarming even if, in truth, she had more than occasionally thought about him. This was not so very surprising given his attempt to lure her, in the plain of day no less, inside a public house. Of course that very brazenness—or was it ingenuity?—made him all the more intriguing. Who was he? One of the Grelleys? She'd noted his accent. Were the Grelleys French? *Gre-lay*? And here he was at it again. She said, "Surely the likes of Monsieur Grelley has more pressing matters."

He was shocked. "Grelley? No, no, I am not Grelley. I am Michaud. I merely work for the Grelleys. But I am hurt, for you disappeared. Into the air. Poof."

Had she poofed? "Isn't that in the nature of angels?"

His laughter revealed a mélange of teeth, straight, twisted, white, stained, and he asked her name.

"Frisadie."

"Frisadie?" He tried it like a sip of wine, testing it musingly upon his lips and tongue, which caused her another not altogether unpleasant fizz of alarm. Returning his hat to his head he adjusted it to the desired slant and then offered his arm. The cheek! He may as well have pinched her. And yet she didn't know how to gracefully refuse, not that she wished to refuse; she was not sure what she wished, perhaps simply to be left alone, but this was so very much more exciting than to be left alone, and yet what if he simply rated her—a lone brown girl—an easy mark? Whirl and walk away? Something in his eyes, however, and in the spirit of the festivities, and in the fact that she was lonely, caused her to accept, and so just like that she found herself strolling arm in arm with a man she scarcely knew. Or trying to stroll, for every few feet he was accosted in the most jovial manner by men seeking his opinion, men eager to banter, men with whom he had ongoing business, men who would begin new business, men who had news to impart, issues to discuss, or who merely winked and nodded. In the half-hour during which they perambulated, Frisadie was introduced to a dozen people, mostly men though a few ladies, none of whom failed to evaluate her and then regard Maxie anew.

Utterly out of her depth, she slid free and walked a little apart, hands once again clasped behind her back. "You are a popular one, aren't you?"

He blew air dismissively even as another set of men, rougher, drunker, called to him. Putting his hand to her elbow he steered her the other way and insisted upon treating her to a seltzer and lime, saying that this time she could not refuse.

Borne along on the wave of his bonhomie, she allowed that seltzer and lime would be most welcome.

They stopped at a cart. There was cherry and rose and anise but no lime. Maxie was devastated, his world collapsed. He put his hands to his head and lamented.

"Cherry will do nicely," she assured him.

"But are you certain?"

"Quite certain."

"We can walk on," he insisted.

How absurd he was, and how much fun. "Not at all."

"Two cherry seltzers, please, and thank you very much, maestro," sang Maxie to the vendor who, apparently familiar with Mr Michaud's antics, grinned and went to work.

Soon they were sipping their drinks and watching kilted Scotsmen hurl the caber, which bludgeoned the turf. When Maxie was spied, the officials demanded he give it a try, and he was presented, amid much laughter, with a billiard cue.

Frisadie asked if it was a celebration of the Queen or of him. He could only shrug as if baffled by all the attention. It was an hour before they completed a circuit of the festivities, and then Maxie insisted she dine with him. Terrified, she stammered that she had to work.

"Tomorrow then. Lunch."

"I'm afraid my time is not so free," she said.

"Time," he said, as if it was but a word and not a very significant one at that. He was earnest and he was perspiring, his suit of purple corduroy far too weighty for the weather. He'd have done well to visit Cran & Sons and have his beard cut and his hair shaped, but his brown eyes were as luminous as forest lakes, and he was persistent and he was well liked and he was genial and he was entertaining and above all he was as intriguing as a box to a cat, and the truth was that Mrs Frame did allow her two hours of liberty in the afternoon and she was desperate for diversion whatever form it took. She rated herself ignorant in the subject of invitations to luncheon yet felt certain that it behoved her to appear to require additional convincing.

"A little lunch," he insisted, as if the diminutive made it both less forward and more appealing. "A bite."

It occurred to her to simply ask, Why her?

He read the question in her eyes and shrugged in response. "Why not?" he asked. "Are you not an angel?"

Angel? Just what was this fellow on about? Should she remark that angels did not eat but survived upon manna? Then again was she overthinking? How tiring her brain was. "I shouldn't half enjoy that," she said.

He took her hand and kissed it, at which she nearly shouted as if it was an electric charge, even as he put his other hand upon the kiss as if to press it firmly in place. "Until tomorrow." He raised his hat and was taken up by a trio of eager gentlemen.

On the way home she scarcely heard the hisses and catcalls from the various men in the various alleys. A man had kissed her hand and the sensation of it remained hot upon her knuckles and radiated all the way up to her cheeks, and she didn't know whether to be delighted or horrified.

That evening in bed, Frisadie wondered what her mother and father would think of her accepting an invitation from a man she scarcely knew. Her mother's words dinned in her ears: *You can't trust them.* She thought back to those first days in Victoria after her father's death on the voyage. Frisadie believed that her mother's spirit, her *'uhane*, had left the body and gone to Lua-o-Milu to be with that of her husband. Frantic at being left behind, Frisadie had climbed the Garry oak in Mrs Mace's yard and, shutting her eyes, jumped, for in Hawai'i the route to the afterlife was to jump from a breadfruit tree. She landed in the roses, which saved her from broken legs, although she spent the next week in agony, trying not to touch the stinging welts and scrapes from the thorns that Mrs Mace treated with liberal dousings of tea tree oil. When she was on her feet again, Frisadie followed her mother's body about the house trying to speak to her, to call her *'uhane* back from Lua-o-Milu, but while her mother paused and looked at her and occasionally put a hand out and settled it on Frisadie's shoulder, she never spoke again.

At eight years of age, Frisadie understood that, Mrs Mace notwithstanding, she was well and truly alone. She was stricken. It was a toothache in her heart. Her feelings veered between panic and paralysis. And yet she was also inclined to order and analyze, having always kept her possessions sorted and arranged, her very thoughts in a row. She went over everything that had occurred since departing Hawai'i as if it was one of the arithmetic problems her dad used to set her. The ship had been a bark called *Cowlitz*, a vast beast of iron and wood, with more rope running in every direction than she'd ever imagined possible. Who could have designed such a thing? Who could operate it? It was populated by a tribe of sailors that her father called deck apes. They swung into the shrouds and ran out along the branchlike booms, shouting and gesturing. Frisadie had kept close to her father who enjoyed standing out on the deck watching the sailors, the deck apes, at work. Then her father had fallen ill. One morning he couldn't rise from his bunk. He turned yellow and smelled awful and then, like that, he was pronounced dead. Her mother's terror and remorse were laced with anger and resentment. She and Frisadie watched as he was carried up on a board to the deck where the captain briefly read from the Bible and then the board was tipped up and her father—the shape beneath the shroud—slid neatly into the sea with a stone tied to his feet. Frisadie imagined his suit of clothes getting soaked as he plunged down and down to stand like a sunken statue on the seabed. Afterward, the sailors seemed to regard Frisadie and her mother in a different manner, with a sort of hungry disdain and what she would later understand was a leering licentiousness.

———

The next afternoon she stood before the mirror hanging from its nail, turned her head to the left and then to the right, palpated her cheeks and brow, frowned, lifted her hair, draped it to one side, then to the other, and then forward over her shoulder. What to do? Defeated, she twisted it into a plain braid and left it that way. Taking a few steps back she appraised the full effect of her attire and couldn't honestly be very impressed. She was wearing the same skirt as yesterday though with a yellow blouse, liberally mended, and wore the same pair of shoes as yesterday—the only pair she owned—and her one hat. In short she wanted to weep. Then she gave herself a talking to. She reminded herself that it wasn't as if she had romantic notions about Maxie. How could she? She hardly knew him and besides he was old, at least thirty, short and hairy and with the face of a pug dog, and then there was his smell of brine and cigar. But what did that matter? She loved that he admired her—that through his eyes she felt attractive, good about herself. Still, she pinched the back of her hand and gave herself a scolding: What are you thinking, rendezvousing with a man you scarcely know? For all his show of manners he's got one thing on his mind and one thing only. Preying on a brown girl he rated easy picking, the filthy bugger; it was what they all thought. The nerve. It was crude and cruel and of course she wouldn't go, though she knew full well that she would.

Creeping down the stairs she listened for sounds of Mrs F, heard none, felt her pulse thumping in her throat and ears, gripped the handrail for fear of falling, then slipped out the door and walked quickly away and then slowed as she hiked up the hill to Columbia and turned right toward the Colonial. A hundred times she'd walked this street but this was the first time she'd ever been going to meet a man, a Frenchman of all things. It made everything new. Did she move differently? Were people looking at her with suspicion, did they suspect, or was she merely Mrs Frame's maid?

Maxie was waiting out front, hands behind his back, bouncing up and down on his toes. As soon as he saw Frisadie he put on a show of the deepest concern and the highest hopes and asked if she liked horsemeat.

She'd eaten it a number of times in Mrs Frame's stews and it was a little on the rank side for her tastes. Then again that could have been due to Mrs F's cooking. "I've heard it can be toothsome."

"It is a specialty of their chef. No one does such a horsemeat cutlet!" Holding the door he bowed her in.

She'd never been in a public house, had not in fact been in any sort of public eatery since leaving Victoria, and was surprised and relieved to find it so subdued, no fights under way, no chairs being thrown or beer mugs hurled or insults exchanged, only the snick of billiard balls, quiet conversation, laughter almost demure; it seemed closer to a private club than a saloon. Maxie ushered her past the lobby where, behind the counter, a man in rolled sleeves observed them.

"Thomas," said Maxie.

"Maxie," said Thomas. "So this is she."

"She this is," said Maxie.

"How comes such a fine figure of a woman to be with the stumpy likes of one such as you?" asked Thomas.

"Life is mysterious," said Maxie.

"Unceasingly," added Thomas. "Will you introduce us?"

"Thomas—Frisadie. Frisadie—Thomas. Thomas is the best of the three Grelley brothers," announced Maxie, pointedly raising his voice that any and all should hear.

"I am honoured," said Thomas, offering his cool pale hand.

"As am I," said Frisadie, then wondered if Thomas referred not to meeting her but to being rated first among the Grelleys. Thomas was thirty or forty; it was hard to tell because his moustache and eyebrows were dense with black dye, perhaps to compensate for the baldness of his skull, which was as perfect as a cue ball. The ends of his moustache extended past each side of his face, his eyes were a pale grey, and he was holding a quill over a ledger.

"Thomas tickles the books."

He twirled the quill, then produced a packet of letters, which Maxie slid into his pocket. "Maynard Link said yes. Fox Gleason is doubtful. The Dillards suggest the banks. Morris Bell wishes a word. And Brother Theodore is anxious."

"Brother Theodore is always anxious," said Maxie.

"It is the way of him," agreed Thomas.

Maxie put his hands to his head and affected dismay. "Is my name Atlas? My poor shoulders can bear no more weight. There is only one thing to do—eat!" With a flourish, he turned to Frisadie and indicated the dining room where a table was laid with white linen and gold-rimmed plates and sparkling stemware. How glitteringly regal compared with Mrs Frame's drab dining room. Maxie held her chair; no one had ever held her chair. And to think she'd contemplated not coming! Painted posts supported the painted ceiling and the walls were hung with Arcadian scenes. The floors were black and white hexagonal tiles, and potted parlour palms stood in the corners.

"What a pleasant room," was all she could come up with.

"I'd do it differently," said Maxie, frowning as if at an ongoing irritation.

"What prevents you?"

"Lack of vision."

She was confused. "Do you not see well?"

"I see just fine. It is the Grelleys who lack vision."

Frisadie looked through the archway to the lobby where Thomas was at his post behind the counter. "But you are deferred to; everyone seeks your advice."

"Yes and no. Sometimes I think they seek my advice in order to do the exact opposite."

A waiter arrived with a basket of sourdough and a jug of lemon water.

"Thank you, Felix."

Felix inclined his head in acknowledgement, then departed.

While Maxie filled Frisadie's tumbler she asked what he'd do differently. He leaned forward to share a confidence. "Get rid of the Grelley brothers."

"Thomas seems amiable."

"Thomas could stay."

"And what else would you do?"

"A separate entrance for the restaurant"—*ress-toe-rahn*—"so that families and ladies aren't forced to walk through a tavern to book a room or enjoy a meal. It makes the wrong impression, puts them off."

"Very considerate of you."

"It is business. And more billiard tables. Right now there are four; there should be eight." He frowned at the paper above the wainscotting as if at a torment that all but made his eyes bleed. "Lambs and flowers." He grimaced. "What would you suggest?"

She? He was asking her opinion? She'd often studied Mrs Frame's establishment, thinking what she'd do to improve it. She appraised the Colonial's dining room. Mr John A. Macdonald had recently vowed to spark the continent to life with hammer and steel. "Railroads. The entire dining room done over on the theme of railroads."

Maxie studied her with a dubious expression and she feared she'd disappointed him, that she was not an angel after all, and certainly not sophisticated, in fact nothing but a tedious lump of a girl, and that he'd made a mistake inviting her to lunch. "I was thinking Polynesia," he said. "Hawai'i. And you, you would be the grande dame, the hostess, the *sine qua non*."

She was confused. Simultaneously disappointed and relieved and indignant. What, he wanted her as a cigar-store Indian? "I've never been a *sine qua non*."

"Would it please you?"

"Am I to understand that you are offering me a position?"

"I would. If."

"If?"

"If these Grelleys had ears that did more than hold up their hats. New ideas are not always welcome."

Felix reappeared bearing two plates. He set one down before Frisadie and then circled around the table and set the other before Maxie. "*Bone apper-teat*," said Felix, withdrawing.

"Why, thankee, Felix me lad," sang Maxie.

"You don't sound very French, Mr Maximilian Michaud."

"The Grelleys call me Max My-chod."

"Either way."

"I 'ave de good eer. If I so desire to employ it," he added loftily.

"You're a chameleon."

"You know what we're up against with *les anglais*." He winked conspiratorially, then brushed a forefinger down the side of his nose.

Frisadie knew that the Québécois were rated well below the English, though whether they were on a par with the Italians and Greeks and Irish, or the French from France, she could not say. Where were the Scots in this? And the Slavs? Then there were the Germans. It was bewildering. They were all white, or whitish, but rated differently, on the basis of exactly what, she could not say. However, there was no secret as to where she herself stood in this hierarchy—the bottom. Yet here was Maxie all boo hoo. She nodded for she felt obliged to reassure him, just as she always tried to reassure Mrs Frame, for that was the way it went most smoothly.

"How is your cutlet?"

Her knife fairly fell through the meat. It was lean and tender and tasted of wine and pepper and something else. "Excellent."

"The secret is pig's blood. It must be sautéed in pig's blood."

"Ah."

"Fresh pig's blood," he added.

"Of course," she agreed, as if there could be any other. Then, at the risk of being thought talkative, she shared an early memory from Hawai'i—one she'd utterly forgotten until that moment—of her father killing a pig, sitting on his heels with the animal across his thighs, embracing it, speaking quietly, the blade hidden, and when the creature was calm, when it had ceased squirming and squealing, drawing the knife out and in one small motion slitting its throat, then tilting the beast to direct the spouting blood into a bowl. Maxie then favoured her with a recollection of his own, of his mother inflating a pig's bladder and rigging a small basket and netting to it and then suspending the contraption from the ceiling because he'd been so enamoured of hot-air balloons at the time.

"It would seem that the humble porker has been formative for us both," she said.

He smiled and nudged the basket of bread forward. "Du pain?"

"Merci."

Tucking a white linen napkin into his collar, he set to. He was wearing the same suit of purple corduroy and what appeared to be the same shirt. His wiry hair was parted severely in the middle, exposing a pale line of scalp, which put her in mind of an article she'd read in *The British Columbian* about medical advances in Bohemia wherein a man's skull had been sawn open and the brain exposed and a tumour removed. She shook her head to dislodge the image of a pulsing grey clockwork.

"It is not good?"

"It is exquisite!" And to prove it she forked home another morsel. "A Polynesian theme," she prompted.

He spread his arms to embrace his vision. "Coconut palms, bamboo forests, dancers in skirts of grass."

"Skirts of grass! You expect me to put on a grass skirt and dance?"

"No, no!"

"What then?"

"I don't know. It is a concept, a vision, *une idée*."

"*Une idée*? Clearly you've picked up some funny *idées* about Hawai'i and Hawaiians on your journey here," she said and looked toward the door preparing to bolt.

Maxie pleaded that he had no ideas, that it was a whim, a fancy.

"A fancy?"

"I didn't come via Hawai'i at all, but overland, on foot."

Frisadie thought she'd misheard. Not that it mattered, for either way his *idée* was his *idée*, no matter how he'd reached it. But now what was she to do, march out in a huff in the middle of the meal, laugh it off? "Are you telling me that you walked across the continent?"

For the next hour, through the cutlet, the cheese, the custard, the coffee, and the mints, Maxie recalled his twelve-hundred-mile trek from Winnipeg to New Westminster, the seas of grass, the rolling thunder of buffalo herds, the Cree majestic on their horses, summer lightning, anvil clouds, skeletons animal and human, the dry wind and hot sun, the evening rite of boot mending, the lone sound of a single shot on the far prairie, the taste of roast gopher, the scent of wild roses, the texture of bread made from ground bone, and the funerals, so many funerals. Seventeen started out and eleven arrived. "One man got it into his head to go barefoot," said Maxie. "He walked with his boots on his hands, clapping them together, clunk, clunk, in time to the song we were singing. We were always singing. Maybe the snake didn't like our song and so bit him to shut him up, or he stepped on it. Either way, we lay the fellow in the ox cart. Our opium had already been used up so it was a loud death, and slow, nine, maybe ten days. We plugged our ears with wax, like Odysseus." Maxie was downcast at the memory. "And since then you've been with the Grelley brothers," she prompted.

"No, I had a café upriver serving the gold miners. Chez Maxie." He affected to shrug at the absurdity but was clearly defiant and proud. The clock tolling four interrupted them and Maxie bunted himself on the brow with the heel of his hand. "Me, me, me! You see, it's what I do, it's why I'm here, to talk. But not a question about you!"

"Me?" What could she have said to match his tales? "I'm afraid I have to go," she said, "though I've enjoyed myself immensely." Which for the most part she had.

"But it's early."

"I have my duties."

He came around the table and offered his elbow and walked her out. En route to the door they passed a discarded copy of *The British Columbian* lying on a table. It was open to the advertisement for the sale of Bostwick's Boarding House. Frisadie's mind leapt to a vision of Mr Bostwick's face if she returned with Maxie, how his tune would change. But what did Maxie want with a boarding house? What, after all, was a boarding house but a hotel in small—reduced in every way, no liquor, no billiards, no crowds, no music? No, she thought, Maxie needed a hotel, his own stage upon which to perform, and there, above the ad for Bostwick's, was an announcement for the sale of the New Brighton Hotel. Frisadie had heard of New Brighton, a holiday spot ten miles north of New Westminster on the Burrard Inlet. She paused and made a bit of a performance of looking at it. Maxie stepped closer to see what had caught her interest and she pointed it out to him, as if to say, Well, well, ask and ye shall receive. He looked away and said he knew. When she observed that he could realize his vision, he put his hands in his pockets and shrugged and said, "But for the small detail of money."

The saloon had become livelier with the in-tide of working men. Many lobbed remarks to Maxie and brazenly eyed Frisadie. Two dandyish fellows in checked suits appeared one on either side of him and set to pounding his back and chattering in French. Maxie moved Frisadie on past and she was relieved to step out onto the boardwalk. The sun had inclined to the west and the light had taken on a richer hue with the ebbing of the afternoon. Chat, so easy for the past hours, became awkward. Maxie seemed suddenly haggard and she, feeling foolish and frightened, tired and out of her depth, thanked him once again and hurried off.

That evening she stumbled through her work, alternately exhilarated and then disappointed. Maxie's Polynesian theme was interesting, but was that all she was, a part of his business vision, a player in a tableau, a coloured skin? Why was she surprised?

The next afternoon Mrs Frame sent her to the market. It had rained but the May sun returned to set trees glittering, boardwalks steaming, and transformed the puddles to mirrors. How rich the air smelled. The market vegetables were firm, the corridors between the stalls earthy and ripe and cheerful; in the myriad sensations she forgot herself and her spirits floated. Yet when she got back, Mrs Frame was waiting in the dining room looking dour even by her usual standard.

"Frisdadie. Join me if you've a moment."

She had many tones of voice, all variations upon the theme of disapproval, and this one bespoke a muted rage that filled her with dread. Mrs Frame made a point of shutting the door even though they were the only two home. She faced the girl and crossed her arms over her lamentable bosom. She wore her standard outfit, a white blouse with frayed cuffs, the neck tight about her creased throat, stained apron over a grey skirt, her hair as ever twisted in a tight bun at the back of her skull, drawing her eyes taut. "Have I treated you well, Frisdadie?"

"Yes, Mrs Frame."

"I see. Or rather I don't see. For I've had a visitor," she said. "Lucinda Bostwick. It seems you've been making inquiries."

Frisadie opened her mouth, but having no excuse or explanation that would mollify Mrs F's indignation, she closed it and looked down and prepared for the worst.

"Two years ago you show up at my door and I take you in. I offer you advice and protection. I feed you and pay you a wage. I should send you on your way, missy."

Frisadie clenched her jaw, upper and lower teeth fitting like a leghold trap, and fought not to squirm.

"Shouldn't I."

Frisadie did not necessarily agree yet nodded that indeed she should.

Mrs Frame drew in a long dry breath and changed tacks. "And just where did the likes of you expect to get the money to buy a boarding house? Max My-chod?" She snorted and shook her head. "A Frog. I'm disappointed. I am. Not half-disappointed. Though maybe for you it's a step up. Well, if your position here don't suit, then fine, you can leave toot sweet. If not, you can stay on—with a twenty-five percent cut in wage—until I find someone with more gratitude, someone who don't go mooching about in the afternoons, which shouldn't be too hard."

FANNIN - 1886

HENRY WOKE TO THE ROLLING ROAR OF hard wheels on a fir floor. Lying in the dark he admired the resonance, which, even at half a furlong, caused such a satisfying sensation throughout his skull. He was lying on his bench beneath a horsehide coat lined with sheep's wool. The bench was a slab of Douglas fir that served as a good corrective for the curvature of his spine, which was apt to cause stabbing pains in his hips and neck. In the throes of such spasms he'd lie panting on the slab and recall the *Stalwart*, in which he'd come up the coast, whose cables and timbers had groaned and strained like the rigging of his own body. Along with the sound of wheels on wood he heard the ringing of frogs and the small heave and slap of waves, as well as a breeze stirring in the newly leafed maples. Isolating sounds had become a means of diverting himself from pain. His many books on mesmerism had advised this. *Put your mind somewhere else*, as if his mind were a hat that he might remove at will, and sometimes it worked. If he put his mind to it, if he bore down on the task, his mind could, if only briefly, trick itself into looking the other way.

He sat up with the care of one uprighting a vase. Light-headedness sluiced his skull and he waited for it to settle, found his lucifers, scraped one against the sandpaper strip on the box and lit his oil lamp, and saw by his watch that it was gone 4:00 AM.

The eyes of his animals gleamed with a preternatural brightness. He'd had their glass eyeballs sent up to Victoria and then across to New Brighton from Germany via San Francisco, but it was not only the quality of the glass, but the fact that he put a piece of lodestone in each creature's skull. Henry's business was still small, but all who saw his work remarked upon the animation of his animals and the lustre of their eyes. His was an art dating to the pharoahs, and if his clothes smelled of fur and feathers and formaldehyde he rated it a mark of distinction no less honourable than that of the incense pervading a priest's robe. His menagerie included the head of a noble black-tailed deer and one of a snarling cougar. There was also a river otter, a raven, a pileated woodpecker, a pair of whiskey jacks, and his ducks.

In the five years since leaving London he had crossed the Atlantic and then the United States and approached every embalming parlour en route. At Roswell's in Brooklyn he had foolishly announced his theory about putting lodestones in the subjects and was laughed out the door. Burnett's in Chicago had taken him on and yet it soon became clear that he would never be allowed to do more than swab floors and sluice drains. When he quit he was relieved that he had discovered enough discretion to have kept his ideas regarding magnetism to himself. In Sacramento a man called Gillings had taken him on but then proceeded to make unnatural advances. In San Francisco he found work in taxidermy. Admittedly, this was embalming's poorer cousin, yet it shared many techniques and he learned to respect it. He stuffed foxes and wolves and eagles, and he might well have stayed in San Francisco, for he liked the hills and the sea and Chinatown and the coming and going of ships, but the tide of people flowing north to British Columbia, the Queen's domain, a bit of England on the Pacific, swept him along.

Seated cross-legged on his bench in his stump house, Henry listened to the swirling sound of rolling wheels. "Mr Black," he said aloud, and considered what a deeply troubled man was the Laird of New Brighton to be roller skating at such an hour. Henry looked to his collection of magnets and lodestones in the glass-fronted cabinet, for he believed that in magnetism there lay an answer to both Black's dilemma and his own. He'd become a student of Franz Mesmer and Maximilian Hell, pioneers in the field of magnetism's wide-ranging effects on the human mind and heart. In the cabinet were four tin hearts, and the lodestones that would fit inside them, wanting only another few days' work to complete. He was putting his faith in them to draw love back into both his life and that of George Black.

He picked up *The Mighty Curative Powers of Mesmerism* from his night table and opened it to a drawing of a fiercely frowning Franz Mesmer, hair and cravat awry, hands raised in a gesture of incantation. The preface spoke of Mesmer's early life and influences, his interest in astronomy and medicine, culminating in his theory of animal magnetism, viz. that there existed a vitalizing energy that communicated between all things both animate and inanimate, and that the skilled practitioner could focus and direct it.

The Monks of the Eastern Orthodox Church, the Singers of Gregorian chant, the Yogins of Hindostan, the Priests of

Tokio, the Indians of New Mexico, from Antiquity unto the Present, all were and still are Adepts at primitive forms of Mesmerism, utilizing both Sound and Gesture in Hieratic Formulas intended to Induce a State of Receptivity.

Receptivity. Setting the book aside, Henry swung his legs down and his bare feet pressed the floor that was simultaneously gritty with beach sand and felted with animal hair. He unbuckled his Heidelberg Electric Belt, stepped out of it and placed it in the cabinet, then rubbed at the red indentations it always left in his hips and thighs and buttocks. He pulled on his denim pants and looped the suspenders over his shoulders and then tugged his boots onto his bare feet. They were good boots; he'd made them himself.

He tugged the peg from its slot and the door drifted open. It was damp and cool in the pre-dawn, it having been a wet April and so far a drizzly May, and at the moment there were both stars and clouds, and a small breeze meandering up the inlet. As always the air smelled of woodsmoke, dried fish, pig shit, and, it being spring, sap. His stump stood high up the slope and had a view of the lights of the sawmill half a mile across the water of Burrard Inlet, while off to his right stood Black's roller skating hall beneath a quarter moon. Carrying his oil lamp, Henry angled his way through the trees across the slope, the frogs falling silent as he approached and resuming their ringing as he passed. The circling roar grew clearer. The hall had been built as a barn, then Black laid down inch-thick fir planks sprung with horsehair and began using it as a dance hall and banquet room and most recently as a roller skating palace.

The sliding door was open. Even as Henry stepped in he had trouble believing what he saw, or rather what he did not see: Black was roller skating in the dark, without so much as a lamp or a candle. Remaining near the entrance, Henry listened while his eyes adjusted. The wheels rolled like stones in a barrel, rumbling low and relentless, as though they had been travelling through the ages, from the past to the future via the present, across steppe and prairie and desert with no destination other than the pure pursuit of speed and distance, and it seemed that the wheels travelled in blindness, as though guided by some other means beyond the ken of Man. Henry had seen blind men tapping along the lanes of London and New York and Chicago and San Francisco, their sticks bobbing like the antennae of beetles, yet even the most confident moved slowly; Black sped, drawn as though by a magnet. Henry heard him cross-stepping into the far turn, skates tapping and scraping and the sound changing as he swung hard around the bend and came plunging toward him. He held the lamp high to be sure Black saw him.

"Henry!"

"George . . ."

Black loomed up out of the dark and shot past in a rush. The noise of the wheels receded to the right and then warped as Black leaned once more into a turn. Eyes adjusting, Henry now discerned Black's gliding shape and imagined a ghost rider, an enigmatic Hermes bearing a message from the Afterworld, or perhaps from the past, from out of the night, and envisioned an entire flock of such messengers hieing through space and time. He found a seat on one of the benches, blew out his lamp, and then leaned his head back against the wall so that the vibration of Black's skates shivered up through his feet, through his pelvis, and up his spine into his skull. He placed his palms flat on the bench on either side of him, shut his eyes, and listened to the wheels rolling around the rim of the hall. When he opened his eyes the hall was a shade brighter, for dawn was approaching and it revealed Black skating backwards in a crouch, one leg out like a Russian dancer.

"You don't think it dangerous? I mean, in the dark?" asked Henry when Black hove to and joined him on the bench.

"Not a jot." Black drew a flask like a card from an inner pocket and for a while they passed the rum, savouring its sweet corrosion in their mouths.

"I miss my girls, Henry. They had lovely warm hands."

Henry felt his eyes simmer with tears. He swirled the last of the rum in the flask, pretended to drink, and then passed Black the final swig. Henry missed them too. Or one of them: Leonora.

Fifteen months earlier Henry had walked into Sanderson's Gunsmith & Metalworks on Carrall Street in Granville intending to purchase magnets. A well-dressed young man no older than Henry himself was studying the pistols, weighing one, then another, spinning the chamber, holding each at arm's length and closing an eye. Satisfied, he placed his choice on the pitted wood counter, a fine weapon with a carved grip and gleaming barrel, and began unfolding notes from a skilfully crafted wallet of oxblood leatherette. He asked for a box of bullets and then invited the proprietor to keep the change, which brought a wide smile to his clean-shaven face. Loading the pistol, the young man raised it to his ear as though to admire the sound of the mechanism, and then calmly, with an expression approaching relief on his handsome though drawn face—the expression of one sighing into a hot bath, not an experience Henry often had and therefore all the more notable—he pressed the barrel to his temple and without word or hesitation pulled the trigger. An instant later his brains and blood were running from the wall and dripping from the ceiling, and the proprietor was no longer smiling.

As for Henry, he backed his way out of the shop and into the street where men and women in rain gear darted about their business in the racketing downpour, which had apparently muffled the shot. Henry looked at the door of Sanderson's, wondering if he had dreamed it all, wondering if, were he to open that door and step back in, nothing would be out of the ordinary. The rain battered his bowler, muddling his thoughts. It ran down his ears and his cheeks and it was only because some drops were hot and tasted of salt and something else that he realized he not only was sobbing but had blood and brains on him.

The shop door opened. The clerk stepped out but stayed under the eave. Frowning, he lit his pipe, puffed until the bowl was glowing, then looked at Henry and spat into the mud and shook his head, then spat once again. He said, "I should've sussed the fellow was touched. I've seen it before and I should've known. Now I got one helluva mess to scrub."

"Does it happen often, then?"

He puffed his pipe and Henry smelled the scent of rum-cured Virginia. "Twice. But they had the common courtesy to go off down the beach."

It had already been a day of some drama for Henry. Until that morning he had resided in the West End boarding house of a Mrs Brille, who had a daughter called Eliza. This young woman had taken a fancy to Henry in spite of—or perhaps emboldened by—his curved spine, because she herself had a humped back. It was not a massive hump, it did not dominate her appearance, and a clever arrangement of her abundant chestnut hair could obscure it, just as Henry, with a little mustering of his fibre, could stand as straight as any man. Eliza had impish eyes and a sensuous mouth and a porcelain complexion and was accomplished in French. Discovering that Henry was in fact rather well read, and intrigued by the Napoleon III beard that he'd begun sporting, she'd invited him to admire her copy of *Gargantua and Pantagruel* illustrated by Gustave Doré.

Henry had expected her to bring the volume down to the parlour. Instead, she invited him to follow her up the stairs into her room. It was mid-week and he knew that Eliza's mother was out, and so, drawn by her hair, her scent, her complexion, her fulsome bosom, and her swaying hips, as well as the frank glance she gave him over her shoulder, he eagerly obliged. Her room was on the third floor, southwest corner, with a tinted oriel window and a vast brass four-poster bed with a burgundy canopy and curtains.

When he asked where the book was she said, "Book? Why, the book is there," and nodded to the shelf. "But first you might admire these." And unbuttoning her blouse she showed him a sight far more enticing than *Gargantua and Pantagruel*, and soon Henry and Eliza were in the brass bed making the beast with two misshapen backs.

Eliza's mother spent three afternoons per week lunching with members of the Women's Relief Society, and on each of these days at each of those times Henry and Eliza went to her room, though never once did they look at *Gargantua and Pantagruel*.

August and September passed. Eliza's room was a kaleidoscope of tinted sunlight in the afternoon, and Henry would stretch and yawn amid the tangle of Egyptian cotton sheets while Eliza planned his future: he would go into the law, or business, or politics, or perhaps even the clergy, for she'd noted that he was a decidedly introspective fellow. Eliza's mother, seeing what was under way, did not intervene because she judged Henry Fannin to be a mild and studious young man with a large potential ready for the shaping. Neither mother nor daughter perceived that while Henry's spine was curved, it nonetheless possessed a tensile strength after the fashion of a hunting bow, whose very power comes from its shape and sinew. He had no interest in business or law or politics, and certainly not in the Church of England. Embalming, on the other hand, was an open field. To preserve the body was to preserve not only the form but, given Henry's work with lodestones, perhaps a spark of the spirit. Or such was the aim of his ongoing research. When he expressed this to Eliza and her mother, they grew alarmed. If he was interested in life everlasting, why was he so dead set against the church? For there was plenty of life everlasting to go around in the C of E, and ample opportunity to conduct funerals if this rather singular interest in the dead so engaged him. Henry did not see himself as a sermonizer, and the prospect of Sunday mornings putting on a frilled robe and mounting a pulpit made him feel absurd. Eliza and her mother were patient. They smiled. Men were children. They rarely knew what was best for them. A little time would tell. But the summer passed and the maples began to turn yellow and then red and then the leaves fell and the rains began and Eliza decided that Henry's time was up; having tasted of the cream, he must now purchase the cow.

"Henry."

He was sitting cross-legged in Eliza's bed. Ignoring her severe tone, he smoothed the sheet and arranged an array of her pins and barrettes and teasingly held a horseshoe magnet above them; each time he did, one or more pieces leapt to the magnet and a small gasp of joy escaped him. As wide-eyed as a child, he invited her to share his wonder.

"I've seen your toys, thank you very much."

He leaned closer as a safety pin hopped bug-like and attached itself to the magnet. "Fantastic," he whispered.

"Henry."

"There is a law at work here. Something fundamental. Something universal. And by the way, they are not toys."

She reminded him that he was twenty years old, and when he reminded her that magnetism was a primal force of nature, she asked him if he could make money with it.

"Money," he said, as if at a comical topic more suited to the panto. "Did I ever tell you about the money that fell from the sky?"

"Yes."

"It was in New York City. My very first day."

"You told me."

"Wandering along."

"Henry."

"And suddenly coins came raining down, pinging on the concrete."

"They were thrown, Henry. Or fell."

"Until I can get a position with an embalmer I can earn a living in taxidermy. It's a solid vocation and I'm the best. In fact," he said, in a rare display of bravado, "I don't think I am going too far to state that I am a bit of a magician."

"Corpses."

"Life."

Eliza strode forward and, snatching the bedsheet with both hands, shook it, scattering metal across the room. Then she tossed his horseshoe magnet out the window. With a cry, he ran naked to the ledge and looked out and then turned and stared in horror at Eliza, who was wearing her yellow robe, her splendid hair rippling to her hips, her equally splendid bosom heaving, her face red, her eyes swollen, chin hard. In a tone beseeching him to understand, she said, "Can't you see I'm trying to help you? Dead animals are disgusting and magnets silly."

He knew that she believed what she said, and that something solid was on offer, a path, a life, a way in the world, and that years from now they might both look back and laugh at his immaturity, even as they sipped their lemon squash on the veranda and watched their grandchildren gambol about the lawn. He knew that he was a nothing from nowhere and that it was obvious what he must do, what any sane man would do, what his father and mother were undoubtedly urging him to do even as they looked on from the other world: grow up and take this opportunity and get on with a proper life. What he did, however, was shout that the magnet had cost him fifty cents. Getting dressed, he ran out and searched the bushes below her window with no luck even as she leaned out and called to him. Looking up, he said he was going to Sanderson's to buy another.

———————

Stunned at the suicide in Sanderson's, Henry wandered aimlessly and narrowly missed being run down by a milk wagon in spite of the clatter of the horses' hooves, the jingling of the harness, and the shouts of the driver. The rain had eased and a chill wind tore the clouds, revealing streaks of blue. Hunching his shoulders and clenching his fists in his coat pockets, he walked the wood-brick streets with two questions dogging him. What could possibly have driven that fellow to such an act? And more intriguingly what was to become of his corpse, most especially the remnants of his skull? Even now it was likely en route in the ambulance to McKeen's Funeral Parlour where the artists would face the mighty challenge of reconstruction. Henry had presented himself at McKeen's when he'd first arrived and heard the usual story: it was a family business.

When he'd somewhat recovered from the shock of witnessing a suicide, Henry returned to the boarding house but found the door locked. He tossed pebbles at Eliza's window and called her name until it opened and his satchel thudded to the sodden ground.

"Eliza!"

An arm thrust the curtain shut.

Henry spent the night by the fire of a Native man who asked him why he'd come all the way around the world just to sit there by the fire with him. Henry did not wish to be contrary, but in point of fact he'd not come all the way around the world just to sit by the fire with him. He didn't even know him. The man poked at the fire with a branch and for a moment Henry was confused, thinking that perhaps he really had come all this way to sit here, that perhaps the fellow had been waiting for him and Henry had been tardy. Then the man chuckled and Henry understood that he was having him on. In the firelight he seemed old. His hair was long and silver and hung in two braids and he glinted with metal necklaces and polished seashells.

"It must have been pretty bad where you're from to travel all this way."

Henry had to think about that. His father dying had been bad. The Barnardo Home hadn't been good.

"What are your plans?"

Henry explained about embalming.

The old man nodded deeply and listened intently. "I'll be put in a tree so the birds can carry me on up to the sky."

Now Henry nodded deeply and listened intently. This was similar to the practices of the Parsi.

"So you travelled all this way to preserve the dead."

Henry wouldn't have put it quite that way.

"Going to be a lot of stiffs. Where will you put them?"

"Crypts, mausoleums, cemeteries."

"That's a lot of crypts, mausoleums, and cemeteries."

Once again Henry was not sure how to respond.

"There money in it?"

"I view it as more of a calling. An art, if you will."

"There's no money in art." He said this with such quiet conviction that Henry was compelled to ask him if he was an artist, and the man exhaled long and then shrugged in a pantomime manner that could only be interpreted as a yes.

The next day, under a clear sky and blustery wind, Henry wandered east along the shore of Burrard Inlet, no clear idea where he was headed, nodding to the tenants of shacks and tents who glared half-feral from bearded faces, suspicious that he intended mischief. It was low tide and the rocky beach seethed with scuttling crabs. An otter slunk into a gap and gulls rose crying at Henry's approach. He was a fool and he knew it, and yet if he felt depressed he also felt free. It occurred to him to return to San Francisco, or go farther south, perhaps New Zealand or Australia. Ships loaded with lumber in Moodyville on the north shore of the inlet regularly departed for Australia.

At dusk he discovered that he'd inadvertently reached New Brighton. He'd heard of it and of Black's Hotel but never visited. There it stood, two floors with balconies, as well as a fish-drying concern and a barn and some shacks, a wharf, a stream, and a great deal of mud. There also appeared to be a crisis, with much coming and going from the hotel, and a distraught female voice keening inconsolably.

The drizzle had resumed. Wet and cold and tired and hungry, he took refuge beneath the hotel balcony in spite of a dank and musky odour. He hugged himself in the chill and grew nostalgic about Eliza's bed and even had second thoughts about a career as a man of God. Perhaps she and her mother were right. Was he not already dabbling with the very essence of life and death with his notions of magnets in bodies? Was the priesthood so very far removed? The dank and musky odour seemed to be accompanied by a heavy breathing. Some drunken dosser? He was considering slipping into the barn for the night when a man stepped out onto the porch and leaned on the railing and let his head hang. He was tall and bearded and about forty though in the gloom it was difficult to say more. Henry stood very still, not sure whether to speak or hide. Then the man raised his head as if sensing a presence and seemed about to discover Henry, who decided it was best to take the initiative and declare himself.

"Good evening, sir."

The man did not respond right away but stood rigid as if he hadn't yet decided how he ought to react, and Henry wondered if he'd have done better to have withdrawn in silence to the deeper shadows. "I fear it is not really a good evening at all," said the man. "Though I thank you." His low voice bespoke strength and gravity. "No," he went on, peering at Henry, who stood below on the grass, "not a good evening in any way, shape, or form, I am afraid."

Henry admitted that he'd heard the crying.

"My daughter," said the man. "Her fiancé has . . . has died." And then he added, "By his own hand."

"Today?"

"Yesterday."

Henry gripped the post at the foot of the stairs to steady himself and thought of the scene he'd witnessed the previous day. What strange fate was this? "Tragic."

They stood for what seemed an eternity in the rain until at last the man gathered himself and said that he had no rooms to offer. "But there is the stump." He pointed up the slope toward the silhouetted trees. "It's actually quite comfortable. Would you be staying long?"

"Possibly. I don't know." He was not flush with money. "A stump?" Henry squinted in the direction he'd pointed and saw only a vague dark shape.

Now the man introduced himself. "Black. George Black."

"The Laird of New Brighton."

"The same. The door is open. Make yourself at home."

"It has a door?"

"And much else. Only take care if you are wont to wander at night," said Black. "It wouldn't do to surprise Lydia. She is old and doesn't take well to sudden movements."

"Lydia?"

"My bear."

"Is she not chained then?"

"Yes, but it is a long chain. She is just here."

Henry peered about beneath the porch and discovered not ten yards off two darkly gleaming eyes and heard again the sound of snuffly breathing. A renewed wail from within the hotel snapped Black around and he stepped toward the door.

"Thank you," said Henry. "And I'm sorry." But Black was gone.

Henry did not like the idea of a bear, even if it was chained, and so, skirting wide around the porch, he hiked off up the grassy slope and found the stump. The oval door resembled a cave entrance. He lifted the latch and, groping about the darkness, discovered candle stubs and lucifers. As he lit the wicks the flames swam up the coved walls like anxious souls, but Black was right, it was a good stump, with shelves and nooks and ledges carved right into the wood, round windows fitted with glass, a plank floor, and a square of flagstones beneath a stove with a flue rising up through the high dark ceiling. The walls had been adzed smooth and smelled of pitch. There was a slab table and a pair of bentwood chairs tipped onto their forelegs against the table on which sat a white jug and ewer and a glazed vase of dried grasses. Henry hung his bowler on a peg and sat looking around his new home, thinking of how that sounded, his new home, and thinking of Eliza and of the fellow who shot himself and the young lady down the way cast into the depths of mourning, and what a strange coincidence it was that he should have come here of all places, for surely the two suicides were the same—how many suicides occurred each day thereabouts unless such acts of despair were common on the margins of empire?—and it seemed that it behoved him to tell what he had witnessed, but he did not know if he was up to it, not at that moment at any rate, or if it was the wise thing to do, which raised the question that what was right was not necessarily wise, so he remained in his chair and listened to the night and heard only the wind in the trees and the waves on the shore and the occasional wail of mourning.

———

Autumn seemed appropriate with its intimations of death. In January New Brighton was all but isolated from the world by deep snow. The boat from Moodyville and Granville touched Black's dock but few passengers stepped on or off; only the seals and otters went about their business unbothered, sliding in and out of the water while tree branches brittle with cold cracked like gunshots and dropped under their burdens of white.

Henry was busy. Within days of moving into the stump he'd got in a stock of hide, and his first commission was a pair of English-style riding boots for Black in exchange for a month's rent. He also repaired a set of Louis heels for Mrs Black and a pair of button boots for Leonora, their grieving daughter, whom he had yet to see except at a distance. Thanks to Black, Henry's name was getting around. Moodyville mill workers began sending their boots across with the ferryman and Henry mended them and sent them back by boat. Officers and seamen from the ships at the Moodyville wharf also began sending their shoes across, and Henry was soon obliged to pay the ferryman a percentage for acting the middleman. The smell of leather filled the stump, complementing the spice of sap. Cobbling was satisfying in its way and it earned him money, which was good, but it was not his first or even his second love.

Each morning and afternoon, regardless of the weather, he made a point of walking an hour along the trails for the sake of his spine. Black too walked, with Lydia. She was large and black and shambling, stank, and was fitted with a strap-iron muzzle, Black explaining that she had become cranky with age and that he never used to employ a muzzle but she'd begun eating the guests' dogs, which had proven bad for business. When man and bear were not out walking, Lydia snored under the balcony and seemed content enough on a diet of fish heads and pork bones. Putting his arm around Lydia's neck, Black rubbed her ears and the beast moaned with such a peculiarly lamenting tone that Henry could well believe she was a woman from a myth condemned to the shape of an animal for having angered a petulant god.

"How old is Lydia?"

"Perhaps twenty or twenty-five. She is a very great lady. You can stroke her if you please," offered Black.

Fearing that it would be judged an insult as well as cowardly to decline such an invitation, Henry pressed his fingers into the bear's thick rank fur and gave her just enough of a rub so as not to appear effete, and wondered what it said about him that he preferred his animals dead. Whenever Henry saw the bear he thought only of what an undertaking it would be to preserve her. She'd require a lodestone the size of a cannonball. Visions of Mary Shelley's monster reared in his mind and he wondered if it might not be wiser in some such cases to skip the magnet and thereby avoid altogether the risk of drawing the life force back into her. Or was this unfair? Was not Frankenstein's monster just as much a victim as a beast?

If the tide was low Henry walked along the shore, a veritable highway of sand that was full of treasures. Occasionally he met Native women clamming and they stopped their work and stared in silence, and, depending upon his mood, Henry would sweep his bowler from his head and offer a deep bow, which might earn him a smile. Then again it might get him cool disapproval. Or no reaction at all. One woman in particular seemed to find him absurd, and she'd lean to talk to her associate, who would nod, then shake her head, and for the remainder of his outing Henry would puzzle over what they must think of him collecting dead animals and, of course, wondered what they must think of a stranger, a white man, appearing in their midst, with no invitation and precious little knowledge of where he was or who they were. During his many months convalescing in the Barnardo Home he'd read many extollations of the British Empire detailing its virtues and glories and the superiority of the English above all other men past or present, and thus the rightness and inevitability that they should be pre-eminent the world over. Where, how, or if he fitted into such a pre-eminence he did not know.

It was on one such stroll along the shore that he found the owl. He knelt on the sand and studied it: a barred owl, the feathers pearly in colour with tan tips and striping, a small yellowish hooked beak, large round flattish face, a thick neck as though wearing a hood, rather elegant colouring about the brows, as though drawn by a lady meaning to bring attention to her features. The bird was fully three feet from tail to head, and Henry carefully thumbed open one of the eyes, discovering it to be big, brown, and intelligent, and for a moment he almost expected it to blink and speak to him in a resonant voice on subjects eternal. Cradling the great bird in his arms, he carried it back to his stump. He had worked on birds in San Francisco and now he applied his skills to the owl. This was to be the first in his collection. The creatures he had "filled" previously had all been for others; this owl, however, was his. He prepared a hollow plaster mould, then took her to the ice-works in Granville to keep her fresh until he could order up a stock of fluid and a set of eyes. When they arrived, he retrieved the frozen bird and with a freshly sharpened knife removed her skin, hollowed out the head with a teaspoon, removed the tongue and the eyes, and then sank her into a blend of alcohol, arsenic, and borax and left her for three days, after which he fitted the eyes and then positioned a small lodestone in her skull, arranged her over the model, and, lastly, sewed her shut, arranging her feathers to hide the stitching. He gave her pride of place on a ledge from which she looked down like an oracle.

Over the following days he never passed the owl without pausing to study her eyes. Was there a glimmer of slowly widening consciousness? Was she watching him? Perhaps she would communicate with him via dreams? He lay a pencil and paper by his bed so as to record any messages. Next he found a young otter washed up on the beach. The circling birds told him it was there before he reached it. The predators had been at it, though Henry could still appreciate the remains of its sleek black fur, needle teeth, formidable paws, and short stout whip of a tail, even if the eyes were gone. He took it home. Then he found a red-tailed hawk. By spring he'd added a raccoon and a mink, all filled and mounted, each fitted with a lodestone in its skull.

One morning Black popped in, leaving Lydia outside nosing a rotting log. The laird was carrying a field hockey stick, holding it across his shoulders and doing twists to the left and then to the right, and was bemused and impressed with Henry's workmanship. "You trap the buggers and then pickle them."

Henry was not a little appalled. Gently he corrected Black, explaining that he walked and he found them, that is to say they *presented* themselves.

Black considered young Henry Fannin, an innocent enough chap, talented in his way and earnest to a fault, his broad cockney accent and wide blinking eyes giving him an ingenuously endearing quality. "They look almost alive," he said, stepping closer and peering into the eyes of the owl.

This excited Henry, for here was the unbiased opinion he'd been seeking. He hadn't told anyone about his use of lodestones, having learned that most regarded magnetism as bunk. He rated George Black a pragmatic man, kind, generous, sincere, but no great intellectual and certainly no mystic, a man more of the body than of the mind. A sportsman, Black raced horses, played field hockey, football, rugger, and cricket, ran sprints, put the shot, enjoyed archery, hosted Sports Day each year on the first Sunday after the summer solstice, and held fortnightly roller skating regattas for the children at which he supplied the skates and treats.

"Do you roller skate?" asked Black.

"I have never roller skated," admitted Henry.

"I tried teaching Lydia when she was younger and more agile but it was no go." Together they considered the bear, which had found grubs. "Leonora is very talented on the skates. Or was." He fell silent as if he'd stepped into a chasm. "She could teach you," said Black slowly, his voice rising and eyes kindling. "It might be good for her. A diversion."

Henry was excited but fearful, for while he was more than a little intrigued by the tragic and beautiful Leonora Black, he wasn't athletic and dreaded appearing clumsy.

"Yes," said Black, liking the sound of it. "I'll talk to her. Come along, old girl," he said to Lydia and went off swinging his field hockey stick, decapitating dandelions.

Henry had yet to have a conversation with Leonora, though he had seen her often. She was tall, like both her parents, slim to the point of asceticism, with long dark hair, and she walked with somewhat rounded shoulders, which he put down to her burden of mourning. With the improvement in the weather she was out and about more, though she never seemed to venture far, often just standing on the porch and staring out over the inlet or up the slope to the stagecoach terminus as if expecting the return of her fiancé from the land of the dead.

While Henry had yet to have an actual conversation with Leonora Black, it did not mean that he hadn't had imaginary ones. This wasn't unusual for him. He often talked to his stuffed animals, greeting his seals and otters and hawks in the morning when he woke and upon his return to his stump when he'd been out. He found his raccoon, Liam, a particularly good listener and often kept up a monologue of his ever-evolving ideas for Liam's benefit. It was inevitable that he talk to a live person even if she wasn't there in the flesh. Sometimes he regaled Leonora with tales of his travels across the continent and at others with his theories about magnetism, which she embraced with greater enthusiasm than had Eliza. As for any amorous visions, in spite of his experiences with Eliza, Henry was too much of a gentleman to advance beyond veils and mists.

When Black had wandered off whacking dandelions, Henry closed the door and considered his animals, his equipment spread on the worktable-cum-bed, and his stove. It was not yet noon and the warm sun poured through his windows, one of which he had enlarged to give him a view and more light by which to work and read. He continued to read widely, his books and magazines and gazettes filling a shelf next to his magnets. His devotion to magnetism had evolved. He had begun to wonder if he could draw the spirits of his mother and father back to life, or to some form of communication. So far his experiments had failed, yet he remained optimistic. One of the problems was that he did not have any personal items, ideally metal, that had been worn by them, which hindered his efforts. Placing lodestones in his animals was a form of research. He had lodestones sent all the way from Australia, renowned for their natural properties, as well as lodestones from Greece and China, and what he could say for certain was that they affected his dreams. When he strapped on his Heidelberg Electric Belt each night and arranged magnets at each corner of his bench and one on his chest directly over his heart, he dreamed vividly of the creatures he had preserved, seeing the world through their eyes, soaring with the birds, hunting with the raccoon, swimming with the otter. This enthused and inspired him.

The morning after Black suggested that Leonora might benefit from coaching Henry in roller skating, a note appeared under his door. A mere slip of folded paper but one as bright as a flame, it was the first thing he saw when he sat up and swung his legs down from his bench. Still wearing his Heidelberg Electric Belt, which fit like an iron diaper, he hobbled to the door and unfolded the note.

Dear Mr Fannin,

Forgive this intrusion, but my father claims that it is one of your lifelong dreams to learn the art of roller skating. If this is indeed the case, I will be at the rink this mid-morning at eleven, as I will be each morning for the remainder of the week. Do feel free to join me.

Yours,
Leonora Black

MOODY - 1859

FRASER RIVER

"I LIKE HANGING MEN IN WINTER. Their necks snap rather than stretch. Quick and clean. Less mess and much more satisfying."

Moody regarded Judge Matthew Baillie Begbie sitting next to him in the lounge of the Hudson's Bay Company steamer *Beaver*. They were chugging upriver toward the goldfields, to interview Ned McGowan as part of their investigation of the murder of one Peter Brunton Whannell. New Westminster was behind them and the banks on either side black but for the occasional fire all the more tenuous for the depths of the surrounding dark. Moody had boarded the night before in Victoria; Begbie had joined an hour ago in New Westminster.

Begbie was taller than Governor Douglas, though slimmer, with a granite goatee and wavy silver-grey hair. He was a dandy, wore a fur-trimmed burgundy cloak and beige kid gloves over the fingers of which he had slid various silver and gold rings, while his high black boots were polished to black glass. Moody knew the judge by reputation and so was not shocked by his remarks. Begbie was contradictory, irreverent and yet serious, anarchic and yet conservative, blithe and yet severe, a connoisseur of orchids and opera, a sketch artist and a horseman, his feet firmly on the ground even if his head appeared to be in the clouds.

"You are a connoisseur of hanging, sir."

Begbie barked a laugh and then grew wistful and then grave as he confessed that he'd had perhaps more experience of hanging than most, perhaps more than any one man should in any given life. "Some say I'm whimsical. I can assure you that in the court of law I am anything but. As for the late Mr Peter Brunton Whannell I've got it on good authority that he was nothing but a carpet knight, a loiter-sack, a quisby, a poltroon, a fopdoodle, a twit, a zounderkite, all of the above and much more. Not, of course, that that justifies plugging him." Word had reached them that Ned McGowan not only had shot and killed the Yale magistrate but had publicly scorned the border as so much fluttering ribbon and worst of all, most shocking of all, he had uttered denunciations of the Queen. "That simply won't do."

"I, for one, look forward to meeting the fellow," said Gosset, joining them.

Begbie did not so much as even register Gosset's arrival, being too busy aligning the rings on his gloved fingers.

Moody had seen little of Gosset since reaching Victoria and had dared hope to be shut of the man. He adopted his father's manner. "We're too small a force to dominate them," he said with a quiet yet stony adamance. There were eight sappers on the lower deck eagerly preparing their weapons, but Douglas had been right in saying that they were little more than a symbolic show. Moody, however, did not wish to have to "use Gosset." He'd deal with McGowan his own way.

Gosset smiled into his pipe as he filled it with tobacco and said that there was more to domination than mere numbers.

Begbie too began preparing his pipe. "The Yankees will be drunk," he said between puffs of port-flavoured Turkish. Settling back he adjusted himself, crossed his long legs, and sent leisurely drifts toward the framed daguerreotype of the Queen.

Moody felt obliged to remind the judge that Whannell had closed the saloons.

"I have every confidence that they're open again and doing a lively business what with Mr Whannell being dead," said Begbie. "Where there are men there is always hooch."

Gosset chortled richly as if he could not have phrased it better. Only then did Begbie discover Gosset and, facing him even as he leaned away for a clearer view, he demanded to know who he was. This threw Gosset, and he blinked and swallowed and croaked his name, "Gosset," then added, "sir."

"Gosset." Begbie repeated the word as if it were some bit of hardware and then observed that he was not in uniform.

"Liaison. Advisory capacity. Incognito. Eyes and ears of the governor."

"Eyes and ears." Begbie was skeptical. He shook his head as if at a list of cannibal trophies.

Once again Gosset's veneer cracked, a reaction that Moody found instructive. So, indifference was the key, easy indifference; the problem was that he himself was rarely easy or indifferent to anything. Once again adopting his father's tone, Moody said, "Frustrated by sobriety or wild with whiskey, it would be foolish to think we can walk in and arrest anyone, much less McGowan, without resistance. There will be blood. If there is blood there will be an outcry, and it will become an international incident with irreversible repercussions. London doesn't want it and Mr Douglas doesn't want it. Therefore we must be shrewd. We will maintain the facade that we are conducting routine surveys of the gold-mining sites and facilities. Nothing more." Moody was trembling by the time he'd finished yet determined not to back down.

Begbie nodded a reluctant acceptance of this argument. "I suspect that McGowan will see through the ruse."

"Very likely," agreed Gosset.

Moody fought to keep his voice from quavering. "McGowan revels in the game. Whether he sees through us or not, he will be intrigued."

"Subterfuge," said Begbie as if impressed by the term. "Well, we will see what your subterfuge achieves." He spoke like a man who occupied an altogether higher plane of existence, a sort of private Olympus, and he serenely smoked his tobacco to the ash, tapped his pipe on his heel, then angled his low-crowned hat forward over his eyes, crossed his arms over his chest, and slept. Soon Gosset too was snoring.

The *Beaver* throbbed its way upriver into the interior. The salon was well appointed with decanters of lime water, tinned biscuits, and whiskey; Moody went to the whiskey and poured himself a double peg. As he drank he looked around. The chairs and couches were deep and comfortable, but Moody was not at ease; he was rarely at ease and now even less so. He poured himself another drink and brooded: so Gosset had heard of Malta. Fearing a repeat of the sickness that had prevented him from leaving Malta for the Crimea, Moody inspected himself from head to toe, inside and out, and had to admit that he had endured a stomach upset after supper with his family last night before departure. Mary had remarked upon his pallor and put her palm to his brow and he had been forced to excuse himself to the facilities where, splashing water on his face, he had recovered in a quarter-hour. Now, however, he felt fine. The whiskey was buoying him. His father had been a great exponent of whiskey, and though he had died at forty-seven Moody did not recall him ever laid low with fever, agues, complaints, or injuries. Even his death had been contained, if not completely decorous; Moody had found him in the barn with the mare nibbling his sidewhiskers. Moody had stood and stared a long while, bewildered by the sight before him as well as his own feelings, a mixture of remorse and relief and confusion.

Now he flexed his hands and tested his limbs, rolled his head about on his neck, stretched his jaw, rubbed his thumb and fore-finger beside each ear to test his hearing, squinted with one eye and then the other at the picture of the Queen, and concluded that everything was in working order. He was not young nor yet terribly old, he was fit and he was experienced and he was ready for Ned McGowan. He raised his chin and assumed his father's demeanour, a man who, if he'd ever felt doubt, certainly never succumbed to it. And yet by and by Moody's kindled spirit dimmed and he returned to his seat and sank down like a wick subsiding in wax.

———————

At noon the next day they dropped anchor at Fort Langley. This was the site Governor Douglas had chosen for the capital, which would be rechristened Derby after the British prime minister. Moody scarcely needed to leave the ship to see that it was a bad choice. To begin with it was flat, the modest hill of the fort not-withstanding. At the very least it should be on the other side of the river. Worse, it was too close to the border, a mere twenty miles, and an invading force could sweep unimpeded right over them.

A hilltop or mountain slope was ideal. How could Douglas have not seen this? More troubling, how to tell him?

Gosset appeared and greeted Moody in his sneering and superior manner, then squared his shoulders and filled his chest as though invigorated by the frosty air. Whistling thinly, Gosset stepped sure-footed down the icy plank and, hands behind his back, strolled off toward a row of clinker-built shops where a puppy, grey-brown, trembling in the cold, appeared from beneath a shed. Gosset halted, frowned, and fished in his pocket for a scrap and knelt and fed it to the sorry hound, tickling it under the chin and behind its ears and making reassuring sounds. Then, head tilted in the attitude of a man on the verge of a decision, he picked the dog up and tucked it inside his coat and continued his walk.

Well, thought Moody, it was easy to feel pity for a hound; one's actions toward people were more complex. Gosset and Begbie were both younger than Moody and yet neither took him seriously, or not seriously enough. Eight years on the Falklands and not a shot fired; he may as well have been a monk on an island monastery. Then there was his year on Malta during which he'd tried everything to be transferred to the Crimea. It had been agony seeing all the troops and ships, the officials and their families en route to the war while he stayed, and then when he finally got clearance he'd fallen ill. He gripped the icy railing, gripped it tightly in spite of the cold, gripped it until it numbed his palms. Evaluating the terrain he thought: *No, Fort Langley was a poor choice for a capital city.* Yet he would deal with that issue when he returned to Victoria, for now he had to move on and deal with the murderer and provocateur Ned McGowan.

They woke the following morning stuck in ice. As on the day before, Gosset joined Moody on deck and stated that McGowan's spies would report their predicament, adding that no doubt word was travelling upriver even as they spoke and an ambush imminent. Gosset cradled the dog nestled inside his greatcoat more tightly.

"No," said Moody, "he's too shrewd."

"He attributes great shrewdness to this McGowan, don't he, Derby?" said Gosset, and the dog rolled its eyes toward Moody.

"McGowan's aim is revolution. He wants an excuse to call upon American forces to defend American citizens. Therefore he needs provocation, and that is something we will not, I repeat, will not, give him, no matter what. There is too much to lose."

"We don't think McGowan gives a tinker's fart for such niceties, do we, Derby?"

Moody considered plucking the mutt from Gosset and dropping it overboard. "We have no choice. We are under orders. And it's not as if we can call up a regiment."

"You have a valid point there," agreed Begbie, emerging from the salon adjusting his scarf and his sleeves. He noted Gosset and the rheumy-eyed pup and seemed unimpressed. "More of a cat man myself."

For the next two hours sailors and sappers attacked the ice with pick and hammer in the blowing snow. By ten they'd made little progress, so Moody declared that they would proceed via canoe and portage. Gosset rated this an agreeable adventure, and while Begbie glowered after the manner of a god called upon to soil his winged feet, he did not debate. They clambered into oilskins and at noon they were ready, eight sappers, Moody, Begbie, and Gosset, who seemed genuinely fearful on behalf of the dog as he handed it over to one of the crewmen for safeguarding. Skidding three canoes off the ice into the water, they began battling wind and current. It proved slow going. In spite of the cold the sappers were soon steaming from their efforts while Moody, Gosset, and Begbie, each in a different canoe, sat wrapped in furs.

By mid-afternoon the light was fading so they dragged the canoes ashore and built fires, drank tea laced with whiskey, gnawed dried venison, then crawled into their tents. Moody envisioned McGowan in a cave enthroned on a chair of human bones like some sort of American Hades, staring into a glass skull observing the progress of the British. In the morning, they boiled pots of snow and then steeped tea laced with more whiskey while watching a tree trunk come coursing downstream carrying a small black bear that groaned pathetically as it paced back and forth along the bobbing and rolling trunk. They watched until the spectacle was out of sight around a bend.

At midday they found themselves alongside a stretch of ice-free water and so relaunched the canoes and pressed onward. In the evening the sky cleared and a gibbous moon threw enough light for them to continue, the illumination turning the river to rippled black steel. No one spoke above a whisper and they dipped their paddles in silence and in this way they moved all night. At dawn they reached Fort Hope. They pressed on. It was ten more miles to Hill's Bar where McGowan was ensconced, and one-half more to Fort Yale where Whannell had lived. They began to see other boats, barges, skiffs, rafts, and canoes, and on the banks encampments small and smaller, sometimes little more than a flap of canvas draped over a branch, a sputtering fire, and a figure so woeful, so bereft, so beaten, so mired in remorse and regret and confusion as to how he had come to such a pass in such a place so far from home that Moody had to look away, for it was as if he was touring the condemned of purgatory. Other camps were livelier. Seeing the armada of three canoes led by the imperious Begbie singing in a fine tenor the cavatina "Ecco, ridente in cielo" from *The Barber of Seville*, men tossed their hats, shouted huzzah, whooped and capered and waved. On one occasion an emaciated fellow, an anchorite or hermit, or merely a fool maddened by fatigue and hunger, ran naked along the riverbank, his belly-length beard rippling like a pennant over his shoulder as he laughed at the folly of men great and small. They reached a cluster of tents where, eager to allay suspicion, Moody called out a hearty greeting, and as men emerged hoisting their suspenders and scratching their parts, he introduced himself and his company and made a performance of innocent interest in their mining operations. They lingered but a quarter of an hour and then, after shaking hands and wishing them the best of luck and of the season, pressed on.

In the early afternoon there was a gunshot. Then another. While Moody dropped and peered through the trees trying to spot the sniper and Gosset crouched and readied his rifle, Begbie strode toward the shots, halted, set his hands on his hips, and shouted, "Stop that at once!"

The shots ceased.

The auburn fringes of the judge's mink collar stood tall in the icy wind and gleamed richly in the low winter sun. He waited as if expecting an apology, and though he frowned he appeared no more seriously troubled than a schoolmaster cautioning rambunctious boys. Satisfied, Begbie turned to the others and suggested they make camp. Moody would have preferred to be the one to issue the order but saw no point in quibbling. That night he shared a tent with Begbie, who took up two-thirds of the space lying spread-eagle on his back and snoring grandly. Unable to sleep in spite of his fatigue and a deep drink of whiskey, Moody once again gauged the state of his body. Feet and ankles throbbing, right knee twisted, lower back clenched, piercing pain in right hip, the rigging of both shoulders strained, hands numb, headache. All in all not too bad. He was the oldest man here but he was keeping pace; more than that, he was leading. Surely his father could not but approve.

Sometime in the night Moody woke to a presence moving about the tent and thought a coon or worse a cougar had slipped in. Cautiously, he reached for the knife he kept on his belt, which was looped to his trousers, which were folded on the floor within reach. He drew it out and while keeping a grip on it he managed to strike a match and hold up the flame. Judge Begbie. Standing like a statue that might have been called *Desolation.* Unsure what to say or do, Moody touched the match to the candle beside him. The judge was oblivious or indifferent to the light and remained in that stricken attitude for some minutes with Moody feeling awkward, even voyeuristic, and wondering if he should snuff the light and say nothing. Suddenly the judge, in nought but his long underwear, stepped out of the tent. The simple interpretation was that it was the call of nature, but there was something decidedly unjudgelike in the judge's manner, and after a few moments Moody crawled on his hands and knees and peered out the tent flap and saw Begbie standing in a patch of moonlight, head down, shoulders sagging. Then he appeared to sob. Moody withdrew, frowning, frightened, utterly at a loss about what to do. Still on his hands and knees, he peered out again. Now Begbie was leaning against a tree, forehead on his arm, chest heaving. The sight was as terrifying as it was intriguing: Judge Matthew Baillie Begbie—weeping?

It was so unheard of that Moody actually speculated Begbie might be rehearsing a role for an amateur theatrical, a cast-down lover, a depiction of despond. Now Begbie pushed himself away from the tree and collected himself, wiping his face with the back of his wrist, clearing his throat, drawing himself up, and marshalling his strength. He turned and strode toward the tent. In a panic, Moody hurried on all fours toward his sleeping bag, but rediscovered the candle he'd lit. He could hardly snuff it out now for it would be too obvious. Begbie swept the flap aside. Moody got slowly to his feet. They faced each other. In the quavering candlelight it was difficult to gauge the judge's expression. Without a word each returned to his bed. Moody pinched out the flame and lay in the dark, smelling the burnt wick and feeling the sensation of hot wax coating his fingertips.

Begbie's voice rose out of the dark. "Did your father beat you very much?"

Beyond the occasional handshake his father had never touched him. "No."

"Mine made me sing."

Had he heard correctly? "Sing? Sing what?"

"Hymns. Upon transgression said offender was banished by the *pater* to the northeast room, ground floor, and bade commence and continue the hymns for full duration of sentence. Three hours for misdemeanour such as sloth, and a full six for property crimes, disrespect, ill grace. Theory being that the Breath of Life must run strong and run pure, and the immortal words of John Wesley be felt through to the marrow. Only thus will said son attain perfect integrity of heart and mind."

"Singing."

"Until the throat bled." Voice thick, Begbie confessed that now, even decades later, the night still brought on terrors that rose like creatures from a swamp.

If they'd been longer acquainted Moody might have suggested Begbie consider marriage—who better than a woman to assuage a man's nocturnal anxiety?—but he feared that it would be presumptuous. He wondered what Mary would make of Begbie and was eager to describe him, especially given her insights into Governor Douglas.

As if reading his thoughts, the judge said, "One trusts one can depend upon your discretion."

"Of course."

"Never beat you at all?"

"Never."

"Extraordinary."

Moody was about to risk a confidence and describe the Arctic nature of his relationship with his parents, but Begbie had begun to snore. Wide awake now, Moody began composing in his mind one of his letters to his dead father but did not get past the opening salutation.

––––––––

They came in sight of Hill's Bar late the following afternoon and were greeted by a shot that pinged off a rock and thudded into a tree trunk. More followed, fizzing past their heads and skipping off the water. Hunching in their canoes they paddled furiously for the far bank and the safety of Fort Yale, where smoke rose in straight serene columns from stone chimneys, Front Street was calm, the snow pristine, and passersby, apparently accustomed to shots from the other side, paused to inquire after their health.

Gold panning had ceased due to the winter weather, which left most men without occupation other than to mend their kits, catch up on their journals, stroll, smoke tobacco, smoke opium, drink gin, drink laudanum, drink beer, visit their neighbours, gamble, or any combination thereof. Moody asked a man in a black bowler hat with a short beard and a big cigar clenched between his teeth who had taken up Whannell's post. The fellow looked confused and answered that no one had taken up his post, and others on the road and on the porches chimed their agreement, saying that he was "right there in yonder abode."

"Then Whannell is not shot dead?"

"Not as of half an hour ago," said the cigar chewer.

Moody and Begbie looked at each other with expressions of confusion and relief, though perhaps in Begbie's case with a hint of disappointment that he might not get to hang McGowan. By the time they reached Whannell's pine-board house the man himself stood on the porch, arms flung wide as if praising the Lord for their arrival and inviting Moody and Begbie and Gosset to come in, come in. Soon they stood about the hot stove removing their steaming outerwear.

"Is there coffee?" asked Begbie.

"There is, there is," cried Whannell. "Barnabas! Barnabas!"

A cripple with a crutch hop-limped to a shelf stocked with stamped sacks, tins labelled with bucolic scenes, glazed ceramic jars, crates and pots and flasks, and set to grinding beans with a mortar and pestle. Begbie observed this with concern and, when he could no longer bear to watch, begged leave to instruct the gimp in the figure-eight motion that yielded, he assured him, the most swift and desirable result. All present gathered close to study the judge's system.

"The key lies in the swivel of the wrist. We do not desire silt nor yet do we seek sand, rather a happy medium." Done, the judge lifted the granite mortar in both hands as though it was a chalice of sacred liquor and, shutting his eyes, inhaled with a shivering rapture that struck Moody as verging on the unseemly. He thought of their conversation last night and envied Begbie's marvellous elasticity of spirit, rising from the depths of despond to the heights of irreverence. It was as if the judge possessed a power of amnesia that he controlled at will.

"Boil it up, lad," cried the judge, sending him reeling with a clap on the back, "and add a few grains of rock salt to smooth the burr."

Whannell proceeded to tell his tale of woe. McGowan had not shot and killed and buried him in a muddy grave but had abducted and jailed him.

"Though now you stand free," observed Moody at the risk of stating the obvious.

"Only after paying a ten-dollar fine! Ten dollars!" cried Whannell. "The dog marched right into this very room, this very room, a government office, my courthouse, my abode, and he and his henchmen took me away at gunpoint. Gunpoint!" Whannell was wearing spurs and a sword, sky-blue trousers, and a red coat with blue braid and gold buttons and lion's-paw epaulettes along with various medals, none of which Moody recognized. His moustache was waxed and his sideburns feathered and his hair oiled and parted in the middle with a curl at each temple. His smell of cologne water stood its own against the fug of wet wool and boots steaming by the stove. "He is an agent provocateur. A Yankee insurrectionist who obeys no law but his own, none but his own."

"You pissed him off," said Begbie.

Whannell was tall but Begbie was taller. Face writhing with frustration, Whannell pointed to the picture of the Queen and reminded them that he was a servant of Her Britannic Majesty.

"You cut off the hooch," said Begbie. "At Christmas no less."

"But there are twenty thousand Americans between here and Victoria. That's no mere mob, sir; it's an army. Would you see them drunk? I made the prudent decision. The prudent decision."

"Well, sir," allowed Begbie, "you made a decision, we'll give you that much."

Having heard only ridicule of Whannell, Moody sought now to be fair, conceding that perhaps Mr Whannell's actions were not utterly without reason under the circumstances, for certainly McGowan had been high-handed and, unless they heard mitigating evidence, outright criminal. "Where is McGowan now?"

The gratitude in Whannell's eyes was almost endearing. "Slithered back across to Hill's Bar like the water snake that he is."

Collecting his coat, Moody stepped onto the porch and looked across the river to Hill's Bar, a low assemblage of plank buildings, tents, and stables set against the backdrop of a snow-clad ridge, very much the mirror of Fort Yale. The snow had ceased and the clouds had risen to a high haze and the light fell grey and muted. "We will stay here for the night and pay Mr McGowan a visit tomorrow. Is it true that he lives in a cave?"

"Only in the summer," said Whannell.

Moody was not sure whether he was relieved or disappointed. The cripple appeared at his elbow with an enamelled cup of coffee. Moody thanked him and took a sip, bitter and granular—the judge had not ground it enough or perhaps favoured it that way—with a touch of citrus and at the same time something smoother running below, like chocolate silt. Moody had developed a taste for coffee while on Malta, encouraged by Mary, who did so very much enjoy a strong cup in the morning. Still, in his heart of hearts, Moody feared it was un-British.

The canoes ground against the bank and Begbie stepped off with such an easy motion that it was as though he had crossed the river in a single stride. Hill's Bar was not impressive; certainly no building stood apart marking itself as the redoubt of an arch-fiend, insurrectionist, or revolutionary. It was unlikely that any of the town's structures was more than two years old, and yet many already leaned to the point of collapse under their burdens of snow.

"You, man," demanded Gosset of a yellow-eyed sot with a mashed hat. "Where is McGowan?"

The man straightened as if the very name McGowan sturdied his spine and he gestured widely with both arms. "Everywhere!"

This earned a laugh from a crowd that had gathered on a porch. The wit now drew out his pizzle from between his buttons and proceeded to piss steamingly against a wall. Cursing him for a filthy beggar, Gosset batted the lout across the back of the skull while Moody, alarmed by the sight of the fellow's scabbed and pustuled member—and marvelling darkly at the infinite variety of crudities expressed and embodied by Man—turned away, calling his company to proceed. By now men lined porches, leaned out windows, stood before tents and shacks and lean-tos, and halted their wood chopping and pan scouring and tobacco spitting to regard the eight red-uniformed Royal Engineer sappers led by the trio of Moody, Begbie, and Gosset.

McGowan's house was not impressive: rough planks, steep roof, shallow-set windows whose whorled grain showed in the sun. Yet if McGowan's house was undistinguished, there was a remarkable assortment of men flanking the road that led to it. If any were meeting with success in *finding the colour* they were hiding it well, and prudently so given the tales of how far men went to take another's poke, from bullying to robbery to disembowelling anyone suspected of having swallowed their gold or inserted it up their fundament. Many a packhorse had endured an exploratory arm searching its nether regions. Three steps led to a porch where a one-eyed man guarded the door. He was not a giant, though he was broad, his demeanour enhanced by his long coat of black fur and matching hat that, along with his square black beard, gave him the appearance of a Tartar. His good eye swivelled about sizing up Moody and his entourage while his blind eye resembled a rotten walnut. Moody was not impressed. Hands behind his back and chest out, he waited and eventually the doorkeeper demanded the nature of his business.

"That should be obvious. To speak with Ned McGowan."

"Who are you?"

"Lieutenant-Governor Richard Clement Moody."

"The law," said Begbie.

"McGowan's the law here," said the doorkeeper.

Moody maintained his calm in the face of such rot and stated that there was only one law, British law, for this was the Colony of British Columbia, and he was its representative, so the man should stand aside.

The doorman's good eye darted about like a frantic squirrel. "McGow—"

The door swung wide and a man half-ran, half-flew between Moody and Begbie and narrowly missed pitching face first down the steps into the muddy slush. Skidding, he turned and drew himself up in an admirable reclamation of dignity, even taking a moment to punch the dent from his felt hat and place it upon his head and adjust it before he aimed his finger and announced in a voice raw with outrage that he would see McGowan at dawn with pistols.

Ned McGowan stood smiling amiably in the doorway. "Now, Cole, you know perfectly well there's no duelling in the Queen's Colony of British Columbia."

"We'll ride across the line."

"You ride across the line, and while you're at it do us all a favour and keep on going and don't come back. Find yourself a San Francisco whore and beg her to take you in and sort you out."

"You're a coward, Ned."

McGowan stepped forward and Cole stepped back. A long moment ensued during which no one stirred and the very air itself, as though a sentient thing that watched and waited, tensed in anticipation. Now McGowan wondered aloud for all to hear why, if he was such a coward, he was on the advance while the brave and big-worded Cole was on the retreat. As if to explore this phenomenon further, McGowan advanced another step and Cole retreated again, much to the delight of the onlookers.

Moody was too stunned to speak, stunned and at the same time fascinated, for he was all but witnessing a gunfight, the raw, gritty, unshucked Yankee version of a duel. It was appalling and it was invigorating and of course it must stop. "Enough!" he shouted.

"More than enough," agreed McGowan, and by way of explanation said he had given Cole the task of watching his bear, Lydia.

"One day he had to watch her, one blasted day, a mere twenty-four hours." Cole began to interrupt but McGowan overrode him. "An easy task, a simple task, a task an idiot could perform. But maybe I was the idiot. Maybe I had it ass over tea kettle and should have had Lydia watch over Cole! Certain as sundown I'd rather lose Cole and keep Lydia. I loved that cub and now she is gone."

As this speech proceeded Cole had begun dissolving himself a step at a time into the crowd and McGowan, spotting this vanishing act, called after him to take his sorry self away and dwell deeply upon his inept and perfidious nature. Moody now felt bound to inform McGowan that only yesterday they'd seen a bear cub on a log floating downriver.

"My Lydia?" McGowan's pained gaze turned toward the river and he agonized as though witnessing the fate of his beloved pet unfold before his eyes: Would she be tumbled from her log and swim ashore and fend for herself in the forest primeval, or would she be swept under by the rapids and drown? Then again maybe she would reach the sea and be shot for sport by some shipboard sharpshooters, or fall into the chuck and be eaten by the killer whales, or then again be trapped and sold to a circus, or perhaps rescued and adopted and enjoy a long and varied life. Her brass collar was scribed with her name to which she responded most benevolently. It took some moments for McGowan to recover, and when he did he shook himself and, recalling his hostly duties, invited them in.

It was a building identical to Whannell's though instead of a portrait of the Queen there was a thirty-two-star US flag as well as skins and pelts and deer skulls lending it a darker and more pagan appearance with the leathery odour of a tannery. McGowan indicated the chairs. There were two dozen, proving that at least one of the room's functions was as a meeting place. He waited until his visitors were settled before taking his own position behind a plain wooden desk on which sat a Mason jar of quills, an ink pot, paper, a stack of gazettes, a bible, a small brass bell, and a well-rubbed stick of arbutus the length and width of a man's forearm.

McGowan was somewhat shorter than Moody, though wider across the shoulders and deeper through the chest, and the hands he folded upon his blotter were thick knuckled and gleamed with gold rings. His reddish-brown hair was combed from just below one ear across the dome of his skull and reached his collar on the other side. But it was his moustache that was his most salient feature, completely masking his mouth and most of his chin. As for his coat, it had a narrow lapel and standing collar and its reddish-brown wool echoed his hair and complexion.

"Can I offer you tea?" he asked, bright and interested, as if tea was as fascinating to him as were gold and politics. "I'm doing my best to become an Englishman right and proper. I have Ceylon as well as Cameron Highlands and Darjeeling, though regrettably I've run through my stock of Assam. Not that that does us a whole shit heap of good today."

"Tea would be welcome, yes," said Moody. Who knew, the crisis might yet be settled amicably after the fashion of gentlemen; and if that was unworthy of the penny dreadfuls his John loved, it was nonetheless preferable.

McGowan tinkled the handbell and a rear door opened and a man appeared. He had the narrowest skull Moody had ever seen, as if he'd spent time—for what offence, who knew?—with his head in a vise. "Randal," said McGowan. "Tea. And are there any biscuits?"

The narrow-skulled Randal reported with grim satisfaction that the biscuits had weevils and not even the rats would eat them. "What about scones?" asked McGowan. "Can you fabricate some scones?"

Randal bared yellow teeth and said he'd nose about but not to get his hopes up, and then withdrew.

"Gentlemen," said McGowan. "You are here regarding Whannell." He set his clasped hands upon his desk, lending the impression that he was presiding in his own court of law, an impression that Moody did not care to encourage.

"He has lodged a charge," said Moody.

"Abduction," said McGowan.

"A serious business," said Moody.

"Undoubtedly."

"You've overstepped yourself," said Moody. "I don't know how it works in the United States, but civilians cannot arrest anyone, much less magistrates, in the Colony of British Columbia. It is tantamount to kidnapping."

McGowan assured them that he was a great believer in the law.

Begbie, seated to Moody's right, said, "You will have to explain the finer points of this belief."

"But it's simple," said the affable McGowan. "As simple as a straight line from point A to point B. Allow me to introduce Mr George Perrier, justice of the peace, Hill's Bar. JP of HB, as I fondly call him." He indicated a man standing by the wall, a plump specimen with an unctuous air whom none had noticed until that very moment. "His testimony," said McGowan, "bears directly on the case. In brief—for I know you are men of affairs and therefore busy—Mr Perrier deputized me and bade me fetch Whannell for questioning. When Whannell refused I had no choice."

"Deputized," said Moody.

"Servant of the Queen," said McGowan. "Won't deny I felt not a little chuffed."

Moody turned to Perrier for confirmation.

"Word for word as the sky is blue." Thumbs stretching his suspenders, Perrier explained how Whannell had unfairly harassed and fined a certain Mr Hicks, an honest man trying to make an honest living as a purveyor of spirits, wines, and ales, a credit to the community and an example of the principles of free enterprise, and if that wasn't bad enough Whannell had then done the unspeakable by closing the saloons at Christmas, an act as unwise as it was un-Christian—for does not the book of Timothy extol the virtues of wine?—and finally refused the summons, precipitating the deputizing of the right good Ned McGowan.

It was a well-rehearsed performance and their pleased manners showed that both Perrier and McGowan regarded the matter settled. Moody could have predicted as much. What he could not have predicted was that Judge Begbie was apparently satisfied as well, for he slapped both hands down upon his thighs and stood, announcing that it was time for elevenses. "How is Hill's Bar accommodated for *les restaurants*?"

Moody stared, so dumbstruck that he wondered if the judge and McGowan might well be in league. Had Begbie been bought? Was it possible that the entire journey had all been a facade? Either way, McGowan was putting on a show of enjoying the renowned Begbie. He smiled widely, offering a glimpse of teeth so white they might have been painted, and explained that they were not yet the parallel of "Paree," but if they rode the current downstream, Chez Maxie served up a tolerable red wine ragout.

Not so easily diverted, Moody stated that there was more immediate business yet at hand, such as a tour of Hill's Bar with McGowan serving as guide. "We have heard of your cave," said Moody, "and should dearly enjoy a look."

"My cave's cold and damp and unhealthy this time of year. Breeds the ague."

"We have heard tales of its Ali Baba splendour," said Begbie.

McGowan regarded the judge with admiration and said that he was flattered. "Well then, hellfire and fire up hell, if there's no way to deflect your interest, it behoves me as a proper host to obey. This way, gents." McGowan took up the club of arbutus and led them out the door through which they'd entered, the Tartar standing aside and the lines of men flanking the path straightening to attention. They headed away from the river up a sloping trail past tents whose occupants stood when they saw who approached, McGowan not once failing to address each man by name. They reached a gap in a wall of scree and stone marked by two upright logs.

Striking a match, McGowan lifted a torch of oil-soaked rags from a rack and lit it and then led them to a door hasped with broad black hinges that he unlocked with a large key. It cried open, the echo bespeaking a sizable cavern. McGowan stepped on in and went around touching other torches in their sconces, a magi sharing the miracle of light, and the room began to expand to an impressive dimension, with a high ceiling receding into the dark and wide coved walls. Completing his circuit McGowan returned to his guests and said, "Call it McGowan's Folly."

The cave was illuminated in an encircling chorus of flame and shadow that swayed and crackled and it all smelled of damp stone, stale air, oil smoke, and hides. Moody thought of a mead hall of old, loud with oath-roaring thanes. As with his office, the walls were draped with bear and deer and coon skins, though there was also a thirty-foot banqueting table, tall-backed chairs, tripod braziers, and at the far end of the cavern not a throne of skulls but a modest desk and chair with an oil lamp. Nearer to hand, at either side of the entrance, tarps had been thrown over what appeared to be crates. Moody took note.

Begbie was turning a slow pirouette while nodding his approval. Holding his finger aloft he said he detected a breeze. McGowan explained that there was a vent and Begbie, mildly, casually, asked after the themes that McGowan and his associates foregathered here to discuss.

"Themes? We natter. Talk of this, that, and the other. Play a few hands of canasta or hearts, sing songs, yes, sing a lot of songs, sad ones and a few, I won't deny, a tad ribald. Just a cool retreat from the summer heat. Who would've known it got so hot this far north?"

Begbie was all smiles. "But this is a temple and you are its oracle."

"Hell's bells! The cave's Mother Nature's doing. I'm naught but a country mouse."

Moody did not doubt their nattering included politics and borderlines and armies. "What do you have in those crates?"

McGowan shrugged vaguely as if he couldn't quite recall. "Supplies."

"Supplies?"

"Hardware."

Moody waited for him to elaborate, which McGowan did not do. No matter, Moody knew perfectly well what was in those crates and he would see the self-satisfied light dim from the man's eyes. Hoarding weapons to outfit an insurrection would see him marched across the border, if not imprisoned.

McGowan chose this moment to discover Gosset and observe that he looked familiar.

"Familiar to what?"

"Your face," said McGowan. "I've seen it before. The eyebrow. Or lack thereof, if you'll forgive me."

"Nothing for you to feel bad about. It's for me to forgive the wench who struck me with the hot pan. And I do, for I deserved it."

"Acting the beast, were you? Do tell." McGowan glanced around, eager to draw the others into the mood for a ribald tale.

"It's a story I do not repeat."

"Admirable discretion, sir." Noting Gosset's ring, McGowan snapped his fingers in recognition, remarking that not many wore them on the forefinger for it got in the way of the trigger.

"I'm left-handed."

"The Calliope Kaffe Haus in Vienna!" said McGowan. "Summer of '50. On the Ringstrasse. No? Budapest?"

Gosset said nothing.

"I could have sworn," said McGowan. "So many strangers out and about pursuing the Queen's business." He winked and stroked a forefinger past his nose. "The dogfights in Bucharest! Spatarului Street. You were backing a chestnut mastiff with a white spot just here." He touched his forehead. "Or do you have a twin?"

"The crate," said Moody.

"Beg pardon?"

"The crate," said Moody.

"Yes," echoed the judge. "The crate."

"Fascinating serpents," said McGowan. "Blue with white lateral stripes. Deadly. Not to be trifled with."

"Not krait," said Moody. "Crate."

"Are your crates so deadly?" inquired Begbie. "Is Pandora inside?"

"Ah, once again the subject is women." McGowan winked.

"Chop, chop," said Gosset.

"Blunt sort of fellow, aren't you?" The warmth went out of McGowan's eyes even as he maintained his smile.

"Direct," said Gosset.

"I've always held the view that digression was the essence of conversation. Anecdote and recollection. Aside and association. The most intriguing details always come from the oblique."

"I hazard that there is more than one source of wind in this cave," murmured Begbie.

But even as McGowan dissembled he went to the crates and threw back the tarp and, after a brief dramatic pause, a magician about to perform his coup de grâce, raised the lid of the wooden box. At first Moody thought he was looking at a corpse, that this crate was a coffin and the cave a burial site, a catacomb full of the bodies of McGowan's victims, and that they were all done for, that the fiend's cohorts were about to leap forth, guns blazing, the infernal racket of shots the last sounds he would hear . . . In fact he was looking at a clown mask, grotesquely grinning red lips, bulbous nose, orange hair, painted eyes, made of some sort of skin, the bladder of a lamb or flap of intestine, the sort of material used in the Crimea to cover amputations. McGowan pulled it over his face and spread his arms as though to take applause.

Still wearing the mask, he described their summer theatricals and extended an invitation to all of them to return at the solstice and see their production of *A Midsummer Night's Dream* in which he, naturally, would take the role of Oberon.

Ignoring this nonsense, Moody reached in among costumes heavy with the odour of mothballs, dug down to the very bottom, and yet found only fabric, shirts, skirts, stoles, wigs. The second trunk yielded similar results; the third, however, was different, for beneath a layer of Hudson's Bay Company blankets he unearthed something better than gold—a stratum of pistols layered in wood shavings. He turned to McGowan who had removed the mask, revealing an expression not of alarm but of delight.

"My collection," he said.

The next layer revealed rifles, then a still deeper layer more rifles, most decidedly antique, but weapons nonetheless. "Collection indeed, sir. I would call it an arsenal," said Moody.

A laughing McGowan suggested that this was unlikely given that hardly a one even fired. "You asked my business plan. I will tell you. A museum. I intend to display these relics." He selected a pistol and, holding it reverently in two hands, presented it to Moody, drawing his attention to a card at the end of a string tied to the trigger: *Duval Flintlock—Nantes*. "No lesser a man than Lafayette himself owned the very same model."

Returning the weapon, Moody picked up another and read the elegantly scribed card: *Sharpe Model 1760*. It was fashioned from what appeared to be a single piece of rosewood with a pair of swan-necked triggers. Moody had seen one in the belt of a Royal Navy officer on the Falklands. The rifles were equally dated, including Spanish long guns and blunderbusses with trumpet-shaped barrels.

"Craftsmanship of the first order, I'm sure you'll agree."

Moody had expected army-issue ordnance but, loath to concede defeat, observed that they appeared in fine enough condition to fit out a small force.

"I saw worse hardware kill scores of good Englishmen in the Crimea," growled Gosset.

"The Crimea? You've seen a bit of the globe, sir. Of course, where there's a will one can turn anything from a wooden spoon to a laundry paddle into a deadly weapon. But these . . ." McGowan was dubious. His eyebrows went up even as his moustache went down. "If there was antique powder and ball to be had, then maybe. Even so they're such cumbrous affairs a man'd be dead on his feet with a bullet 'tween his eyes before he could fit his priming rod. You've seen the newest models coming out of Philadelphia? Six shots in a rotating chamber. No, these antiques are for display, public edification, nothing else." He grew confiding: "Damn. Men hereabouts are a bottomless resource of woe-is-me sob stories and outdated hardware, and they're all strapped for coin. I perform a public service by unburdening them of such useless ironmongery. Better they be safely stowed with me than in the hands of rummies and malcontents. I put it to you, sirs, that I do as much to preserve the peace as any lawman, perhaps a darn sight more."

But Moody had had enough. "You Americans affect to prize plain speaking. Well then, I ask again: What's in this for you? Scrap iron? A dusty display of old hardware? No. I will tell you: to engineer some excuse for American forces to storm the border. Fifty-four forty or bust. Once in possession of British territory you foresee yourself awarded a governorship."

Even the ambiguity of the torchlight could not mask the hardening of McGowan's face. Then he was smiling again. "Skeptical as you had ought to be. I admire that. I have heard—"

Moody cut him short. He felt churlish and unmannerly and ungrateful but it was time to let McGowan as well as Gosset and

Begbie see who was in charge. "The Colony of British Columbia is sovereign territory. The border is set."

"Border? Strong word for such an evanescent thing," mused McGowan. "A border is as fanciful as a sentence and as easily erased and revised unless backed by iron. But then," he hastened to add, "we know what your compatriot Mr Bulwer-Lytton said of the pen and the sword."

"President Buchanan well knows where the border runs," warned Moody.

"President Buchanan is a great and fine man," said McGowan. "We were at school together."

Moody remarked on the divergent courses of their respective career paths and McGowan, eyes like brads, was obliged once again to take refuge behind his moustache. "Yes, well, he was always the more studious, was Bucky."

They reached Fort Hope that evening and dined on a beguiling ragout at Chez Maxie. Begbie ate with gusto. Perhaps it was the food and the bottle of pumpkin rum, but he did not share Moody's gloom at McGowan's having slipped their grasp, asking, after all, what the man had done aside from amass a hoard of useless hardware rusting in a damp cave, to which Moody could not help responding that it was not what he'd done but what he intended to do, with or without the iron.

"To condemn a man for his thoughts would be to kill a good many," mused Begbie. "He knows we know and that is enough." Anticipating further debate, he added, "I'm afraid that, for the nonce, it will *have* to be enough."

Moody didn't like it. It seemed that Begbie was choosing an odd time to be letter-of-the-law and laissez-faire.

Gosset didn't like it either. He dug the point of his hunting knife into the tabletop and said that McGowan was laughing at them. "He and his confreres."

"Confreres, is it?" said Begbie, picking his teeth with a silver pin.

"I propose slipping back upriver tonight and bleeding the bastard." Gosset flashed his blade upward.

Moody was intrigued and yet felt obligated to warn that it would only incite the Americans to act.

"There'd be no inciting. Only revenge. They'd think it was that sorry bugger he ran off for losing his bloody bear."

Moody hadn't considered this. Later, when he was sure everyone else was asleep, he sought out Gosset who, wide awake, admitted that he had indeed met McGowan in a certain house in Munich, adding that McGowan had rallied the women to take up arms and toss the madam out the fourth-floor window. "It was a revolution. The man's an anarchist, plain and simple." He insisted that there was still time for him to return upriver and deal with him. "I can do it." He added in a cold tone, "It is the reason I am here."

FRISADIE - 1865

NEW BRIGHTON

THEY WERE FORCED TO STEP DOWN FROM the coach and hike the last hundred yards to the top of the hill. Maxie offered Frisadie the benefit of his elbow even though he was in no fit condition to be offering anyone help, having been, as he phrased it, "drunk as a toad" the previous evening, and so it was she who supported him. They reclaimed their seats in the coach, which had three benches, two facing forward and the foremost facing back, with three passengers per bench. Maxie and she were on the rearmost, he having paid extra to be spared the awkward intimacy of interlocking their knees with those people on the middle seat. The jalousies gave fresh air and a partial view while blocking the mud flung by the horses. Yet the coach pitched and rolled like a ship at sea and at one point he gripped Frisadie's knee to steady himself and seemed about to topple into her lap, something to which in other circumstances she'd have felt obliged to raise an objection. Instead she stroked his arm and asked if he was inclined to *mal de mer*.

"I am very much inclined to *mal de mer*," he croaked, his eyes stricken and his face, or what was visible of it through his beard, a sickly grey.

"You're not going to . . ." She swept her arm upward from beneath her chin, meaning vomit upon her.

He groaned and shut his eyes and shook his head. "I will try not to."

"Your efforts in that regard are most appreciated," said Frisadie.

The journey from New Westminster to New Brighton was ten miles of rutted road and sand-covered logs. In spite of Maxie's condition Frisadie was ecstatic. It was an adventure, the farthest she'd been from Mrs Frame's boarding house since arriving in New Westminster. When the cloud cover broke and the sun burst through she sat forward, face to the slatted window, for the salmonberries gleamed like nuggets of gold and ruby, the lowly skunk cabbages were the purest yellow, and a scatter of black-tailed deer reared and fled from the thundering carriage.

"Perhaps we'll see a wolf or a cougar," she said eagerly.

"I hope to never see a wolf or a cougar," croaked Maxie.

It hadn't been easy persuading him to go to New Brighton and look at the hotel; even when she'd laid out the numbers he was reluctant. He had eleven hundred and forty dollars; with her five hundred they could make the purchase and have operating capital besides. He said he couldn't take her money, while she countered that in point of fact she'd be taking his, and furthermore they'd be business partners. Wasn't he eager to escape the Grelleys? Wasn't he smarter than they were? Wasn't he ready to be his own man and realize his own visions for a hotel? He muttered that the Grelleys really weren't so bad and she reminded him of everything he'd said to the contrary, admissions that he seemed to regret.

"It is a great risk," he'd said, suddenly timid.

This was disappointing. Where was the man who'd walked a thousand miles across the prairie shooting buffalo? "We should at least take a look," she'd countered, "for if nothing else we will enjoy a fine outing." In fact she'd not been without her own skepticisms regarding this New Brighton Hotel venture. However, she did not see any other way forward. The reception she'd had from Mr Bostwick had been disheartening. The notion of a young Kanaka woman going into business on her own was clearly an alien if not outright absurd conceit altogether too vast for his brain. If she needed a partner then it had to be Maxie as she knew no one else; certainly Mrs Frame would have scoffed had she suggested it to her.

Now Maxie opened his eyes, for they'd hit a stretch of level road and the stage travelled more easily.

"I have a good feeling," she said.

"You are young," said Maxie, as if good feelings were a fault of youth that time, in its awful wisdom, would correct. "How old are you?"

She lied and said twenty-two.

"Twenty-two," he said, as if recalling an impossibly distant past.

"One would have thought that a man so worldly wise as yourself would have learned his capacity for drink. Do you often get as drunk as a toad?"

"No, sometimes I get pissed as a newt."

Frisadie thought, but did not state, that he was certainly the colour of one, and clammy as well, and in sore need of a bath. Where was the charmer from the other day? She hadn't told him of her conversation with Mrs Frame, fearing that he'd think her desperate and reckless, which of course she was.

They approached some Natives walking single file along the road: two men in dark suits and hats, two women, one old, one of middle years, and a child, wearing blankets and carrying haversacks. As the carriage passed, the Natives paused and turned to watch even as Frisadie leaned forward to look at them. In seconds they were gone, but as with a photograph an impression was left in Frisadie's mind. She knew very little about the indigenous peoples. None had ever stayed at Mrs Frame's establishment; indeed no one of any colour had so much as stepped in the door. Still, she often thought of the various people she saw in the street. What paths had led them here? She recalled the anger and indignation of Hawaiians at the influx of *haole* so brazenly strutting about the town, her father arguing with her uncles, admitting that yes, they were loud and they stank and their teeth were bad, but insisting that they knew things, important things.

Soon the stagecoach crested a ridge and Frisadie beheld Burrard Inlet. It was a broad glitter of dark blue water with forested mountains on the far side soaring to caps of snow even though it was May. The driver whipped the horses and the wheels drummed the logs as they traversed a bridge. The road approached at an angle across the slope leading down to a gravelled terminus with hitching posts. There was a chorus of groans as the passengers extricated themselves from the coach. Some made for the wharf where a lighter would take them across to a schooner loaded with lumber bound for Australia, while others, less desperate or adventurous, dispersed along the beach or the tall grass that was bright with clover and daisies and dandelions, unfolding chairs and putting up umbrellas.

The New Brighton Hotel was a rectangle of grey logs chinked with mud and mortar, with a low roof quilted with moss and mulch and a chimney of river rock. All about stood stumps, clusters of nettles, roiling clouds of mosquitoes and flies and midges, and large bees lumbering about the wildflowers and salmonberries.

Frisadie could not deny that the building wasn't as impressive as the setting, nor did it equal the sketch in the newspaper ad. Still, she was eager to see it in the best light. Maxie, however, who had seen the place when it was new, was shaking his head at the sorry state into which it had fallen. When they reached it, he pulled a bone-handled knife from inside his coat and without so much as a word stabbed one of the logs as if he'd make the place yelp. He prised at the wood and then inspected the wound.

"Well," he allowed, "it's not rotting. Yet."

"You see!"

He was dismissive.

"Grump."

"Naïf."

She laughed at him and it was all she could do to keep from catching his hand and skipping as they mounted the wobbly deck that overlooked the sea. There was a broken window, a sagging eavestrough, garlands of reddish lichen, a brimming rain barrel busy with bugs. The words New Brighton Hotel had been burned into a plank of yellow cedar suspended above an open door.

"Who could not fall in love with a place that has the words *new* and *bright* in its name?"

Maxie, for one. He glowered at her and she laughed at him, and such was her joy that he felt bad and saw himself from her perspective and was bewildered as to why he was so sour—had he become old before his time, set in his ways and fearful of change?—and did his best to wrestle his mood into shape. Rolling his shoulders, straightening his coat, he stepped to the door and in a big voice called, "Hocking." There was a silence during which Maxie was all too eager to turn and leave.

"Michaud. At last. I knew you would come."

Maxie sagged visibly.

Frisadie whispered, "You know him?"

He muttered that indeed he did. Exhaling like a convicted man entering the cell he'd be occupying for years to come, he stepped into the gloom that was slashed by shards of light that pierced the gaps in the log walls. Frisadie followed.

"Where are you hiding?"

"I am not hiding."

They looked up to discover a man crouched on a rafter. He appeared to be naked but for a loincloth and a feathered cape.

"You have been smoking the hashish," said Maxie. "I thought you quit that decadent habit."

"I believe I have unfurled the rose, petal by petal, and reached the inmost bud. And for your information, I can smell the gin on you from here."

Ignoring that, Maxie said, "Hocking, this is my friend Frisadie, who believes we should buy your establishment. I suspect that, like you, she is not of sound mind."

"Ever the skeptic, Michaud. You want vision."

"Plus funds and luck and much else," added Maxie, as if his life were a testament to fruitless labour.

Hocking hugged his knees and rested his chin upon his arms and said, "As contradictory as ever, Michaud. The sullen sprite. Master of misery—"

"Hocking," Maxie growled. "Come down. You are not a pigeon."

"And yet those Grelleys are vultures," warned Hocking. "They feed on your soul like the eagle sent by Zeus to feed each day on the liver of Prometheus."

"Exactly what I've been telling him, sir," said Frisadie.

"Then you are wise as well as beautiful."

"Three years and this place is already ruined," said Maxie, staring about in disgust. "What have you been doing? How have you let it get into such a state?"

"Perhaps if you'd come in as my partner as I'd asked it would have turned out differently," said Hocking. He did not sound bitter but philosophical.

"The time was not right," grumbled Maxie.

"Ah, timing," said Hocking as if he had much to say upon the topic.

As Frisadie's eyes adjusted she saw that the hotel was indeed in a state. There was a general decrepitude, as well as debris and branches and shells and overturned furniture in a corridor leading to rooms whose doors were off their hinges.

"What have you been doing?" Maxie demanded. "Or rather *not* doing?"

"That is difficult to say. I am a bewonderment even unto mineself."

Hocking stood and stepped to the next rafter, and the next, reached a wall ladder and descended, then went out onto the balcony. Maxie and Frisadie looked at each other. Maxie's expression asked: What more proof do you need of the madness of this venture? Frisadie was not so easily deterred. She took his elbow and guided him out to where Hocking stood with his wings folded cape-wise across his chest, resembling an owl in contemplation.

"Do you think you can fly?"

"In spirit if not in body," he answered. Then he added that if they bought the hotel he'd include the wings.

"Keep your feathers. How have you come to this?"

Hocking drooped and leaned against the railing and admitted that he didn't honestly know, that it had come upon him stealthily, like a shadow in the night. "I think it's the rain." He put his fists to his temples and groaned.

"Why did you come here then? Everyone knows about the rain."

"And the forest," said Hocking. "The trees. They loom like Druids."

The firs were certainly imposing, thick, dark, towering, almost sentient, as if aware of their power to dominate and exulting in such terrible strength.

Maxie was not unsympathetic. He knew Hocking. A remittance man, third or fourth son of some earl, well educated, well mannered, well and truly lost, but eloquent and loquacious and generous when in funds. He had stood Maxie many a pint in the Colonial's taproom. "What will you do, go to the desert?"

"I was thinking Tahiti. Or Hawai'i. I need to lie in hot sand; I need to bake the chill from my bones. It could take a few years. How much can you pay?"

"It's not just money," said Maxie.

"Ah, Michaud," said Hocking as if counselling an adolescent. "It is always just money. You can have it for fourteen fifty. You could make a go of it. Your stories, her looks."

If Frisadie was charmed and flattered and terrified, Maxie managed to withdraw into himself like a threatened tortoise and ignore Hocking's remark and all it implied even as it excited him. Shoving his hands deep into his trouser pockets, he hunched his shoulders and exhaled long and hard and weighed it all out. On the one hand he had his money and his position with the Grelley brothers. On the other there was a young woman and a tumbledown hotel. At last he shook his head. Even when Hocking dropped the price by another fifty dollars Maxie remained adamant.

"Fourteen hundred," said Frisadie, trying to make Maxie appreciate what was being offered.

"You're out of your depth," he said, louder than he'd intended.

"I'll thank you for not being so rude, Monsieur Michaud."

"You should thank me for being sane. While you . . . *vous êtes folle! Malade dans la tête!*"

He may as well have slapped her face. "Malade in my *tête*?"

He opened his arms and shrugged as if the evidence was plain. Frisadie made a show of gazing around to take in this supposedly plain-to-see evidence but saw none, only Hocking looking on in the gravest concern. No amount of talking could shift Maxie. On the journey back to New Westminster, Frisadie was too frustrated to speak while he, she suspected, was guilty but relieved. The fearful grump in him had won out. She sat as far from him on the coach seat as possible and stared out the window at the impenetrable trees that spun past. How could a man who walked all the way from Winnipeg to make his fortune balk at going the last ten miles to New Brighton? Where was all his talk, his vision, his—what was the French?—*élan*? "Well," she said, "I suppose it is back to the glories of pots and pans and rats."

"You're young. There's time."

"Time? It seems to *moi, monsieur*, that as *folle* as I might well and truly be, I must make my own time and everything else. And depend upon it," she said, turning to him, "I mean to do it."

They stared at each other, Maxie all too conscious of the other passengers listening in, Frisadie not caring. It may have been 1865 and the American Negro free, and by extension a new world of opportunity opening up for all the coloured races, but Frisadie was all too aware of what was going on in the white heads that were watching. Still, she lowered her voice and leaned closer to Maxie as she asked, "Why did you pursue me that first afternoon in front of Grelley's? Why? And at the May Day fete? And then inviting, *insisting* I have lunch with you? Why? A taste of brown sugar?"

He recoiled as if slapped and she saw that she'd hurt him and she felt tears burn then blur her eyes but firmed her jaw and awaited the answer she felt more than due to her but it did not come.

At the Columbia Street depot they shook hands.

"Good day to you, Mr My-chod."

"And to you, Miss Fizzy."

She walked away briskly, head high, determined not to look as defeated as she felt, convincing herself that it was better this way, for quite plainly she had misjudged Maxie; he was a millstone, a ball and chain, old and tired, all talk and no gumption, and who knew, maybe worse. They were all against her and she wondered how she could have been taken in, what with their lewd gestures and remarks. No, they never let you forget, not just the English but the whites, all of them, you can't trust them. As she walked toward the boarding house two men coming toward her grinned and elbowed each other, then made kissing sounds at her as they passed. That their faces were as brown as her own only made her feel more alone.

As soon as she stepped in the door of the boarding house Mrs Frame said, "So, you and your fancy man were out and about, were you? Coach rides and the like."

"We went to New Brighton for an outing.

"An outing? Building sandcastles, were you?"

Frisadie saw that there was no point in explaining. Mrs F was determined to suspect the worst and it would seem she was justified. She went up to her room as though mounting the scaffold, tied her apron on and stood in front of the mirror trying to calm herself. Her heart racketed in her chest and hammered in her ears so she took deep breaths the way Mrs Mace had always advised, but it did no good.

For the next week she avoided the Colonial. Mrs F gloated supreme and asked where her sugar man was now, even making a show of peering at Frisadie's hand. "What? Not put a ring on your finger? Not rescued you from my despotic rule?"

She did her best to take her in stride and turned her attention to the lodgers, listening in on their talk, hoping for some tidbit of financial wisdom that would see her through, but this was like expecting poetry from pigs. How differently her life would have played out had her father not died on the voyage. Her mother would be alive and Frisadie would . . . well, she'd most certainly not be at Mrs Frame's. What a fateful decision her father had made. But then he'd been a man on the move, ever alert to opportunity and eager to make his way. His employers at the HBC had recognized that, and what with the closing of the post, they did not want to lose a trained and talented employee who knew the workings of the firm. The voyage from Honolulu to Victoria had taken twenty-seven days. He died on day twenty. "When will Father return?" Frisadie recalled asking her mother the first night at Mrs Mace's house, not quite grasping the permanence of death. They lay on cool coarse sheets that smelled of some sort of bitter herb. Her mother assured her that they would soon return to Hawai'i and all would be well. Then she added, to herself as much as to her daughter, "I told him you can't trust them." In the morning, Mrs Mace's maid served salal-berry scones and Hawaiian coffee. It was spring. There were daffodils and hummingbirds, and the air smelled of woodsmoke and sap. Occasionally there were shots. *Puh! Puh!*

"Is there a war?" Frisadie had asked.

Mrs Mace laughed. "The men are hunting. Last week a black bear was shot just there." She pointed through the French doors across the yard and over the fence to the dirt road.

"Was it very fierce?"

"I believe it was ill."

"I would like to see a bear," she said, straining to see out the windows and all around. The trees were enormous. Fir, cedar, Garry oak, arbutus.

Contrary to her mother's intentions, they did not board the next ship back to Hawai'i. They had no money and were in debt to Mrs Mace, and Frisadie's mother fell into a despond that would turn out to be a living death by despair. Frisadie avoided it only by virtue of her naïveté, ignorance, and youth. Not that she skipped forth to gambol with the other children in the neighbourhood. Her introduction to life in Victoria, circa 1857, was a slow assimilation under the wing of the iconoclastic Mrs Mace, who took her to tea, to the markets, and on Sunday drives over the rutted roads. She became known as Mrs Mace's project, her ward, her orphan, her pickaninny, and as long as Mrs Mace lived she was safe.

The last conversation Frisadie recalled her mother having was trying to persuade Mrs Mace to lend her the funds to buy their passage back to Honolulu and Mrs Mace benignly refusing, smiling the smile of the supremely insightful and proclaiming that destiny had brought them here to her door.

———

One, two, three, you are free; four, five, six, beware of tricks; seven, eight, nine, this life is mine. Frisadie decided to negotiate with Hocking on her own. She had less than half his asking price but it didn't hurt to talk, for surely a man so eager to sell would be more than willing to deal. On a humid June morning she rushed through her duties, avoiding Mrs Frame's crow-like glare, thinking: *Dismiss me, don't dismiss me, do your worst, our days together are numbered.* Then she set out for the coach depot, the smell of the river rank and metallic, the horse droppings rich, the mosquitoes and flies eager. She followed a roundabout route that took her past the Colonial, not sure why, not sure whether she was acting against her better judgment or following it. There was no sign of Maxie and she mocked herself for a weakling as she made yet another circuit about the streets for a second pass. No sign of him. Hardly surprising as Maxie was a late riser. Drunk again, no doubt. Feeling like a fool, she hurried to the depot because the stagecoach left at nine. By the time she got there she knew that it was for the best. Who needed a reluctant partner? For all his initial charm and bonhomie, Mr Maxie Michaud had turned out to be a grouch forever finding fault, a black cloud, an éminence grise, the human embodiment of a bell dully tolling the gloom to come. She shouldn't have been so surprised, for people often put up false fronts, wearing bright masks to hide the fear. It was the way of it at the boarding house where the loudest men were inevitably the most frightened, the back slappers, the charmers, the jokers always the ones found weeping in a corner in the middle of the night.

Maxie was waiting by the coach. For her. That much was plain by the way he was scanning the crowd. Frisadie halted. It felt as if the bottom had dropped out of her belly. Her arms hung limp and her handbag very nearly slid from her fingers. No. Not him. Not now. Yet she also felt joy. Indignation and joy. Nonetheless, she turned away, resolved to walk off. But he was at her elbow.

"Miss Fizzy."

"Mr My-chod. Off somewhere, are you?"

"Your Mrs Frame said this is likely where I'd find you."

"She did, did she?"

"As brittle as a dry stick, that one," he said.

"But as sharp as a splinter."

"Just so," agreed Maxie.

"Can I be of service, Mr My-chod?"

"You need a partner."

"And pray why is that?"

"Because I'm an idiot."

"I'm afraid I don't follow your logic, even if I agree with your reason."

"I'm sorry."

"Is that so?"

"It is."

"Do explain the sudden change of mind."

"It was not sudden."

"You've been cogitating between drinks, have you? Weighing it all up?"

"I have."

"You look as if you've slept a month in that suit."

He regarded his suit of purple corduroy and even he had to admit that it was overdue for a brush. "Very nearly."

Frisadie noted that his eyes were caged in red veins and his breath smelled of oil of turpentine. "Are you suffering a congestion?"

Pressing his palm to his chest he admitted to a touch of an ague.

With studied indifference, Frisadie suggested that perhaps some sea air would be preferable to these river vapours.

"Exactly what the doctor recommended," said Maxie. "I talked to him yesterday and that is what he said, yes, exactly what he advised, sea air. He said, 'Maxie, you need . . .'"

She boarded the coach while Maxie, still jabbering, followed her on in. Not three hours later they were shaking hands with Hocking, having settled on a price of twelve hundred and fifty dollars. Sans feathers.

———————

Maxie believed that they could salvage the rotting bedding by arranging it on the grass and letting the sun work its purifying miracles; Frisadie insisted on burning the lot for it was torn and stained and stinking and hopping with fleas, and no amount of smoking or boiling or treatments with Reckitt's Bluing could save it. Maxie said that he'd slept on worse, and she said no doubt he had and then reminded him that this was a hotel and that as surprising as it might seem, people were not paying for bedbugs and mildew.

Maxie did his best to accept this irrefutable argument. Battling his habitual dread of spending, he managed to smile as he cautioned, "Though you realize of course that it will have to be ordered from Victoria, or San Francisco, and that it may put a"—he shrugged and winced ever so slightly—"small strain on our budget."

Frisadie thanked him. "Your concerns are duly noted." Then she informed him of an estate sale that week at Wren's where the list included six full sets of pristine bed linen, fresh horsehair mattresses, eiderdowns, and pillow slips, at which he regarded her with something between awe and despair, and yet if he felt the urge to weep or moan or argue he masked it manfully. They worked fifteen-hour days for the next month. While Maxie scraped the moss from the roof and replaced the broken windows, then washed the new glass with vinegar, Frisadie burned the hotel's old bedding, set out the Hawke's Rodent Remedy, scrubbed the floors with sand, then sluiced everything in vinegar while purifying the air by boiling cinnamon and ginger. Maxie dismantled the bed frames and painted them with egg whites and quicksilver against vermin, cleaned the brass with rape and rottenstone, flushed the drains with chloride of lime, and shored up the leaning deck, even as he battered his fingers with the hammer and saw. Frisadie oiled the furniture and the walls and ceiling, replaced the curtains and restrung the blinds. The tableware was chipped and cracked and stained, the cutlery twisted and blackened as though it had been used for digging the garden or mining coal, except that there was neither garden nor coal pit. She said they'd have to buy everything new and Maxie, unable to contain himself, shouted that they didn't need caviar dishes and sauce boats and pickle plates.

"Do feel free to eat with your fingers, Mr My-chod. And by the way," she said, holding up a ream of the hotel's curled and mouldering stationery, "we'll need to order fresh notepaper and envelopes."

Maxie gripped his beard and fought not to twist it from his face, while she shook her head and said that she'd heard many stereotypes about many peoples renowned for their penny-pinching, from Scotsmen to Jews to the Chinese, but none could match that singular creature called Max My-chod. "You must spend money to make money," she reminded him. "It's called investment. Isn't that what you said the Grelley brothers wanted: vision, boldness, confidence?"

What a figure she was. He surprised himself by shaking his head and laughing. Then he performed a courtier's bow.

"You're mocking me," she said.

"Not at all, I assure you."

"I'm an adult. Nineteen."

"You said you were twenty-two!"

"A strategic untruth."

He stepped forward and took both her hands and held them. "You are a formidable creature, you know."

"Am I?" She felt flattered and frightened. She thought he might kiss her. She'd not have taken it amiss.

He, however, remembered her accusations that he'd merely been after pleasure and made a show of looking around. "What do you plan on doing with that?" he asked, releasing her hands and pointing to the wooden pineapple she'd sawn from the newel post of Mrs Mace's house and that was now sitting on the mantel above the fireplace.

"I plan to leave it right where it is. Do you have an objection?"

"None at all."

"Very well."

Naturally they had to advertise. And just as naturally it behoved them to have a new name for a new hotel. In Frisadie's opinion it only made sense. Seaside Inn, Oceanview, and the New World all seemed old hat. She thought of the *New* New Brighton Hotel. Or the *Bright New* New Brighton.

"Maxie, what do you think of the Sand Dollar Inn? Or the Inn by the Sea? Or the Edge of Empire Inn? Or . . ." Struck by inspiration, she said, "Château Maxie!"

He put on an innocent expression and considered it the way he'd considered her name the first time he heard it. Beneath the genial musing she could see his mind was also considering yet another expenditure, for of course there would be costs for paperwork, signage, letterhead, and more. She gave up on a name change. Still, they ran ads in *The British Columbian* as well as *The Daily British Colonist* extolling the virtues of their breathtaking setting, bright rooms, pristine linen, artful decor, and world-class cuisine, and of course their stock of beverages guaranteed to satisfy any and every thirst. Inevitably, they debated the size and placement of the ad, Maxie observing that the back page had been good enough for the Grelleys and Frisadie countering that that was exactly the point: they were better than the Grelleys. Maxie could not refute this and conceded.

The ads worked. They were booked up even before they opened on July 1 and there was a gala atmosphere from the get-go. Guests sensed they were there at the start of something big, the gold and silver bunting Frisadie had hung to enhance the mood hardly necessary. They had six double rooms and offered three meals a day plus elevenses and high tea, meaning they worked non-stop. By the end of the first week even Maxie agreed they had to hire a skivvy and a cook.. The stocks of food and liquor went down at a terrifying rate. Every third day they were being resupplied from New Westminster. But they were making money. Maxie saw this and soon was gung-ho. All summer they were full, and if they thought it would level out in the autumn they were wrong. As the weather cooled they bought more quilts, hired a woodcutter, and kept the fireplace blazing. Gin and tonic was replaced by hot rum. The maple leaves turned from green to gold to red and drifted past the windows. The rain began and yet still the guests arrived and they liked to sit out on the deck under umbrellas and comment upon the Natives that often angled their way up from the beach across the grounds and into the forest. In general the remarks were benign, though occasionally some fellow would stamp his foot as though shooing a stray dog. Maxie would feign not to notice and Frisadie's face would burn with shame and confusion at her own silence.

Late November finally saw a slowdown and they had a few weeks to gather themselves, but with Christmas business quickened again and at midnight on New Year's Eve, Maxie, Frisadie, and their ten guests spilled onto the balcony beating pots and pans beneath a glitter of stars reflected in the inlet's chill black water.

"The frozen trees sparkled and the snow-covered ground glistered," intoned Harry Hearne. "Or is it better the other way round?" Frowning, he embarked upon a different arrangement. "The trees glistered and the ground sparkled?" He was writing the hotel up in the *Daily British Columbian* and was particular about the rhythms of his prose. Palm over his heart, he gazed up and recited: "The glistered snow trees sparkled frozen . . . frozen treed the snow glistered . . . glistering the treed snow . . . snow treed the glistered glistened—begad, I'm pissed." He got down on all fours and, groaning, pressed his face into a patch of snow to cool his brow and freshen his brain. Once he was sufficiently cooled he climbed to his feet and retrieved his tumbler of hot punch from the railing, then proposed a toast.

"To the remarkable couple—Maxie and Popo, the Acadian Argonaut and Polynesian Pocahontas! May you live long and flourish!"

A speech was called for and Maxie, who had shed the last of his misgivings and mustered a wholehearted enthusiasm for the hotel venture, recounted yet another story about his journey from Quebec to the coast, this one concerning two Scots living in a sod house near Moose Jaw brewing beer from beets and buffalo hide. He was happy. They had worked hard, and though they had, in his view, spent far too much, they were also well on their way to recovering the expenditure and moving into the black. Perhaps most satisfying of all was the day in December that the Grelley brothers had paid them a surprise visit and went away impressed, Thomas Grelley in particular making a point of giving Frisadie a wink and a nod of approval. There had also been a couple of visits from one Gregory Barnes of the Hotel Victory in New Westminster, an establishment rated even higher than that of the Colonial. The manager of Hotel Victory was slim and stylish and good-looking and well spoken and bore about him the dignity and restraint of the well bred. Gregory congratulated Maxie and he congratulated Frisadie and seemed utterly sincere in his celebration of their success. And now, thanks to Harry Hearne, there would be a newspaper article endorsing them.

It was three in the morning of January 1, 1866, when Hearne and the others took themselves off to bed. One couple, well travelled and of worldly views, lingered to remark: "Mrs Michaud, you and your husband are splendid hosts. So relaxed and natural."

"Thank you so much," said Frisadie, not sure exactly what she meant by relaxed and natural, and not sure how, or whether, to explain that she and Maxie were not married. In the end she opted to say nothing.

Maxie came to the same resolution and merely smiled. When he and Frisadie were alone he turned to her and offered his elbow and said, "Well, Mrs Michaud?" Entering into the theatre of it, she took his arm and observed that he seemed very relaxed and natural, and in that way they proceeded along the corridor to their room, where Maxie opened the door and bowed her in.

At first they'd had separate rooms, yet as business prospered and demand for space grew they'd found themselves bunking in together. The Japanese screens dividing the room had maintained a pretense of propriety and eased any awkwardness. As the weeks passed, Maxie would occasionally place his palm against the small of her back and once, after she collapsed exhausted on her bed, he knelt and slipped her shoes off and rubbed her feet. Rubbed them long and slowly and deeply and it was all Frisadie could do not to groan aloud. This became an evening ritual. He worked his fingers between her toes and pressed his thumbs into her insteps and heels, then gradually his hands worked their way up her ankles to her calves and the backs of her knees, where he halted. At first Frisadie was relieved that he went no farther. Having him rub her legs was intimate enough, perhaps too intimate; after some weeks, however, she was not sure if she wanted him to halt or to continue on up over her thighs. She took to rubbing the back of his neck and shoulders, even if only for a few moments. How satisfying it was to feel his body relax under her touch.

Guests regularly remarked upon their compatibility, and it was true that they were comfortable when silent while at the same time never lacked for conversation; they could be profound, then grave and then silly and even lewd. It was routine for Frisadie to sort his hair and straighten his collar or lick her thumb and smooth his moustache. She grew fond of his scent of brine and cigars and Pears soap and saw the beauty of his pug's eyes, large ears, and thick wrists. If he had been too forward when they'd first met, he had since discovered a decorum that reassured her.

When they were both inside the room in the early hours of that New Year's Day, Maxie closed the door with a certain resolve, a certain deliberateness that couldn't be ignored, so that Frisadie became alert and curious and eager as he turned to face her with an expression that said they had arrived in a new place at a new time in new circumstances that merited new action. He took her in his arms and in seconds they were beneath the eiderdown.

Afterwards, they lay side by side on their backs holding hands and it was strange and it was peaceful and most important of all it seemed to Frisadie right and inevitable, and she thought of her life thus far as having reached a milestone, a viewpoint on an ascending road from where she could gaze out and take stock and perhaps a well-deserved moment of rest. When Maxie's breathing deepened and she was sure he was sleeping she wept a little, not sad, not joyous, but relieved, feeling as though she'd finally left one Frisadie behind and moved on to inhabit another larger and more significant Frisadie, and that it had happened at exactly the right time and in exactly the right place, and that perhaps there truly was such a thing as providence. She thought of her mother and father. She wasn't sure what her mother would think of her and Maxie. Her father would see Frisadie and Maxie and the hotel as a unit, an accomplishment, an incontrovertible place in the world, exactly what he had hoped to achieve by taking them from Hawai'i to Victoria to take up his position with the HBC.

It was nearly dawn before she slept and when she woke Maxie was already up and about the hotel, and Frisadie took the opportunity to scrub the blood from the bedsheet. It proved a long day. She dropped dishes and bumped guests. She and Maxie scarcely had a moment to exchange a glance or a word, though that night they lay together again. Love was nothing as she'd imagined; certainly the act itself was less misty and ethereal and flotatious and more tangibly physical than she'd expected, closer to an entranced form of wrestling, a humid struggle, all flex and thrust and sinew, that seemed to take place not in a bed in a snug room but on a raft on a wide river rushing toward a waterfall. How large she felt, how substantial; she had responsibilities, land, and, so it seemed, a lover who would soon be her husband.

Through January and February and into March they were often snowed in and guests were rare so they had the hotel to themselves. They let the help go with a promise to rehire them come spring and in the meantime did what little jobs they could, such as hunting down and stanching leaks, while the rest of the time they spent in bed or in front of the fire, watching the snow fall, listening to the silence, discerning faces in the trees, identifying the voices of owls, barred, great horned, and screech, as well as the cries of ravens and gulls and eagles and kingfishers, laughing at the barking of seals and admiring the pods of whales that came up the inlet blowing great spouts of vapour from their glistening black backs. Time slowed and they studied the progress of icicles lengthening from the eaves, the transit of the daylight, the rise and fall of stars, and read to each other. They agreed that Mr Dickens had wit and brio, decided that they would have liked to have met Mr Sterne, felt a great warmth for Mr Goldsmith and admiration for Miss Austen, and acted out the speeches and sword fights from *The Three Musketeers*, Maxie quicker on the thrust and parry but Frisadie enjoying the longer reach.

Come mid-March the rain set in and the snow was reduced to slush and then mud. One afternoon Maxie slipped on the porch and hurt his hip and elbow and wrist all at once, while Frisadie scalded herself making him a poultice of comfrey. They were out of rum and laudanum so spent a miserable night. In the morning, however, the first day of spring, as if on cue, the rain ceased and the sunlight bored through the slate-grey clouds and a rainbow arched from one side of Burrard Inlet to the other. As they lay together in bed, Maxie put his good arm around her waist.

"I'm happy."

"In spite of all the torments I've put you through."

"Because of them."

Surprising herself, she asked if he didn't feel the lack of children in his life. She didn't know where the question had come from, for she'd rarely reflected on motherhood and certainly did not pine for the sound of pattering feet and twittery voices. Not quite yet, at any rate. Maybe it was the fact that she was now nineteen and on the verge of tipping into her third decade, or it was the season, the birds chirping and frogs singing, a new crop of mice skittering about the hotel at night, and the fact that it was only the two of them in what suddenly seemed a great and cavernous place.

"Children?" Taking the idea as a cod, a lark, an engaging absurdity, a bit of repartee, Maxie lit on the idea that he could put them to work around the hotel.

Hurt that he saw it as so absurd, though relieved that it was not the start of a battle, she said, "You could give them little porter and maid uniforms."

"And not have to pay them!"

"Though you should feed them," she cautioned.

"Bread and jam and tea."

"Beef tea. You must keep their strength up. And besides, there are now child labour laws."

"Laws. There were no such laws when I was growing up. Very well, beef tea it is."

"I think you'd make a fine father."

He mused. "That would require a mother."

"Yes," she said, going suddenly very still, "I suppose it would . . ."

With a laugh he hugged her tighter as if the whole business was as splendid as it was ridiculous and she was a capital companion.

By May they were full again and so it continued all through summer and autumn, which diverted Frisadie from the fact that she was living in sin. Not that she was a devout Christian. Some of her earliest memories were of attending Sunday morning services in Honolulu but not really taking in much of their meaning, the grave-toned sermons passing over her head. It had been more an occasion for the family to dress up as *haole* in uncomfortable *haole* clothes. As for Mrs Mace, she had spent her Sunday mornings in bed nibbling cinnamon toast and playing patience or reading the biographies of great women, serenely unconcerned about how Frisadie spent the Sabbath, and as for Mrs Frame she was as indifferent to God as she was to the Queen, demanding to know what any of that lot had done for her. Still, the substantiality Frisadie initially felt at being in business with Maxie began to seem tainted, especially when she noticed female guests studying her finger for a wedding band and asking probing questions.

But the hotel was a success. She and Maxie were a team, a phenomenon, a destination in and of themselves, and she worked hard at not dwelling on the state of their—what was it, arrangement, partnership, liaison? Neither contradicted guests who assumed that they were married though neither ever offered the assertion.

One rare quiet October evening as the gold and red leaves drifted down from the maples, she was reading an article about cotton prices in Manchester in an old copy of *Punch* and Maxie was reading his newspaper when he looked up and said, "I love you."

She looked at him, curious, surprised, elated, her mind racing over those three words, and wondering what he meant by "love," for it had as many aspects as a well-cut diamond. Or so she'd read, having never actually seen a diamond, well cut or not. Struggling not to gush she said, "And I love you, too."

With that he smiled and went back to his paper, murmuring that Bismarck was destroying France.

Fearing that a rare moment was passing, that an alignment of minds and moods was about to drift apart and be lost, she suggested that perhaps they should go there. "To Paris," she said. "When the troubles are over."

"Paris is a great city," he said, not looking up.

"The City of Love," she added. As his response was to merely turn the page of his paper she cleared her throat and said it again. "The City of Love."

He didn't answer. Moments passed and she frowned as though standing on a dock watching a boat departing downriver.

———————

The following spring they completed an expansion, pushing out a wall and adding three rooms, purchased six palm trees, had some rattan furniture made, and contracted Monsieur Juste Lefoy, recently arrived from San Francisco, to do a Polynesian mural.

Monsieur Juste positioned Frisadie a few feet from the window, first standing and then sitting, head raised, head lowered, turned à *droite*, turned à *gauche*, and dashed off sketches. Occasionally he adjusted her sleeve or collar, lifted her hair, and arranged her hands; he discovered a speck on her shoulder, which he brushed away. His breath smelled of tobacco and coffee and brandy, he wore his hair shoulder length and tied with a ribbon, had a goatee and an earring, and his nose, which she often saw up close each time he inspected "her lines," was long and thin and looked especially fragile. He wore a beret, a paint-spattered smock, fingerless felt gloves, and stitched Moroccan slippers. His sketches took two days, then there followed two weeks during which he completed his mural.

He and Maxie conversed in French, Maxie suddenly quite the connoisseur of painting, and he and Monsieur Juste embraced often and pounded each other on the back regularly. Frisadie couldn't see what they were admiring. What she did see were images of herself that were neither accurate nor complimentary. Certainly she wasn't that plump, was she? Either way, she was not so terribly fat that Monsieur Juste missed any opportunity to run his hands over her curves every chance he got while making appreciative noises. Nor did he miss any opportunity to run through their stocks of wine and beer and brandy. He was a thirsty little Frenchman.

The guests enjoyed the spectacle of Monsieur Juste for he brought an air of sophistication, being a genuine Parisian, and many remarked upon his use of colour and form, the play of light, the depth of vision, atmosphere, and symbolism, noting the positioning of this tree and that banana. Revelling in his celebrity, he spoke of Delacroix and Géricault as if they were old friends.

As for Frisadie, she was happy the day he announced that he was leaving. With hugs and tears and vows of eternal devotion, he boarded a ship for Victoria intending to carry on to Hawai'i and Cochinchina. For weeks afterward the hotel smelled of linseed and turpentine. They never heard from him again, except via Hocking who sent a letter from Honolulu where he'd had the great good fortune of meeting Monsieur Juste and lending him five American dollars. Hocking included a photograph of himself posing on the balcony of an impressively large tree house and invited them to come stay. Frisadie asked Maxie what he thought and he laughed as though she had an imagination worthy of Monsieur Jules Verne.

"If we went by balloon, maybe," he said.

"You'll fly but you won't sail."

He saw that as patently obvious. "Of course. I suffer from *mal de mer*, not *mal de l'air*," he said, enjoying his rhyme.

That winter the palm trees died and in March the murals began to glow with some sort of luminous mildew that turned the many images of Frisadie green and yellow. In the central mural, made up of five sections, a figure that was supposed to be her was seated upon a keyhole-backed throne of cane. There was no doubting that it was a regal image, an attempt at depicting some sort of barbarous regality, her head high and gaze direct, but was that blood on her lips from feasting upon long pig? The other four, two on either side, showed her brandishing a knife, sleeping on a bed of leaves with her knees parted, laughing in the sunlight, and basking with her eyes closed in the light of a full moon as if, primeval creature that she was, she enjoyed some animal communion with the base forces of nature.

"Monsieur Juste was not a *very* great artiste," she observed. "Nor a *very* deep thinker."

Maxie said nothing to this for he was too busy complaining of rheumatism and headache and gout and briefly of double vision. If Frisadie touched him the wrong way he squirmed as if she were a mosquito buzzing in his ear. One morning, on that second winter, with yet more snow spilling down out of the grey, she again suggested they shut the place for the season and take Hocking up on his offer. There were ships in the inlet, they could be in Victoria the next day, and according to the shipping log in *The British Columbian*, a vessel was departing for the Orient via Honolulu within the week.

With strained patience Maxie reminded her that his stomach was bad and he'd likely die a prolonged and grisly death en route. She noted that doses of ginger tea were said to work miracles. He indicated the mural and observed that they had Hawai'i right here.

"I look like a green-faced bullock."

He didn't debate it.

"So you agree! You not only let that man insult me but paid him to do so!"

"It's not that bad."

"So it is bad, just not so *very* bad."

"What is the problem?"

"Juste was a charlatan! I hate that thing. It's ugly and insulting and I'm going to paint over it."

"It is a rustic vision," he informed her as if she was too simple to grasp its essence. Then, angry and indignant, Maxie said, "Paint it over, don't paint it over, tear it down and burn it, it's up to you." And he snapped open his newspaper and raised it like a shield.

She was tempted to fetch a splint from the fire and touch it to that newspaper and watch him leap. If he was angry and indignant, she was more so, and not only due to the mural. *Did it not occur to him that they were being judged? Or more to the point, she was being judged?* It was all very well for him to dance the horizontal jig, but what about her? He'd be celebrated while she'd be excoriated. Had he no concern for her reputation? "Maxie . . . Maxie! Am I your whore?" That came out more bluntly than intended though she let it stand.

The newspaper fell from his grip and he fought for breath as he searched her face for the person he thought he knew, the person who'd clearly been replaced by a stranger.

———————

Harry Hearne, New Westminster's own Grub Street Shakespeare, reappeared in May, commissioned by *The British Columbian* to update "their story" in what he called "a feature." Hearne resembled the drawing of the rat on the box of Hawke's Rodent Remedy, pointed nose, small eyes, thin lips, bad complexion, stringy sideburns, and a moustache composed of but a few alarmingly long and glistening hairs. None of this seemed to detract from his self-regard. He proceeded to nose about the place, notebook and pencil at the ready in case the muse whispered in his ear. Taking Frisadie aside he asked after her "formative years" in Hawai'i and Victoria and New Westminster. What authority that pencil gave him, not merely the authority of authorship but of a commander inspecting troops. By virtue of that pencil he was judge and jury, tweaker of noses, attacker of evil, defender of virtue, and maker of reputations.

"Give him a good lunch," said Maxie. "And a bottle of stout. He likes stout."

He most certainly did like stout. Mr Hearne stayed two nights gratis and enjoyed numerous chops and all too many bottles of stout, as well as eggs, rashers of bacon, and cups of coffee laced with brandy while lying in bed with his notebook. In this he and Monsieur Juste were birds of a feather. Eventually he returned to New Westminster and wrote up his impressions.

Picture a spring morning. A day liberated from the Dread Demiurge Labour. A pleasant coach ride through verdant forest a-glister with sun-shot dew culminating in a vista— nay, a buena vista—of sea and sky and mountains. Thus you are arrived at New Brighton!

And there in the very centre sits the eponymous hotel. But it is more than a hotel! It has by now become an institution, a destination, a fulfilment. How fitting that it waits at the End of the Road, there to welcome travellers of every stripe. For this is the New World, where men of all station rub elbows, exchange views, breathe the same salutary air of the great west coast of North America!

Here, too, you meet Maxie and Popo. The little French- man and his Polynesian Pocahontas. As intrepid as any voyageur, Maxie Michaud will regale all who have ears to listen with tales of his journey from La Belle Province to New Westminster, the final twelve hundred miles of which he and his fellow Argonauts walked. Shall I repeat that? Walked. Trod. Plodded. Yea, like Sisyphus they rolled the boulder of hope, begirding their loins with the sinews of faith in the Western Dream!

Where else can the runt of the litter come to stand shoul- der-to-shoulder with nearly any Englishman? The little Frenchman worked hard. He befriended Frisadie—Popo— wandering lost in the street. There was an immediate affin- ity. Two souls, seekers of solace, driven to free themselves from the hobbles of paganism and Old World superstition.

He, a Papist Frenchman; she, heir to sea-roving cannibals who slaked their bloodlust by feasting upon human flesh. But the gleam of something higher animated their eyes. They are exemplars of diligence, and the New Brighton Hotel is their ziggurat, their pyramid, their Taj Mahal!

Maxie and Popo offer hospitality to all who would escape the dinning hecticity of New Westminster, of Seattle, Portland, San Francisco, or any city even further afield! Their cuisine is second to none. Ragouts, fishes, beef, fowl, game. Their wine list commendable. The decor simple, as befits the setting, the fire comforting, the rooms snug in winter and airy in summer, whilst just across the inlet Red Indians dance their dread rites!

When you are settled before the fire with a port or an ale, with Popo standing by as stately as a totem pole, ask Maxie for one of his stories.

"You wan' de sto-ree. Hokay, I tell you de sto-ree. You go jus' sit dere an' Maxee he tell you a good wun."

And he will.

The article continued for two more columns of such suppurating prose.

Frisadie had read it twice and was not overly surprised. Polynesian Pocahontas? Very well, she was at least a queen. But that accent? She watched Maxie churn as he stared off out the window toward the mountains.

Finally he said, "The *maudit anglais* bastards never let you forget, eh?" In a rage he grabbed up the paper and shredded it and flung the tatters. He stood and looked for something else to destroy but had to settle for punching his palm. "And the bastard Hearne thinks he's done us a favour. The English." He spat.

Frisadie saw no point in observing the irony that Hearne was Irish, though whether a Proddy or a Catlicker she wasn't sure. "No," she agreed, "they never let you forget even when they think they're your friend. It's a fact of life, like being a humpback. Or a woman, or being a woman of—"

But he cut her off. "Not even when you succeed do they let you out from . . ." His English failing him in his anger, he struggled for the word.

"Under their foot."

He stared as if she was somehow to blame. "It's better to be ignorant," he announced. "Better not to notice at all. To be like this—" He held his hands alongside his temples as though they were horse blinkers. "You don't see, you don't care."

"But you do care," she said. "You care because it hurts. Because it can't fail to hurt. No one can be so blinkered. No one with any dignity."

"How do you go on, then?"

"Maxie, you go on because there is no alternative, but you are wary and defensive and bitter and alone and somehow guilty and so you learn the art of appearing one way and feeling another, of saying one thing and believing another." She felt calm and cold even as tears glistened on her cheeks. "Besides, I'm not convinced about the wisdom of wilful ignorance. Ignorance is a false bliss."

"False bliss?" Maxie seemed genuinely perplexed and wondered if bliss could be false. Was sugar not sugar?

FANNIN - 1886

New Brighton

HENRY LOOKED UP FROM LEONORA'S NOTE WITH round, fearful, enraptured eyes. He consulted his watch, the crystal scratched in spite of his carrying it wrapped in a cloth, and saw that it was just gone eight. Three hours. What exercises could he perform to prepare himself for roller skating? What could he do to not merely safeguard his dignity but earn her respect? He stood on one foot, then the other, squatted in a skater's crouch and pumped his arms. Should he put it off until tomorrow or the day after lest he appear overeager? Unless of course to delay would seem rude . . . Unstrapping his Heidelberg Electric Belt, he hung it on its nail in the cabinet and then positioned himself in profile before his mirror and studied the state of his hunch, filled his chest with air, and straightened himself until he stood as stalwart as a Prussian. When he exhaled he drooped again. Over the years he'd tried every exercise and contrivance. For a time he'd slept with an overturned soup plate under his spine. When that proved too painful he tried a deflated football, yet that did nothing so he resorted to a felt pad, which was comfortable and effective, rendering him square shouldered and ramrod spined as long as he lay still, but he was a restless sleeper and forever rolling side to side and from shoulder to shoulder, often waking on his stomach. Now, before the mirror, he took deep breaths to calm himself and expand his chest but had to stop when he grew light-headed.

Rereading the letter, he observed the neutral tone, which was only proper, while noting that the penmanship was more constrained than he might have thought, no flairs or curlicues, no tails to her *y*'s and *g*'s, though given her recent trauma, flourishes would have been unseemly. He counted back from the present date of May 27 to October 5. Just shy of eight months since her fiancé's suicide. Was she emerging from the gloom?

He ground his coffee beans with his mortar and pestle and boiled them up but the very scent of the brew twisted his stomach. He managed a mug of water from the rain barrel and a bite of bread, then applied himself to a pileated woodpecker he'd recently found, yet he could not sit still, so he pulled on his boots and strode up the slope past the post and telegraph office and out along the New Westminster road. He walked fast, the alder and maple in full broad leaf casting deep shade over the beaten dirt while salmonberry and nettle and salal and honeysuckle thickened the underbrush. The sight of bear prints made him about-face and proceed briskly home, rapping a pair of stones together to scare off any predators. It was of course possible that George Black had taken Lydia for a walk but he wasn't taking any chances. In his heart he was a city boy; give him a thug with a knife, a lout with a stick, rather than a bear.

He'd never said a word to Black about having witnessed the suicide, and now, ready to meet his daughter, he was once again tormented by the fear that he had been not only wrong but cowardly. How had he let this happen? It was lodged inside him like a bone in his throat. Back in his stump he studied his posture again, arching backward and stretching his chin toward the ceiling and his arms over his head. He did some side twists and pinwheeled his arms and shook out his hands and jogged on the spot. He then combed his hair and beard and wished he'd had time to visit a barber, for his Napoleon III, which had once delighted Eliza, had grown long and scruffy and disreputable. He went at it with his straight razor, trimming and shaping, and then shaved with extra care, succeeding in scoring his cheeks and throat raw. He found his other shirt, a gift from Eliza, red with black pinstripes, which she'd said lent him a bold and upright demeanour, and yet now he wondered if it was too bold and upright for this occasion, a touch obvious, so he took it off, then in an anguish of confusion put it back on, scrubbed his hands and fingers and pared his nails, lamented his lack of cologne water, wondered what was the point of it all, scolded himself, reassured himself, called himself a fool, a git, a muggins, plucked a few of the longer hairs from the backs of his fingers lest he be thought apelike, and just before eleven stepped into the roller skating palace.

He'd seen Black skate and he'd seen the children he taught tumbling like puppies, but Leonora Black was a gazelle, a figure from a ballet, a sad swan gliding slow as an elegy.

"Hello, Henry."

"Miss Black."

"Leonora."

"Leonora."

She paused before him, toe of one skate pressed to the floor like the still point of a compass. She wore a long pleated skirt of pale grey, a shiny black belt and a tan blouse with a ruffled white collar and cuffs. Flushed and smiling, she breathed deeply with the happy exertion of skating. Noting her height advantage, Henry stood as tall as possible without being too obvious. Exaltation and terror spun inside him until he feared he'd pass out; he wished he hadn't come but wouldn't have left for the world and thought that if he died now he'd do so halfway to paradise.

"Are you experienced?" She read his hesitation and promptly offered reassurance. "Not to worry. Relaxation is the key. Breathe and relax. Relax and breathe. Here are some skates."

She indicated a trunk that stood open displaying some two dozen pairs. "You can choose tried-and-true metal wheels, new and improved vulcanite wheels, or old-fashioned wooden ones."

"Which would you recommend?"

"At the risk of streaking Daddy's floor, vulcanite." They both noted the long black marks striping the wood. She glanced appraisingly at his feet and plucked a pair she thought might fit.

He sat on a bench and, from habit, found himself evaluating the workmanship of the skates; the stitching was tight, the grommets and nails neat, the laces frayed with use, but in sum a solid bit of work. He pulled them on. Stiff and heavy, the felt inlays packed down with use.

"Good?"

His toes were pinched painfully and his heels hurt but, not wanting to be a complainer, he said yes, they were good.

With a nudge of her toe she sent herself gliding backward out onto the floor, tracing a reverse circle. "Now you."

Alarmed, he said, "What, skate in reverse right off the bat?"

She laughed and apologized and said he could skate forward or backward or sideways, whichever he chose, whichever felt more natural, that it was important that it feel natural. How delightful to hear her laugh. How slim and willowy and lithe and lissome she was. How could that fellow have killed himself, what demon of despair could have driven him to such an act? Clearly he'd been unbalanced.

He stood, wobbled, threw out his arms for balance, then pushed with his right foot and, leading with his left, came very near to plunging face first but, extending his arms like wings and more importantly bending his knees and working his thighs, he regained his balance and was off. If there was one thing aside from shoemaking he had learned at the Barnardo Home it was balance, for all the time he'd been forced to walk with a bible on his head had trained him to maintain perfect posture and alignment. Ha! At a stately pace he and Leonora circumambulated the floor. What easy strides she took, hands behind her back, each musing step as relaxed as if she were strolling barefoot in summer grass. Henry laboured to mimic that ease. Unused to the motion, however, he soon felt the exertion in his legs and fought to stand tall and not give in to his hunch. She glanced at him with concern and he, seeing this, forced himself to stand taller, to imagine a string attached to the top of his head pulling him upward. He laughed, or tried, and nearly fell but she caught his elbow, and for the next circuit they went hand in hand, Henry breathless with exhilaration. Leonora knew the delight of the beginner discovering the freedom of skating and laughed as well, and they did another round and then another, at which she let go and without breaking stride turned and skated backwards just ahead of him and called out: "Most impressive, Mr Fannin. Rarely have I seen anyone take so naturally to the wheels. Remember to breathe, and use your thighs and knees like buggy springs, and of course pump your arms! Yes! Excellent! Well done!" She raised her hands and applauded.

Henry grinned, and in grinning his mind left his body and soared ahead and he congratulated himself, imagining all manner of scenario from the acrobatic to the romantic: he and Leonora skating into the sunset, he and Leonora skating under the stars, he and Leonora skating a waltz on a dance floor, he and Leonora skating down the aisle of a church . . . and yet while his mind flew, his body, not wishing to be left behind, launched itself after and he began to fly—or fall—and only by dint of agility did Leonora avoid a collision, sidestepping Henry as he plunged past and skidded chin first across the floor, striking the wall and collapsing like an accordion. The pigeons and swallows nesting in the rafters fled from either end of the barn while Henry lay stunned, the slam of the crash having blanked his mind.

Or rather the waking portion of his mind. The other portion, the mind that was alive in dreams, was soaring across rooftops, past cathedral spires, crenellated towers, fields, forests, mountains, and then over the sea toward the setting sun and then on into the rising stars, the rolling moons, and spiralling planets, further into the radiant dark where he saw others like himself, not their bodies, for they had no bodies, but their fires, their spirits, soaring and then sinking.

Henry woke lying with his head in Leonora's lap as she wiped his bloody chin with the hem of her skirt. His first wish was to remain there forever basking in her concern, and at the same time he wished to escape, to run away and never see her again, even as he wondered at the state of his chin, which burned and felt scraped to the bone, and feared for the state of her hem stained with his blood, and of course what must she think of him, and furthermore what would she report to her father and that remote and forbidding creature, her mother?

"Have you ever been in a hot-air balloon?" he asked.

"A balloon?" Studying Henry, she wondered if he'd injured his brain. Deciding it best to placate him, she made a show of thinking about the question as if it could be distinctly possible that she had forgotten a flight in a hot-air balloon, and after a moment said, "No. I do not believe so. Have you?"

"No. But I think it would be great fun."

She said, "You have suffered a blow."

He agreed that he had but was sure he was fine. He sat up, rubbing the top of his head, and then touched his chin; the wound throbbed and burned and stung. "I hope I haven't damaged the wall of your father's barn."

She laughed in relief and delight that he was able to joke and assured him that the wall was fine.

"My father and I used to read about the French balloonists."

She nodded deeply at this, for clearly it was deeply meaningful to Henry. Then she cautioned that floor burns were liable to infection and that he should apply garlic.

"I was doing so well."

"You were," she assured him. "Can you stand?"

Henry stood and, by an act of will, mastered his dizziness and skated off and back and then halted, toe planted just as Leonora had done.

"Bravo," she said.

"Same time tomorrow?" he asked, adamant to appear both serene and spirited.

"If you are quite recovered."

"I will be fine." Then he clarified, "I am fine."

"Then tomorrow at eleven it is. And you will tell me more about French balloonists. And do remember to apply garlic to your chin."

They shook hands and bowed and parted.

If he was anxious before their session, afterwards he was ebullient. As he worked on the pileated that afternoon, cleaning and washing and filling then sewing it, he went over every minute with Leonora and concluded that all things considered, in spite of the fall, he'd acquitted himself well, or reasonably well, or respectably, or certainly not half badly, or had he been pathetic? He leaned his head on his hand and went over everything again. No, for a novice he'd done fine. The fall undoubtedly detracted from an otherwise stellar performance but all in all he had nothing to be embarrassed over, much less humiliated about. Or did he? Perhaps she didn't want to skate with him again and was only being polite inviting him back?

That night his chin ached while the smell of garlic on his wound burned his nostrils. In the morning he was anxious once again and walked out the New Westminster road. He'd have walked the beach but the tide was high and besides it would mean having to pass the hotel and he didn't wish to meet Leonora before their scheduled time in case it created awkwardness. At a quarter of eleven he was at the barn. At ten to eleven Leonora arrived. The lesson went well. A few minor tumbles but always quick and laughing recoveries, and in the main he felt good and he could see by Leonora's expression that she was impressed by his toughness and tenacity, his resilience and his spirit. He cross-stepped both clockwise and counter-clockwise and even succeeded in skating, albeit briefly, backward.

"You're a prodigy," she said. "You display *sprezzatura*!"

"It's the instruction," he assured her.

They unlaced their skates, set them in the trunk, and went out. The afternoon was brilliant.

As if confessing, she said, "It's the speed. I love the speed. Like horse racing but better because it's your own strength. You are the horse. Horse and rider at the same time."

How flushed and vibrant she looked. Henry could hardly keep from staring.

"Do you dance, Henry?"

Dance? She was asking if he danced? He knew nothing of dancing other than the names, the cakewalk, the foxtrot, the cotillion, the polka, the gavotte, the mazurka. He'd seen sailors do the jig and men had danced in the street in the freezing rain when news came of General Wolseley's victory over the Ashanti. But there'd been no dancing at the Barnardo Home. The closest the boys came to dancing was in their boxing lessons, wherein the bent-nosed instructor shouted at them to *hop, hop, hop on your filthy bloody toes and keep moving, moving, moving!* "I'm afraid I haven't had much opportunity."

"You'd be a natural, I'm sure."

Henry saw himself whirling around a palm-court dance floor with Leonora in his arms. It was a giddy vision. It felt more than a little untoward. How his mind capered. He also noticed they were walking down the slope toward the hotel and he hoped and at the same time feared that she'd invite him to tea.

"It's Lady Mars," said Leonora, slowing her step. The foreboding in her tone could not be missed, nor could her ironic emphasis on the term Lady.

A buggy and two fine horses stood by the main entrance. The horses were black, their manes braided with silver thread, livery shining, the buggy also black and trimmed in silver paint. A uniformed driver sat up front, in gloves and hat, while Lady Mars, a woman of profound dignity, was poised like a trophy on the leather seat, a small black terrier in her lap, its silver collar glinting in the light. She was talking with Leonora's mother, who appeared to be paying her every deference. As Henry and Leonora approached, the dog bounded from the buggy and ran yapping at them in a great show of bravado. Lady Mars shouted, "Gustavus!" and the terrier came looping back to her, but misjudged and ran under the horses, startling them, and the disoriented dog veered off under the hotel porch where Lydia, lying in the shade, put out her paw and trapped it like a cat pinning a mouse, at which Gustavus squeaked once and was dead.

Leonora cried, "Oh God!" and ducked beneath the porch and scolded the bear, which rolled onto its back and paddled its legs while Henry retrieved the flattened hound, its glazed eyes goggling in shock even as Julia Black and Lady Mars shrieked. George Black bounded down the steps and they all stared at the limp figure of Gustavus in Henry's arms. Lady Mars swooned across her buggy seat. Julia Black cried for salts; her husband turned to race back up the steps but the driver already had a bottle under the nose of his mistress. Turning to Henry, Julia Black demanded to know what he'd done. Her husband tried to intervene but she told him to *do please shut up* and he did. Leonora, however, was not so easily cowed.

"He?" said Leonora. "He did nothing."

"He provoked the dog."

"We were forty feet away."

"It smelled him and his vile profession."

"Oh, Mother, please."

"In India there is a word for such people—untouchable."

Too shocked to speak, Leonora could only raise her arms and let them drop.

Henry lay the animal on the hotel step, looked to Leonora and thanked her for the skating lesson, nodded to George Black, bowed to Julia Black and then to the slumped figure of Lady Mars, and finally turned and walked with all the dignity he could muster up the slope to his stump, where he sat very still like a boy bravely undergoing unjust punishment. Mrs Black's disapproval was no surprise, for she'd never acknowledged him except insofar as to turn away whenever they were in sight of each other. Her aversion to taxidermy was by no means unique, but he didn't understand how a man as affable as George Black could have married such a shrew.

"Henry . . ."

Leonora. He leapt up. He'd have invited her in but feared it smelled of leather and fur and worse, so he stepped out and pulled the door shut behind him. Did he too stink of hide, of carcass, of death? Had he merely grown used to it? She stood with her arms crossed tightly over her chest, shame and rage tightening her face.

"Behold, the mother," she said.

Down the slope Lady Mars was being helped up the steps and into the hotel by her driver and George Black, while Julia Black guided the proceedings as if the old woman were a priceless antique.

"Do you have anything to drink?" Leonora abruptly asked. "Something strong?"

Henry was no great drinker, though he did keep a few bottles of stout for when he felt rundown, ale for when he was parched, claret for his digestion, rum for insomnia, and whiskey for his throat. He opened his door and ushered her in, sniffing the air as he entered, gauging it for odours, and could not deny there was a sturdy smell of hide. If Leonora noticed, she was too polite or distracted to comment. Henry drew out a chair for her and fetched the whiskey and two short tumblers, giving them a quick wipe around the rims with his sleeve. She took hers neat, and as she sipped she looked around the stump, observing that he'd definitely given the place character. Character? Henry considered the word. There was character and there was character. Idiots and eccentrics were said to *be* characters. Then again, men of wit and mettle were said to *have* character. "May I?" To his terror, she stood and began inspecting the creatures on his walls and shelves, paying particular attention to the birds, peering closely at the eyes. "Wonderful," she said.

"I had wanted to be an embalmer," he announced, feeling reckless. "Indeed," he added, "it remains a goal toward which I do yet continue to yet to hope to aspire, as of yet." He coughed to cover his stumbling syntax.

She turned to him, frowning and smiling in bemused intrigue at this singular fellow. "You don't feel it somewhat . . . if you'll forgive me . . . ghoulish?"

The thought had never occurred to him. "I'd always thought more in terms of exaltation," he said, pronouncing it *eggs-ole-tie-shun.*

"You are from London," she said.

"Jacob's Island, Bermondsey. And you're American."

"Chicago. Originally."

"Your mother seems out of her element here."

"She is very much out of her element here. She belongs in a city. She is only really at home surrounded by concrete and glass."

"And yet."

"Exactly," said Leonora.

"I don't understand," said Henry.

"Nor does she. Which is why she blames my father."

"Who is Scottish."

"He is."

"They seem—"

"They are. Very much so. Ill matched. My mother is not introspective. She is intense and acute and observant but not as regards herself. They met in Chicago where she decided that she was in love with his pioneering spirit. It appears that she was wrong."

"They could leave."

"My father loves New Brighton. He loves his bear."

"Does your mother roller skate?"

Leonora's laugh was a soaring bird.

Henry shrugged and smiled. "And you?" he asked. "Do you love New Brighton or do you also wish to return to Chicago?"

"I don't know. A little of each. Some of both." She grew troubled.

Henry saw that he'd cast her into a despond.

"And you?" she asked, changing the topic. "What of your family?"

"Dead." He instantly regretted the bluntness of the word. "Gone. Some years back, my dad. My mum I never knew."

"I'm sorry."

He shrugged.

"I suspect I don't really know mine either," said Leonora. "But I do love her."

"Of course."

"That is, I think I do." She frowned and finished her whiskey, then extended her glass for a refill.

"It's not exactly Redbreast," he said, topping her up.

"Believe me, I don't drink for the taste." She discovered his magnets and lodestones in the glass case. "You're also a geologist."

He considered leaving her with the benign misapprehension that he was a mere rockhound, an admirer of pebbles, yet he was more than that, and he began explaining his interest in magnetism and the theories about its various properties, its influence upon the human heart and mind and spirit, on both the living and the dead. He told her of his interest in contacting his mother and father. "I sometimes have this impression, this sense, that they are adrift in some limbo, awaiting a signal or safety line to be thrown to them, and that I must act quickly or they will dissolve into all the other souls, merge like mist into mist."

This troubled her and she frowned and asked if it worked, and he confessed that he'd not really had ideal conditions for proper testing. Pensive, she looked off out the stump's window and with a pang Henry knew she must be thinking of her late fiancé. He didn't want her to be thinking of him and at the same time berated himself for being so selfish.

"If you had something of his . . ."

She turned with an expression on her face he'd never seen before, pained, frantic, even a little hostile, and spoke in a high, hard voice her mother would use. "Why would I want to draw Frederick back when he so desperately wanted to depart?" Chin trembling, awaiting an impossible answer, perhaps pleading for such an answer, she set her glass down and went out. Henry went to the door meaning to say something, to call her back, but as he had no idea what words could possibly accomplish that, he could only watch her descend the slope, her back, normally so straight and tall, suddenly as bent as his own.

The next morning at eleven he went to the roller skating palace but Leonora did not appear, and for the three days following there was no sign of either her or Black. He wrote her a note.

Dear Leonora,

I'm so sorry to have caused you upset. Please forgive me. I do hope we can continue our roller skating, at your convenience of course.

Until then I remain,
Yours,
Henry

He went up the hill to the post office and bought a half-cent stamp and dunked the brush into the pot and carefully wiped it across the back of the Queen's profile and then positioned it on the upper right-hand corner of the envelope and passed it to the postmaster who looked at the address and then looked at Henry and did not ask why he didn't walk down the hill and deliver it himself, but simply franked it and put it in the bag.

MOODY - 1859

Victoria

JANUARY 25, OVER A MONTH PAST THE winter solstice, and Victoria was unseasonably balmy and the days already perceptibly longer. Snowdrops showed in Lady Douglas's flower boxes, the grasses were unbending themselves, and the salal leaves greening. James Douglas drew Moody's attention to the calendar on which he marked the sunrise and sunset each day along with the weather and phase of the moon. They were standing in Douglas's study, which faced southwest and even on a winter afternoon like today enjoyed a fulsome light.

"We gain approximately ninety seconds per day at this latitude. Though the sunrise and sunset are skewed. The sun will set later while rising at the same minute for two, sometimes three days in sequence."

The shape of the earth and its orbit, thought Moody, though he did not say.

"This is due to the shape of the earth and its orbit," said Douglas. "Any schoolboy worth his chalk and slate knows this." He smiled thinly. "You are circumspect, sir."

Moody's face burned beneath his beard. With Douglas you could never win; either you said too much or said too little. "Not in all things," he murmured.

"Not with McGowan. Begbie says you were masterful." The governor did not smile but his manner was approving and he seemed to re-evaluate Moody, who felt so elated that he thought he might lift off like a hot-air balloon. "Now," said Douglas, with the heartiness of a hungry man who had endured the pre-dinner speeches and was about to tuck into his steak and potato. "Now is the time to transform Fort Langley into Derby."

Moody had been fearing this moment, but honesty was paramount and he forced himself to speak with calm and with clarity and above all with humbleness. "With respect, sir, I spent some days at the fort on my return and could not but conclude that it is perhaps less than an ideal setting for a city, most especially a capital city."

The lines on his brow shifting like faults in the earth's crust, Douglas pivoted from the calendar, put his fist to the small of his back, and frowned weightily at his lieutenant-governor. Moody maintained eye contact and breathed evenly. They had taken tea, the fire was damped to a clean glow, and Douglas, eager to spend an hour refining schemes for the new capital, glowered now at plans thwarted. He asked for Moody's reasons.

He'd known of course that Douglas would be irritated. The impatience of the Colonial Office was already stretched to breaking and here he was straining it further; therefore he had practised his explanation like an actor rehearsing a soliloquy, Mary coaching him on his delivery and deportment, reminding him that what Douglas desired, what they both desired first and foremost, was a capital city, a proper capital city, secure and strategic, and while Douglas may well smart at criticism of his location, a city he would get. Jolly him on through the rough patch, she'd said, to which Moody replied he might as easily jolly a bear or a troll. She shook her head and said *praise him, for no one, high or low, male or female, is indifferent to praise.*

And so Moody began by acknowledging the virtues of Fort Langley. The proximity to the river was of course its chief advantage. In this the governor had shown wisdom. Locating the fort at the top of a hill, such as it was, was also shrewd. As he spoke, Moody monitored Douglas's reactions, the measured breathing, the flared nostrils, the heavy eyelids, the corners of the mouth drawn down as if by curtain weights. Then, as if starting across uncertain terrain, he began to consider the drawbacks, or, as he phrased it, the advantages that could be yet more advantageous, which were two. Sensing impatience, he plunged ahead. "First of all it is too flat."

"It is on a hill."

"I fear it is but a low hill. More of a hump."

"A hump? You are a fine geographer, sir."

There was no turning back now. "And second, it is too close to the border. American cavalry could overrun it in an hour."

Douglas was silent. Then he said, "Not if it was on the other side of the river."

Moody conceded that that would be better. "Still, it is not a wide river, vulnerable to mortar and gunfire, and could be forded at many points."

"I assume you have an alternative?"

Moody grew more confident when Douglas settled himself in a chair and put his fingertips together and composed his features in an attitude of polite attention. Moody too sat, leaned forward and spoke with heat of a location farther downriver, on the north bank, only a few miles from the sea. "We could have readier access to the ocean, enjoy the river as a barrier, and the advantage of higher ground. Cavalry would stand no chance."

"It is forested?"

"Heavily."

"There will be significant labour involved in clearing it."

"If we begin in spring it will be done by fall."

Douglas mulled. "Construction on such terrain will be difficult. It will be slow and it will be expensive. The colony must pay. You must bear that in mind. This is business. The world has changed. Countries and colonies are now investments. London is tightening the purse strings."

"I see a splendid city on a river of gold," said Moody.

"You may very well indeed, sir. Intrepid Spaniards saw cities of silver throughout South America. But there is a problem, for allotments have already been staked and claimed at Langley."

"These can easily be traded."

Douglas pressed himself deeper into his chair, gripped its arms, and shut his eyes as though taking in the panorama of Moody's vision, either that or enduring a pain. When at last he opened them he said, "Very well. Begin."

"Thank you, sir."

As Moody was leaving, Douglas asked, "By the by, whatever became of Gosset?"

Moody had been wondering the same thing. "He undertook an . . . an initiative and has not to my knowledge been heard from since."

Douglas did not ask for details; instead he sank his chin into his collar and, frowning, cogitated.

In the seventy-six days from January 25 to April 10 it rained seventy-six days. The capital of the Colony of British Columbia, not Derby but New Westminster, was baptized in a rain that did not mist or sprinkle or drizzle but fell in a deluge that could only cause Moody to conclude that the Lord, once again, was testing his mettle, that eight years on the Falklands had not been enough, that more pain and patience was demanded. The rain hit so hard it bounced, was so loud it deafened, and filled the air with such density that it was often dark at noon and all but impossible to breathe. And yet work proceeded. Drenched men felled trees that shrieked as they tilted and crashed, taking with them the canopy that had offered at least some protection from the pelting water. The Fraser River swelled brown with the muddy runoff and men slipped and cursed and sweated, moving like wraiths amid the smouldering stumps to cut, limb, peel, and then hand-mill the logs into planks slated for the houses great and small, the government offices, the boardwalks, and the monuments that would comprise a capital city.

In the meantime the Moodys lived in a tent that leaked. The pots set out to catch the drips ticked and rang like so many erratic clocks and bells and gongs. The entire family developed a cough, the twins wept and fought and wept some more, John was irritable and bored and scratched himself raw; Mary, pregnant, had a rash and some of her hair fell out, while Moody discovered a golden fungus growing between his toes.

A Native calling himself Raymond appeared every few days with salmon, eulachon oil, and advice. They ate the salmon as steaks and in stews and burned the oil in their lamps, meaning they lived in a miasma of fishy-smelling smoke, all of which made Raymond's advice, which was that they should have stayed in San Francisco, or better yet in England, all the more pointed. Raymond was in his thirties and spoke with such a decorous calm that Moody could not take umbrage or embark upon a defence of empire but could only pay him his money and wish him a good day.

For the first time in months, Moody found himself composing a letter to his father, not with pen and paper but in his mind.

Dear Father,

But he could get no further.

By April there was the addition of mosquitoes, which whined all night keeping everyone awake. The children whimpered and scratched until they bled while Mary as ever suffered in silence. She knew rain; she'd been brought up in the northlands where mist and drizzle and fog swept in from the sea all autumn and winter and spring and often throughout the summer, and the appearance of the sun was always an event. Here, in New Westminster—or the mud and stumps and smoke that would become New Westminster—she felt she was turning into an amphibian, for everything in their tent was damp and mouldy, the walls dripped, the air was moist, and even the very water itself felt somehow wetter. She recalled their year on Malta with its hot stone and dry wind, radiant light, and joyous flowers. She'd have given anything to go back but said nothing to her husband.

And there was the dog Gosset had adopted at Fort Langley. When the *Beaver* had reached Victoria no one wanted the beast, so Moody had gathered it up in a rare act of spontaneity and taken it home. The children christened her Hilda and while her weak bladder did not endear her to Mary or Moody she mewled so piteously when tied up outside they were obliged to take her in and endure her contributions, such as they were. Soon enough she was under the covers with John and the girls, diverting them from the weather and boredom as they undertook the challenge of training her. Should Gosset make a claim upon her when he returned he'd plunge irredeemably in John's eyes, something Moody would relish.

While this went on in the tent they called home, Moody slogged about the mud and the bush, twisting his knees and ankles while monitoring the work and encouraging the men. He wrote letters and reports and oversaw plans and drawings and orders, coordinating everything to the best of his abilities. As he worked he scratched his welts and his rashes and adjusted the wrappings around his knees and ankles. The appearance of some startling forms of pink and orange mildew in his boots made him recall Charles Toll in Panama City. Would he soon be rolling on the floor and frothing at the mouth? At his desk in the halo of lamplight, with his long beard and a blanket over his shoulders, he resembled a medieval monk. Mary worried about him for he was exhausted and progress was slow, and she knew he felt guilty at condemning them to such a life; more than once he suggested she return with the kids to England and each time she said no even though she wanted to say yes, or even suggest—for the good of the children's health—Malta. To divert herself she became involved in various committees, including one for the Queen's Birthday.

She said to him, "Mr Moody, there must be celebrations. Not in Victoria, but here, in New Westminster. It is expected. There needs to be a site suitable for games and parades and assemblies. It is the social event of the season and it behoves us to be ready.

The governor will be here. Begbie will be here. Upward of two thousand people will be here. Are you prepared?"

"Mrs Moody, you are adding yet another job to my list," he said wearily and leaned his head on his fist.

"No, Richard. Clear your list and throw your energies into this one job."

"Mary, I'm behind schedule as it is. Now you want—"

"Mr Moody, it isn't what I want, but what Douglas expects and what a capital city must be."

"Mrs Moody . . ." But he left off.

Fulsomely pregnant, Mary Moody wore a black cashmere shawl with gold threading about her shoulders, a tan turban on her head against the chill, and a thick wool scarf even while indoors. Her eyes were red veined from the smoke and all the more piercing because of it. She was observant and she was shrewd and she watched the world from her own angle and it was a valid one. Moody knew this and valued her opinion all the more because of it. He remembered his Machiavelli: "The first method for estimating the intelligence of a ruler is to look at the men he has around him." To this he would add: *and women.*

The children overheard this discussion of the Queen's Birthday—as they overheard everything in such close quarters— and John asked if there was to be a gala. Moody looked at him and at Abigail and Amanda, and at the dog, which seemed equally expectant, and finally at his wife, who for all their reduced circumstances was the picture of decorum, and said, "It would appear so." At which the children huzzahed and Hilda barked and piddled.

The next day he hiked about the mud and the stumps and settled upon a high and comparatively level expanse that could, within a few weeks, be readied. Yet while the improving weather should have made work move faster, it actually slowed because men began quitting en masse to rush back upriver and resume panning for gold. Even so, by the third week of May the site was functional. The day before the event Moody was gratified to see the river filled with boats. He noted the Natives who paddled upriver in their canoes and then let themselves drift back down, regarding the activities on the smoking, steaming, tent-clustered embankment in silence. He recalled stories of the ghosts of Roman legions marching through old houses in England, condemned to tramp for eternity from nowhere to nowhere. He frowned and grew inward and felt forlorn, as though witnessing the passing of a people from the sunlit world to a dusk land, and he knew that in some ways, perhaps many ways, he was if not wholly then certainly partly responsible. Looking at the site with its congealing mud, heaps of brush, and smoking fires, he knew that what he saw could as easily be called a grim desolation as a glorious beginning. Once again he thought of that first evening with Governor Douglas and his rueful musings on the inevitable misinterpretations of historians who would one day consider them. Some historians regarded the French Revolution as a disaster while others rated it a triumph. Moody grasped that he himself could be rated a knight or a knave, a visionary or a villain, and that the truth lay somewhere in between.

He tried describing this to Mary that night in bed while the kids murmured and sniffled and snored and the lamplight hovered like a conscious presence there in the tent; as usual she was far ahead of him, she understood, and said that his concerns were of course completely natural, and yet went on to caution him that, be this as it may, now was not the time to balk.

"You've come this far," she said, "and must stay the course."

He agreed that there was little alternative.

"Still, you are troubled by ethics," she observed.

He nodded, then shrugged. Ethics. How elevated that sounded.

"Shall I tell you what Amelia Douglas said?"

He waited.

"She loves her husband yet she finds herself torn."

"Torn."

"The peoples native to this land, and all of the Americas, are being overrun."

"And her very husband—"

"Exactly. He is complicit."

"But Governor Douglas's own mother—"

"A Creole."

"Making him—"

"Of course."

"And yet he marches in step with empire. Indeed leads the advance." He shook his head. "We are all living contradictions."

Mary put her hand on his chest. "I can feel the beat of your heart."

"I blame the Falklands," he said. "I never used to think so much. So much time alone. And the relentless Atlantic wind."

She took his hand and positioned it on her pregnant belly. After a moment he felt a kick and he tried to imagine the fetus, his son or daughter, living, evolving, soon to enter a world of such unrest.

"How does Lady Douglas resolve it? Did she say?"

"She cannot."

"And does the governor feel this as well?"

"The governor does not say what he feels. Do you ever miss Valletta?"

"I miss it now," he said.

The following day Moody stood on a platform and addressed the crowd, speaking with passion regarding the glory that was Britain, the eminence that was Her Majesty, the honour of being a servant of empire, the accomplishments of Governor James Douglas, and the bright future of New Westminster in particular and the Colony of British Columbia in general.

"It is 1859 and Britain is pre-eminent the world over. We rule the seas and we are on every continent. Much has been achieved yet more must be done. But is work not our purpose?" he asked. "Do we not thrive upon industry?"

Cheers and hats went up and sappers huzzahed and Moody felt gratified at the response even if he suspected that it was all show, even if he suspected in some corner of his mind that the antics of man were dubious at best and barbaric at worst and that they were all of them caught in the gears of some dread engine. It also occurred to him that no man liked tossing his hat into the air because it inevitably landed in the dirt.

Afterward, the Royal Engineers fired salutes, sailors danced, marines paraded, and young men ran races, hurled the caber, boxed, and wrestled while the children made mischief and the ladies strolled and ate pudding or sat in the women's enclosure and sipped tea and nursed their babes. Mary observed with approval as Moody was accosted on all sides by representatives from committees urgently seeking reassurances and schedules, commitments and prognostications. Through all of this Moody glimpsed Judge Begbie laughing with the Frenchman, Maxie Michaud, and envied their easy manner as they smoked cheroots, sipped cider, and swapped stories. How tired he was. So much gaiety about and such gloom within. At one point he'd have sworn he saw his father in the crowd, watching him with a stony expression.

The next morning it rained as Moody and Douglas toured New Westminster, the water cascading off their hat brims and sluicing from their shoulders. The fact that it was warm only deepened their discomfort as they perspired in their gear. Moody gazed upon his city-to-be through Douglas's eyes and saw only puddles and ditches and mud. Later that day the rain eased and the mosquitoes swarmed and a mule driven mad by their stinging ran into the Fraser and drowned. The body drifted past the *Beaver* while Moody was seeing Douglas and his party aboard. The governor's daughters, Martha and Jane, ran to the rail to look at the corpse rolling and sinking and rising while Douglas said nothing, though Moody felt certain he regarded it as an omen.

That night Moody lay awake while Mary spoke longingly in her sleep of the sunflowers in Valletta. She was lying on her side with a pillow between her knees. What a different world Malta had been, arid and stony and hot, and yet only four weeks' sail from England. Mary had blossomed there. Their room had looked west over the harbour and in the evenings they sat on the balcony amid the clay-potted flowers. How long those evenings were, how rich the range of colours in the sky and on the sea, how fragrant the foliage and bright the birds.

In June Mary was delivered of a stillborn child, a boy, and was bedridden for a fortnight, the first week of which she lay with her head turned toward the tent's grey wall and stared in silence until the demands of her children drew her back to the world.

Moody felt sick. "It is 1860," he said. "There is the telegraph and photography and electricity and steam power. There is surgery and inoculation. How can this still happen?"

His wife said nothing to this. She had known from the start of their courtship that should she marry him she'd end up in some such place as New Westminster, in the Crown Colony of British Columbia, the far edge of empire, raw, filthy, rain soaked, ripe with disease, dwarfed by mountains and trees and ocean, amid the mad and the driven, the wild and the drunken, and that her love and loyalty would be tested. But was her maiden name not Hawkes? Was the hawk not a bird of power? She had three children and a husband who was making nations and history, and it was her duty to be strong.

In July John came down with a fever and was bedridden, shivering and sweating, pale and lethargic. One morning he looked at his father from eyes red and swollen and yearning and asked, "Where's Mr Gosset? I miss Clive. Why does Clive not come see me?"

A note arrived from Governor Douglas requesting Colonel Moody present himself in Victoria for an interview at his earliest possible convenience.

"You have cleared a field and built a camp," stated Douglas. "And it has cost a pretty penny."

"The celebrations for Her Majesty's birthday were a success," murmured Moody.

Douglas ignored that and observed how in six months and tens of thousands of pounds Moody had achieved a surfeit of stumps and mud. "Were we in the business of stumps and mud, we would be rich indeed. But we are not in the business of stumps and mud.

I see no streets, much less avenues, and certainly no buildings of any consequence, nothing to attract men of business and industry. Where is the grand plan, where the capital of which you spoke? Settlers need roads. They need access to the town, to the port. It all seems rather stillborn. Reports are that you have scarcely a man at work."

Moody mumbled about the lure of gold, to which Douglas rejoined that he must simply lure them back, to which Moody responded that they must be paid to return, a difficult thing when the budget was spent.

"Hire Chinese," said Douglas. He set his massive hands flat upon his desk and sat back, square shouldered and tall, and considered Moody, an experience not unlike being measured by an unhappy bear. "Perhaps it is Victoria that should be the capital," he said at last, not without a hint of grim satisfaction.

With this thought riding like grit under his eyelid, Moody departed, Ingemar opening the door for him and closing it behind with decided emphasis. Standing a moment on the porch, he looked around thinking that it seemed an eternity since their arrival in Victoria on Christmas Day. How different Douglas House looked now, abloom with flowers, the trees in leaf, the warm brine of low tide borne on the slow wind. Moody was strangely at peace. He thought: *The governor has lost faith in me.* He thought: *The governor has crumpled me up small.* He thought: *Am I calm because I have achieved the failure I have always secretly expected?*

He dismissed the carriage that had brought him direct from the wharf and walked along with his hands clasped behind his back and the sun hot on his neck. Had not the same occurred to him on the Falklands, big plans, small budget? There at least he'd had the advantage of low official expectations. If only he were a poet he might have employed his time composing epics while the rain lashed and the wind blew and the seals barked. Walking along the Victoria waterfront, Moody recalled the view from their rooms at Malta: the warships, the walls of the fort, the scent of history in the very stone. He passed a butchery where a man in a bloody apron leaned in an open doorway, carcasses hanging on hooks on either side of him. His arms were crossed and he smoked a stinker and watched another man beat a dog, which, strangely, did not howl or whimper but bore its punishment—just or otherwise—in silence, only the report of the strap on its haunch audible in the afternoon. A little farther on a group of men were boarding a tender. Among them Moody recognized McGowan, who waved and smiled, delighted to see him.

"I am leaving!" called the American in high humour.

"But your cave."

"Take it! It is yours."

Moody actually laughed. How invigorating, he thought, to board a ship heading south. He envied him. "What will you do?" he asked, oddly pleased to see the scoundrel.

"There are rumours of war in the States. I am needed."

"On which side do you stand?"

"War is complex," said McGowan, as if loath to show his cards.

"There is north and there is south," said Moody.

"You espouse the doctrine of the excluded middle," said McGowan.

Moody was unfamiliar with any such doctrine. He said, "Lines must be drawn."

McGowan said, "Lines shift like the sands."

"Principles . . ." began Moody.

"Philosophy," said McGowan, and smiled. "We are each of us servants of empire."

Moody's dubious expression could not be mistaken.

McGowan, standing by the boat, laughed in delight. He wore the same suit as before. Perhaps it was the only one he owned. "There are as many empires as there are men. That is the difference between our two peoples."

How clear and confident the man was. And how wrong. "It sounds like anarchy."

"Not at all. It is the sound of freedom."

Moody could only shake his head and smile, for here was a man untroubled by doubt. What an enviable, if dangerous, state of mind. Did he never know remorse? Did he have no secret self? "And your bear? Did you ever hear word of your pet?"

"Ah, sadly, no."

"I am sorry," he said, and he truly was.

"Yes, she was a good one." Then he brightened. "But it don't do to dwell on the past. Milk under the bridge." He gestured grandly and looked about. "What a splendid day."

Moody too looked about and saw that indeed it was.

"You should really ask the US of A to annex this fine land, Colonel."

This was so absurd Moody barked a laugh. When he asked, Whyever for? McGowan declared it would be for the mutual benefit of all, which caused Moody to say that it would only benefit the Americans.

"But do you not see?" cried McGowan. "We are all Americans if we so choose!" He then hopped nimbly aboard the boat. "Good luck to you, Colonel!"

"And to you." Moody was about to turn away when he called, "What of your museum? What of your collection?"

"Sold!" he shouted, as though to the highest bidder. "They were all worthless anyway." McGowan waved his hand, and that was when Moody spotted the ruby ring on his finger. They were still close, only a few yards distant, and McGowan saw what had taken Moody's attention. "Your Mr Gosset remembered me after all. Returned to pay me a visit and left a token of his esteem." McGowan's smile grew brighter while his eyes darkened.

FRISADIE – 1867

New Brighton

TWO DAYS AFTER READING HARRY HEARNE'S ARTICLE, Maxie announced that he was going to Quebec. It had been seventeen years, he said. He'd be gone four months, maybe less, maybe more, depending upon the travel, first south to San Francisco by sea and then east via train.

Frisadie managed to suggest, casually, reasonably, that she go with him, adding that they could return via Europe and the Far East, visit Hawai'i and say hello to Hocking and look up her relatives. She even managed a lighthearted tone though her voice quavered in terror and her throat felt like rope.

He seemed angry as he reminded her yet again that for him sea journeys were impossible, and more importantly the hotel needed someone reliable and that therefore she had to stay. "I don't look forward to all this travel," he assured her, "especially the boat to San Francisco." He made it seem as if the whole business was an unwanted obligation, a chore put off too long, that he'd been badgered beyond endurance. His gaze prowled the room as he spoke. At last their eyes met and he looked sad and furtive and then managed, with enormous effort, to smile and say, with forced heartiness, "We are good."

Good? What did he mean by good? Was that a statement or a question? Was this a reference to their moral standing, their efficiency? When Frisadie inquired whether or not he'd write he said he'd be back before the letters arrived.

"Still," she said, offhand, gazing at the degraded mural of herself on the wall, "a note from San Francisco. So that I know you're safe, so that the guests know. I've heard rumour that there's unrest among the tongs."

"And what has that to do with me? Come."

He opened his arms and with reluctance she went to him, and he embraced her and said that she had to be strong, that she was young and smart and brave and beautiful, and that he'd be back soon. She clung to those words even as she clung to him, and then she stood back though she held on to his hands. Everything about Maxie was thick, his fingers, his wrists, his forearms, his chest, his neck, his nose, his eyebrows, his ears, and all too often his mind.

The day after Maxie left, Frisadie forced herself through a regimen of chores so as to exhaust herself and help her sleep that night rather than lie awake—which she did anyway. Was it possible that they'd been together over two years—two years that didn't seem half as long as that one night? She reflected that she didn't honestly know if she even loved him, not really, even if she'd said she did, because she couldn't be sure she knew what romantic love felt like, and she supposed that if she could doubt it, then she didn't really feel it, at least not judging by the descriptions she'd read in novels of all-consuming, all-encompassing, unconditional, enrapturing, elevating, transporting, exalting love. Not that that made her feel any better about his departure. She'd overheard lady guests with their chairs drawn close speaking of loving their husbands while not being *in love* with them. There was brotherly love, the love of God, the love of nature, the love of food, of dancing, of music, of animals, the love for one's children. So many voices speaking the word *love* made her wonder if those various loves had their own shapes and colours, blue love, red love, grey love, green, even black. Then again, maybe love was best measured in purity, like silver, ninety-two point five percent pure, whereas everything below, say, eighty percent indicated only a passing fancy, a momentary infatuation, and was unfit grounds for marriage. Of course she understood Maxie's bitterness over Harry Hearne's article. Still, Maxie could *pass*. No Québécois, no Irishman, no Slav, however disdained by the English, could ever know Frisadie's experience. Lying alone in bed each night over the following days and weeks, she envisioned Maxie assuming a new life in the cafés of Montreal, regaling old friends and new, both male and female, with his stories. No doubt there would be many romantic temptations for him—hotelier, raconteur, adventurer—just as there were for her. There was no shortage of men who offered Frisadie their compliments, and she wouldn't deny being tempted by one or two splendid young Kanakas who frankly regarded her and asked what she was doing here among the *haole*, and were surprised to learn that she wasn't the maid.

Early one morning a Native woman appeared on the deck. Frisadie was up and about in the dining room and, sensing some presence, had looked out the French doors to see her staring in. She seemed about her own age, solid, composed, bemusedly curious, like someone on a stroll who pauses to note an unfamiliar bird or flower. Her hair was braided in two long plaits and she wore a shawl. She did not acknowledge Frisadie even when their gazes met. After a few long moments of eye contact—during which Frisadie felt frozen, judged, confused—she simply turned away and descended the steps. Though Frisadie never saw her again she occasionally thought of her. Had the woman known Oliver Hocking? Did she recall New Brighton before it had been cleared? Should Frisadie have invited her in? What would the guests have thought?

The summer rush of guests diverted her. Even with the hired help the days were long and exhausting, what with putting on the charm and the chatter. At night she lay awake, and when she did sleep she had dreams, or visions, or visitors, that is to say one visitor: the ghost of her mother. She lingered off and on for a week. Frisadie would wake in the night to see her sitting by the window staring out, or she'd be standing at the end of the corridor at dawn, or looking into the mirror in Frisadie's room even though she cast no reflection. Only once did she look at Frisadie, and when she did she said, in the dry voice of one who hadn't talked in eons, that she missed Frisadie's father and the warmth of the sun, because where she was it was cold and grey and sad.

This did not jibe with the Hawaiian view of the afterlife, meaning that this mother figure was only an emanation of Frisadie's distressed mind. In her loneliness she'd been thinking of Hawai'i and her parents and the many uncles and aunts and cousins she vaguely recalled. Her father had been stout and tall and always dressed like a European in a coat and boots in spite of the heat, was always sweet with orange cologne, spoke proper English rather than pidgin, had a large smile and loud laugh, though his eye was often wary because he'd had run-ins with *haole* who didn't approve of whatever it was they thought he was up to. He and her mother had argued a lot, he having turned out to be more restless than she'd expected, talking often of distant cities, in particular San Francisco and Victoria, places that at the time meant little to Frisadie but were enough to terrify her mother. The day they boarded the *Cowlitz* a crowd of relatives and friends saw them off. The tears and the wailing frightened her so much that her father assured her that they'd be back soon, that they were merely going for a boat ride. She knew he was fibbing because his eyes were rainy and her mother's face cloudy and the others distraught, and Frisadie clung to her parents, her father to her left and her mother to her right, as the ship, massive, pungent, strange, all iron and brass and smoke, vibrated with noise and activity that she couldn't understand other than to know that it was bad.

———————

Also bad was the fact that she discovered she was pregnant. She'd missed her monthly before but this time there was no mistake; she could feel it in her belly, she was with child. Her thoughts flared in every direction. Some were streamers of joy, most the smoke of attacking shellfire. She tried convincing herself that Maxie would be happy but was not successful, indeed was almost relieved that she had no address to which to direct a letter to him. But would she write if she had one? Stunned, she went through the following days like a sleepwalker, preoccupied, inward, stubbing her toes on chair legs, knocking her shins on the fire screen. If she'd felt isolated before, now she was well and truly alone, a world of one—soon to be two. She thought ahead to what was in store for her. If Maxie reacted well, then all would be fine. Judging by his reaction to her hints about children, however, she could not be optimistic, in which case she should terminate. She was not so unworldly as to think this was either simple or safe. Mrs Frame had often spoken of fallen women dead on the abortionist's table. Was it possible that her life had come to this so soon? Where was the ghost of her mother now? She lay awake in bed at night trying to conjure her back but failed. Was her mother punishing her? Was the world punishing her for having got above herself?

What heroic effort it took to mask this catastrophe and appear amiable and accommodating to her guests and attend to their crises: soup that was not quite hot enough, tea too weak, beef that was overly peppered. One morning a lady who insisted on wearing her parrot-feathered hat at breakfast spat her rosehip jam onto her plate and cried: "It's not jam; it's nuffink but red sand. Where's the manager?"

"I am the manager."

"You?"

Rarely had Frisadie witnessed such rage and incomprehension in a pair of eyes.

———

One balmy Sunday in autumn, when the season's business had tailed off, a family of three arrived on the coach and strolled about the grounds. The man and woman were tall and slim and the daughter, about five years of age, fair and willowy and silent. The adults seemed tense. The man, dark bearded and athletic, in black linen trousers and stitched vest, pointed here and there with his stick as though appraising everything he saw. Presently they entered the hotel and asked for tea, which was promptly served. Frisadie couldn't but note it was a tense affair, the woman coaching their daughter on the niceties of table manners—*No, Leonora, like so. No, Leonora, like this.* When they'd eaten, the man, in spite of dark looks from his wife, became conversational, questioning Frisadie about the New Brighton: how long Maxie and she had run her, what changes they'd made, the volume of business, the earnings of the hotel versus the dining room, their plans, if any, for the future, and then apologizing if he was overly inquisitive, which his wife stated he was, very much so. He smiled affably as though she'd not spoken at all and plowed on, "But I like hotels, my dear. I like a good crowd and bonhomie."

Frisadie allowed that the business could be exhausting and his wife, triumphant, said, "There! Do you see?" while he said that in his experience people kindled him, at which point the young girl spoke up and asked about Lydia, causing the mother to shut her eyes as if in pain. Tossing down her bunched napkin she stood, declared that a bear was not a pet, that it belonged in a zoo, or its skin on a floor, and directed the girl to come along, and the two of them went outside while the man, breathing a long persevering sigh, poured himself another cup of tea and began to hum "Barbara Allen."

———

Day by day Frisadie monitored the state of her belly. She cradled it and stroked it and studied it; she closed her eyes and went within as old Mrs Mace had once advised and tried to feel the being growing inside her. For a time she was able to reassure herself that the changes were too subtle to show. As a precaution she began letting out her frocks in her room at night, picking apart the seams and resewing them lest the help notice anything. It occurred to her to put on a show of overeating and then throw the food out the window into the forest but the subterfuge was just too sad and too desperate. Torn between defiance and despair, she watched for Maxie's return even as she dreaded it.

It was four months before Maxie arrived. No letter preceded him. One moment he was absent, the next he was present. And he wasn't alone. Thérèse Colette Marchand—now Thérèse Colette Michaud née Marchand—was broad across the hips and half a head shorter than Maxie, her complexion mottled, her upper lip darkly furred, her eyebrows meeting above a snub red nose, and her hair thinning. But Frisadie knew from the picture gazettes that her travelling outfit was *de rigueur* and *à la mode* and *au courant*. Then there was the wedding ring on her finger, a ruby embedded in gold.

She was cordial. She moved to embrace Frisadie, who held her hips well back even though her pregnancy was not yet blatant. Thérèse Colette pecked her on either cheek, then stood away, still holding on to her hands as she viewed her, observing over her shoulder to Maxie, "Elle est encore plus belle que tu ne le disais."

"Mais oui," muttered Maxie.

And then to Frisadie, "You must show me everything, my pet," as if implying that they were a team and she would be rolling her sleeves up and mucking on in alongside her. Yet if that was her intention it would have to wait, for it seemed she'd suffered on the journey and even now was plagued by a rash on her neck and cracks at the corners of her mouth, and a touch of the palsy. She announced that she was *très fatiguée* and said to Frisadie, "Popo, s'il vous plaît. I will bathe, but the water must not be too hot, then again not too cool, with three ounces of lavender salts, then I will take lunch, beefsteak and asparagus and a glass of beer, after which I will nap. The pillows, they are goose down? I must have goose down, or duck, but not chicken; chicken feathers are a torment. Thank you, my pet, you are such a treasure. We will be great friends, you and I." And she pinched her cheek.

During this performance Maxie did not exactly avoid Frisadie; he simply didn't seem to see her, his eyes dry and his gaze distant, or he was a different Maxie altogether, as if the man she'd known hadn't returned, had stepped off the stage and allowed an actor to stand in for him. She'd seen something of this before in the way he shifted from English to French; it wasn't merely the language but his voice that changed, his face, his entire manner, even, it appeared, his very mind and, it would seem, his heart.

Frisadie sent the maid to sort out the room, which had been their room, the room she and Maxie had shared, the room in which they had made love, the room in which she had been impregnated, and then she retreated to the one farthest along the corridor where, seated on the side of the bed, hands folded in her lap, just beneath her gently swollen belly, she watched herself from afar. She was feeling strangely calm and oddly remote, as if she was becoming smaller and smaller, receding into the distance—a distance that gave her a new perspective and a clearer view of what had to be done. She thought, *Well, girl, this is the new Order of Things and you can simply flow along or you can make a scene.* The one was impossible and the other too tedious to contemplate. Had she suspected this the very moment Maxie had announced that he was leaving? Had she merely denied its inevitability?

With a groan she stood, for there was only one thing to do. She straightened her frock and cleared her throat and then took a deep breath and stepped out of the room. To the right she heard Thérèse Colette splashing in the bath. She went the other way, toward the dining room—empty—and continued on out to the balcony where she found Maxie leaning on the railing, smoking a cigar and looking out over the grassy slope and the inlet. Maxie turned as Frisadie opened the door and stepped onto the deck. His eyes went wide as he gazed past her as though seeking Thérèse Colette's protection.

"A word, Mr Michaud, if it isn't too much trouble."

He took his cigar from his mouth. His gaze cut left, then right, as if seeking an escape. He took a step back, met the railing, and stiffened.

Frisadie crossed her arms over her chest and, as she did so, couldn't help wondering at him that he didn't see, didn't sense, that she was carrying his child. On this, however, she did not dwell. Instead, she demanded: "Explain."

His mouth opened, then shut.

"Well?"

His eyes looked like greasy windows. She could see a shape—him—lurking within.

"Is this some joke?" she asked. "An example of French humour? Is she"—she pointed back into the hotel—"an actress?"

"Change," he blurted. "Things change. It is the way of the world."

"Change?" For a moment the word lay like a mustard seed on her tongue. She didn't know whether to weep or sneer. "You mean you changed. Because apparently you have many faces. And different stories come from each one. You're a liar, Maxie, a two-faced liar."

His face twitched. "I fell in love."

She maintained a smooth expression even as the blade entered her heart. She thought she might fall over. Everything beyond Maxie blurred.

He became despairing. "It's complex."

"You mean it's *complexion*, Mr Michaud."

"Stop calling me that. Be reasonable."

"Reasonable? Fine, let us be reasonable. Let us reason, shall we? What do we reasonably do now? Do you expect me to be reasonable and stay here as, what, the maid? Or should I be reasonable and vanish?"

He was breathing hard. There were tears in his eyes. "I'm sorry."

"Well." She laughed, or tried, for it staggered in her throat. "That makes me feel so much better. So very much better." Then she sobbed.

"Fizzy . . ."

"Don't call me that." Stepping away, she dragged the back of her wrist across her eyes. "You knew from the moment you left. You went off to find a wife. A *white* wife. So that, what? that Harry Hearne—*Harry Hearne*, Maxie—would approve? So he'd forget you're a Frog and write more respectfully next time? Have you already invited him for another visit? Is it all arranged? Are they going to make you an honorary Englishman?"

He turned away and gripped the railing.

Pale-grey gulls spiralled above the ice-blue inlet. A chill breeze shook the last leaves from the maples. What a black shape Maxie was. A silhouette. A figure of wood, dry, desiccated. His heart—if he had one—a burl. Yet it was done. It was over. They were through.

Maxie turned and said, "I'll pay you out, of course. Your entire five hundred, and more. Don't worry. Trust me."

Too tired to mock the word *trust*, she studied him to see if he saw the irony. He did not. Of course he didn't. She said, "All part of being reasonable, is it? Pay off whatshername. You know, the one who came up with the hotel idea, the one whose bed you shared, the one who spent the past months working all but alone."

Face writhing under his beard, he said, "We'll get the papers in order immediately. Take out a mortgage to get the cash." There was no need to state what they both knew: he'd put in the majority of the money, he was white, male, and therefore he was in control. "In the meantime . . ." His voice was a croak and he looked as if he might be sick.

Frisadie's spine was wilting under the weight of her heartache. Behind her a trail of lies and ahead of her, darkness. She looked at Maxie with resignation, her lips compressed, her jaw tight, offering him one more opportunity to . . . to what? Blither more excuses? Was now the time to tell him? To play her ace? Ace? Is that what the creature inside her was? She felt sick. With nothing left to her but a penny of dignity, she turned and went into the hotel, packed her old carpet bag and on the way out took the wooden pineapple from the mantel, hiked on up the hill to the road, where she paused and looked back at the hotel, the beach, the wharf, the inlet, all chipped blue glass in the pale November sun, the densely forested slopes on the far shore, and then, the morning stage having departed, began walking the ten miles to New Westminster.

Frisadie took a room at the Barclay and sent word to Maxie that he could contact her there to complete their financial settlement. For three days she lay on the bed or sat by the window, mind all but blank and any thoughts she did have meaningless and erratic. Staring out at the street, she counted the number of bearded men versus clean-shaven men who passed in the space of an hour, and then the number of men who had only a moustache, the number of women who walked alone versus in the company of men or children—few, very few—the ratio of dogs to cats, crows to pigeons, and concluded nothing other than what she'd already concluded the day Maxie returned, which was that her mother had been right: *You can't trust them.*

But what of her child? She lay on the bed and cradled her belly, discreetly rounded, and tried to think, tried to cut a path through the thicket of her future, if she had a future, and on the fourth day, driven by desperation, by the plain and simple fact that she had no alternative, she bathed, changed her clothes, fluffed her blouse, turned to the right and turned to the left evaluating her profile, sucked her belly in, let her belly out, poked at her hair, and emerged upon the cool clear morning. She'd had no word from Maxie so she rode the stage to New Brighton, staring out the window the entire way, saying nothing to the other passengers, two of whom, women, regarded her—a black—with crow-eyed rage. When she strode down the sloping lawn toward the hotel, she viewed her home of nearly three years in a new perspective. Had she actually lived there? Had she all but made the place? Yes, and now the building itself was desecrated. How foreign she felt climbing the steps to the main entrance and opening the glass-paned door. Did the air smell different? Dung? Mothballs? Perhaps a hint of vomit? To her relief, Monsieur's Juste's mural was gone, only the ghost of a rectangle remaining. Thérèse Colette had had the good judgment to remove it, something she herself had not. She walked to the desk and pinged the bell and a strange man appeared. Thin face, high hair, long sideburns, and a none-too-clean collar. He halted, unsure how to react.

"Where is Mr Michaud?"

"Monsieur Michaud and his wife left for San Francisco yesterday."

She walked back up the hill as the stagecoach was disappearing around the bend, its wheels splashing through the puddles, and into the forest and was obliged once again to walk the ten miles to New Westminster.

———————

Presenting herself at the Hotel Victory, New Westminster's finest, Frisadie asked for Gregory Barnes, chief assistant manager. The desk clerk seemed alarmed. He was young, slim, pale, fidgety, with a sorry moustache and spots on his brow. When Mr Barnes emerged—the panelled door to his office so highly varnished that the gaslight rippled like water over the moulding—he hesitated; it was only a brief hesitation, yet during that half second Frisadie saw his mind race and she feared that he didn't recognize her out of the context of the New Brighton, that here, now, she was but some anonymous brown face ready to waste his precious time. Then he smiled.

"Frisadie."

"Gregory."

"You're looking well."

"Am I?"

He seemed bemused by her response.

She wondered if, in spite of her situation socially, physically her body was blooming.

He looked past her. "Where is he? Eh? Where's old Max?"

"I'm afraid I'm alone."

He seemed confused. Then he understood. "Shopping spree!"

How hopeful he was; how bad she felt for disappointing him. "Not exactly."

Inviting her into his office he held a chair for her, then took his place behind his desk, a broad affair with inlaid wood and stacks of paper in trays and memos on spikes, and then sat forward, hands folded, in an attitude of eager interest. "Still away, is he? Off in old Montreal?"

"No, he's returned."

"Ah." Gregory was Maxie's age, though with a younger and healthier bearing, his straight dark hair parted in the middle, with curls at each temple, smooth forehead, bright blue eyes, a heavy moustache, a commendable chin, clean collar, and glinting fob. He appeared much restrained compared with the occasions on which he'd visited the New Brighton when, admittedly, he'd been in drink. Frisadie briefly explained her reduced circumstances. It was a grim epiphany, but he grasped the situation. "Ah, I see." He expelled a big breath of air as if having suffered a personal blow. "Nasty. I'm so sorry. Well." He sucked air through his teeth and regarded her. "I'm so sorry."

"So am I."

He widened his eyes and assumed a suitable expression of remorse and yet resolution. "A job." The word sounded foreign to him, like a pebble in his mouth.

Frisadie did her best not to wince. "I was thinking more of a *position*. You know my qualifications."

"Of course. Only . . . so you and Max . . ."

"I'm afraid so."

"Gad." His gaze roamed the office seeking an escape from the awkwardness.

She gripped her handbag in her lap and tried to sit taller, for she was feeling pathetic and absurd and foolish at having inflicted herself upon him, and it was all she could do to resist running back to her room.

"It's just that," he confessed, "I don't really have anything . . . suitable. I mean, I wouldn't dream of insulting you with a . . . a *maid's* position."

She smiled bravely. "I had rather thought I'd moved on."

"Of course! Absolutely!" He tapped his blotter and frowned around as if seeking a solution there on one of his shelves. "Do you . . . need a loan?"

"No!" she lied. She'd been to the bank and been informed that the New Brighton Hotel account had been frozen; without Maxie she could do nothing.

Gregory was relieved, and for the next few minutes he made noises of bewildered but reassuring concern until the torment was unbearable, at which she took pity on him and stood, sucking her belly in while discreetly fluffing her frock.

"If there's anything I can do," he said quickly. "I'll ask around. Keep my eyes and ears open."

"Of course."

She tried two more of the city's better hotels. In one she was ushered out as if caught trespassing; in the other she was offered the scullery.

So, Mrs Frame's expression said, you are back where you belong, down among the women. As sharp eyed as she was shrewd and suspicious, her gaze went straight to Frisadie's stomach. But it was not Frisadie's belly that betrayed her but her eyes, which ran with tears.

"I have nowhere else to go," she said, maintaining a strong gaze, elevated chin, and steady voice.

Mrs Frame's face twisted, first with the desire to sneer, then with the desire to laugh, then a reluctant wave of concern smoothed it over. Still, she would have her moment. "Well," she said, loudly, gazing about for witnesses, neighbours, passersby, anyone who might share her *schadenfreude*, "look how the mighty have fallen."

Frisadie said nothing. Best to let Mrs F drink her fill of the dark wine. Better the dignity of silence. This seemed to work, for eventually the older woman sucked her teeth and cleared her throat and finally stood back, allowing Frisadie to enter. It turned out she'd timed it right, for it just so happened there was need of a chambermaid, the last one—Was there no end to foolish and ungrateful young women?—having run off with an *Eye-talian*. When Frisadie stood in her old room the full weight of circumstance crushed her. Until Maxie returned she was penniless. She looked out at the river as she used to do and watched the mud-grey water flowing to the sea. Such reflection, however, was not permitted for very long.

"Frisdadie!"

"Yes, Mrs Frame!" Tying her apron, which fit much more snugly than before, she hurried down to the kitchen.

The lodgers she'd known previously had all moved on, but the current crop greeted her with familiar delight. Her reputation, it seemed, had preceded her. It was Popo this, Popo that, more tea, Popo, more potatoes, Popo, will you be my Mathilda McGee, Popo—so sang one who fancied himself an artiste and a tenor.

> *Come polish the key to my heart, my dear,*
> *Come polish the key today,*
> *For you are a lock and I am he*
> *Who will make you his come May.*

After a fortnight and no word from Maxie, Frisadie again went to New Brighton and was again informed that Mr Michaud had yet to return, though this time she managed to catch the stage-coach back to New Westmister.

Apparently she embodied such a figure of broken docility that, after glutting herself on the gravy of Frisadie's fallen state, Mrs Frame was moved to pity, and one day she deigned to offer her a cup of tea, cold, of course, the dregs of the morning pot, but sweetened with a lump of sugar—from which she'd first picked the ants—and proceeded to offer wise counsel.

"Frisdadie, you won't believe it, but I'm here to tell you that you will survive. You likely don't believe it, but you will. Look at me."

She lifted her gaze from the tabletop with its frayed red-and-white check cloth. While she had finally begun to show, Mrs F had become even leaner, a stick dried in the sun, hardened, cracked, desiccated, but apparently retaining the sap of human feeling, for she embarked upon an impressive series of tales from her own life and times that featured a good many bad men, a few of whom had promised marriage. Unfortunately, the one who proved honour-able and finally did marry her was also the weakest and he died.

"Seventeen years and not a day goes by that I don't miss him. Now, as to you, young miss. What are your plans about that?" She jutted her chin at Frisadie's belly.

"I have money owed me. I will work until the last moment, then pay you for room and board." Seeing the slate-eyed look of the older woman, Frisadie spoke quickly, assuring her that she'd stay out of sight. "I promise that I will be no trouble and bring no disrepute to your house."

"Trouble." She pronounced the word as if to say she knew every side of trouble. "Disrepute." That too seemed to bemuse her. "Does the Frenchy bugger know?"

Frisadie shook her head.

"Why?"

"He doesn't deserve to."

"Or doesn't deserve not to," she muttered. She pushed out her lower lip and brooded awhile, then said, "Well, it's your decision. Right, drink up that tea, for there's good sugar in it."

Frisadie nodded and did as advised.

Mrs Frame began giving her more responsibilities—perhaps seeing in her, in her newly humbled state, a creature who could at last be moulded to her specifications—and as reward gave her a raise that brought her wage back up to where it had been before she'd betrayed her. She dropped ha'pennies in Frisadie's hand like the Queen bestowing royal favour. Though Frisadie was not ungrateful, the burlesque of redemption cast her down so low that she entertained the darkest thoughts. As one of her responsibilities once again included rat killing, she took a new interest in the proclamations on the label of the Hawke's Rodent Remedy. *Efficacy and Clemency! The Twin Virtues of Strychnine and Opium! Brisk and Benign!* She thought how in other circumstances she'd have begun squirrelling away pellets in a jar and when the time came do herself in, but of course that option was now impossible. She was, it appeared, condemned to carry on.

In the meantime she remained a dogged, if dour, reader of copies of *The British Columbian* left by the lodgers. There was an article on one Ives W. McGaffey of Chicago who had patented what he called "a sweeping machine" guaranteed to relieve chars, maids, and other menials of the drudgery of time-wasting labour with broom and pan, thereby freeing them for other, more edifying chores. There was a report on a certain arithmetician called Luca Pacioli, the father of double-entry bookkeeping, and a photograph of his face, in an advertisement for the new Barnes Business College. She learned that Mr Lewis Carroll had followed up *Alice's Adventures in Wonderland* with a poem called "The Hunting of the Snark," that Queen Victoria was to be crowned Empress of India, and that sardines could now be had in tins. But all this was nothing compared with the news that the New Brighton Hotel was for sale. Frisadie was all set to make her third return to New Brighton when an announcement followed that Maxie Michaud and his good wife had sold the New Brighton Hotel to a George Black and would be moving to New Westminster and taking up residence in the top floor of the Colonial Hotel. Callers were invited to leave their cards.

The very idea of having to see the eminent Mr and Mrs My-chod out and about in New Westminster in their own fine carriage, drawn by fine black horses, Thérèse Colette in a plumed chapeau and pigskin gloves, a fur collar and gleaming brooch, drove Frisadie to her bed. She lay on her side with a pillow between her knees. She was eight months pregnant and felt as if she'd eaten a piglet whole. While her face burned with rage and shame, the baby, ever more active over the preceding weeks, rolled and thrust. In mounting discomfort and despair, she remained there all morning and when Mrs Frame came stomping up the stairs at noon she found her in the process of giving birth.

Frisadie recognized Maxie's large looping handwriting. Fearful, eager, she cut open the envelope. It was a short letter, a note, and it made no mention of finances, only asked her to visit him. She was suspicious and she was angry. What was he up to? Was Thérèse Colette behind it? Frisadie looked to Kai—Kaimana, "power of the sea"—sleeping soundly in his crib. To her relief he was as dark as she was, perfect and beautiful, and she did not know how she could ever have doubted wanting him. Show him to Maxie? Let Mr My-chod see what he'd given up, make him suffer in the knowledge that he would never know his son? Or would he count that a relief? She sent a note saying that they could meet at the bank to sort out their finances and made no mention of the child. He responded with a note saying please. She sent a note questioning the wisdom of meeting him, to which he responded by begging her to see him. She said he could see her at the bank. He said that he was too ill to go to the bank, that he was all but bedridden, that time was running out, that they had to talk and could they please cease with these infernal letters? She said that all he had to do was stop writing and—Hey presto!—the infernal letters would cease. He wrote one word: *Please.*

Before leaving the boarding house she stood before the mirror debating how much effort to devote to her appearance. On the one hand she didn't want Maxie thinking she was getting herself up for his sake; on the other she didn't want to look forlorn. No, the best punishment would be to look serenely indifferent, as though he was but a shadow from the distant past, scarcely to be recalled. It occurred to her to invent a suitor, better yet a fiancé, a man of means, yet in that case why would she still be working for Mrs F? She opted for a tan skirt and white blouse and wove her hair in a French braid, the better for Maxie to see that even if Thérèse Colette what's-her-name had white skin—or whitish, for in truth it put Frisadie in mind of a fungus—her hair was burnt grass next to Frisadie's black silk, and she was as squat as a toad.

As Frisadie was leaving, Mrs Frame gave her a shopping list. She had spotted the letters travelling back and forth.

"You'd best get your money from that two-faced little Frog eater."

"I intend to. Will you watch Kai?"

"Of course. And get more rat poison," she said. "There's still rats. That's your fault. You're too kind, too kind by half, and that won't do. It's how that Froggy bugger snookered you in the first place. Rats smell kind hearts. There's your problem in a nutshell."

"Thank you, Mrs Frame."

"You're welcome."

She bought Stilton, mustard, chutney, salt, soap, walnuts, figs, and the Hawke's, and carried the hemp bag over her left arm while in her right was a furled umbrella. If men ogled her she didn't notice, for she was older now and ballasted by weighty business. She was feeling frightened but strong. The birth had gone well, six hours of pain blurred thanks to a good dose of laudanum that Mrs Frame had stashed for emergencies. To Frisadie's immense relief, Mrs Frame had proven an able midwife and furthermore she had taken to Kai and quite doted on him. As for the lodgers, Mrs F terrorized them into keeping any and all remarks to themselves. Frisadie reassured both herself and Mrs F that soon there would be money—unless of course Maxie and Thérèse what's-her-face were out to gouge her. Was it possible? She walked faster. How light her body felt now that she'd given birth, how free she felt even if burdened by doubts regarding Maxie's motives. The cobbles of Columbia Street glistened in the spring drizzle and the horse dung steamed.

Approaching the Colonial she looked up at the wrought-iron grilles and ornamental balconies of the third floor, half of which Maxie and Thérèse Colette—did she really require, did she really merit, so many names?—were apparently renting. No doubt they'd seen a tidy profit from the sale of the hotel, some thirty-seven point five percent of which, by her calculation, was rightly hers, not to mention the more difficult to calculate value of her hours and effort. Did they plan to buy her off with a token to forestall legal action and a bigger settlement? Did Frisadie smell the influence of that toady little dragon squatting on her hoard? Pulling open the door, she walked straight to the reception desk, ignoring the billiard players and card players and the drinkers who all turned to stare. Thomas Grelley was in the very same spot, in the seemingly very same clothes she'd last seen him in a thousand days previously.

"Mr Thomas."

"Miss Frisadie. Or should I say Popo?"

"You should not."

"Then I won't."

"Then I thank you."

With his quill he indicated the marble stairs. Frisadie lingered to observe that he was looking well, and he responded that appearances were deceiving. She said that she was sorry to hear it, and he said he was sorry to say it, then asked her to pass his regards on to Maxie, for he'd not seen him in five days.

"Is he ill?"

"More in the heart than in the body, I suspect."

Frisadie went up the wide shallow steps, turning this statement for its meanings. The wooden hand railing was sticky, on the first-floor landing flies were drowning in a brimming spittoon, on the second floor came a woman's shrill laughter and then a loud slap that silenced the laughter, and on the third lurked the odours of cigar and vinegar. The runner was threadbare and the gas lamps in their sylph sconces whispered like conspirators. Maxie and Thérèse Colette occupied room three hundred. The gold card read *Michaud* in elaborate indigo cursive. Frisadie took a deep breath and nearly gagged, for the air was dense with dust and the stained-glass windows at either end of the corridor apparently did not open. She lifted the brass ring in the lion's mouth and tapped once, then stepped back holding her umbrella and bag, fearing that the thumping of her heart, so deafening in her own ears, might well be audible to the entire floor.

"Come." Maxie's voice came faint though unmistakable in its mix of gravel and velvet.

The brass knob was loose and as she pushed, the heavy door creaked on its hinges. At the New Brighton she'd never have let such things go. As soon as she saw the view, however, she forgot the hotel's flaws, for the panorama south over the river all the way to the pale silhouettes of the islands beyond was spectacular, if not as raw, wild, or immediate as that of the New B. Maxie was looking distinctly unspectacular, seated in a wing chair, his feet in felted black slippers burred with dustballs, propped on an ottoman. Frisadie shocked herself by laughing, because he was wearing a robe with palms and camels and atop his head, a fez, as though he was someone's idea of a pasha.

"You look like an organ grinder's monkey."

He didn't know whether to be relieved by her laughter or indignant at the insult, so he merely stared. He said, "You are looking well."

She regarded him. He seemed to sense no change in her—did not even notice the size of her swollen bosom. "You are not."

"Nor do I feel it."

Maxie had shrunk so drastically that she was frightened. And then satisfied. Good, he was in pain. Holding her bag and umbrella she waited for him to state his business and, more to the point, pay her the money she was owed.

"Miss Fizzy."

"Mr My-chod."

He winced as if such aloofness was uncalled for. "Please." He indicated a matching chair, buttoned oxblood leather with its own ottoman.

"Do you have my money?"

"Yes, yes, yes!" he said impatiently. "Now please. Sit."

"I went twice to the hotel."

"I'm sorry."

"No word. Oh, he's off to Frisco and by the by the account is frozen."

"Will you please sit?"

Reluctantly she sat. Between them stood a hammered brass table crowded with smudged blue medicine bottles with blurred labels, a spoon, a plate, a tumbler with fingerprints all over it, a bunched napkin, spent matchsticks, cigar stubs. The room smelled stale and smoky, and in spite of the warm weather there was a fire in the grate and a supply of split wood in the box.

"First of all, thank you for coming."

She nodded once and left it at that.

Weighing her reserve he concluded that he had no choice but to proceed. "I'm a fool."

Not about to debate the point, Frisadie gazed off around the suite, noting the patterned wood-block floor, the India rugs—burned and gnawed—the flocked red velvet wallpaper above the yolk-yellow wainscotting, the ball-and-claw furniture, the well-stocked liquor trolley. Maxie was quick to offer her a drink and she was just as quick to shake her head; this was no social call. He frowned into his beard, which, along with his ears and eyebrows, needed trimming, a courtesy, an intimacy, that she used to perform. She let the silence harden and wondered if his woman was waiting in another room ready to make an entrance should Maxie botch the job of buying her off.

"Frisadie—"

"Your good wife is well?" She spoke loudly so that Thérèse Colette Whatshername might hear if she was indeed lurking in another room and be compelled to show herself.

"She is in New York." He stated this with a grimace, as though revelling in his humiliation.

"New York?"

He nodded and looked off out the window.

"And why aren't you with her? I understand that you accompanied her to San Francisco. Braving the ocean voyage," she couldn't keep from adding. "Was it a pleasant cruise?"

He turned to her, his eyes red, face haggard, shoulders low. "I was seasick the entire way. Both ways. It nearly killed me."

"I'm sorry."

"No, you're not."

"No, I'm not."

"Come back to me."

Had she heard correctly? If her heart now leapt it was so weighted with rage and resentment that it plunged right back down. But the real reason it had leapt was that it meant she could say no, that she could hurt him. "I'd rather eat crushed glass. Just pay me my money and let me go."

"I was bewitched."

"No," she said quietly, "you sought her, you travelled all the way across the continent in search of her, your white wife."

He collapsed forward and put his face into his hands, a sight that caused Frisadie both pain and satisfaction.

She found herself gripping the arms of her chair. "But I'm curious. Why didn't you at least get an English wife, I mean, if you are so desperate for their respect? Certainly you could have dredged one up. Gone down to the dock and had your pick from the immigrant ships. Washed her down and dressed her up."

He lurched upright. "I don't know. I clearly don't know anything, do I? I'm a stupid man. A stupid, stupid man!" He stared in agony at the stamped tin ceiling and said that Thérèse Colette was soon to depart New York for Paris. "And Prague, Vienna. Then Rome. And Stamboul. And Beirut. And Damascus—" He flung his hand and then let his head loll to the right and looked at Frisadie so bereft, so woebegone, that it almost moved her.

"And you are here," she observed quietly.

"And I am here," he whispered, as though as bewildered as she as to how it had all come to pass. "We could begin again," he said, pleadingly. "I'll marry you. Now. Today!" He slid to his knees and groped for her hands and began kissing them.

She pulled free. "You're already married."

He looked up at her. "We can be together."

"Maxie," she said, as cold and sad as a burdened god, "we *were* together."

He sobbed and insisted that it wasn't too late, and he groped again for her hands but she crossed her arms and shook her head, and he slowly climbed to his feet and sank back into his chair and leaned his head on his fist.

"Not too late?" she said. "What clock are you consulting?" Contrary to the rage she felt she sounded calm. She wanted to reach across and slap him for having destroyed everything. "So," she said, "your wife has turned out to be as sly and two-faced as yourself. What a good match."

Maxie's eyes flared like a fire in a wind and she feared she'd overstepped, but he nodded that it was true. His robe had fallen open, exposing his pale chest, and she saw how old and sick he looked.

"You're ill."

"Dying, I hope." He seemed to wait—and desperately hope—for her to contradict him. As she did not, he asked, "And you? How are you?"

She was tempted to say that she was already dead, that he and his wife had killed her, but instead informed him that she was muddling along, which was all one could expect in this place with its malarial river and malodorous men, its bigotry and prejudice and ignorance and inequality. "I think I'll have that drink after all." She went to the trolley and lifted the various bottles and decided upon the one that looked the most expensive. "Redbreast. Single pot still Irish whiskey," she said, reading the label. She poured three fat fingers into two glasses.

"Good choice," said Maxie.

"In whiskey, if not men."

"Yes," he said. "Yes, sadly so."

He held his drink as though warming his hands on the heat of the liquor. Then he held the glass under his nose and inhaled, lowered it, and grew wistful. He extended the glass toward Frisadie's as if to toast. She stared at it and then at him and asked what they were drinking to.

"Angels."

"And devils," she added.

"Fine. Where there are angels there must be devils."

But she refused to clink glasses. That was too much. She drank and held the whiskey in her mouth and savoured the fire. After a few moments it softened and seemed to eddy around and, tamed, grow sweet. Only then did she swallow. She retrieved the bottle and poured them each another measure, then set it on the table with the medicines. She thought of the Hawke's Rodent Remedy in her bag and had a vision of them dying together, Popo and Maxie, tragic lovers, then thought of some poor maid discovering them, saw Harry Hearne writing up their obituary in his florid and racist prose, considered Mrs Frame's reaction—would she feel betrayed, grimly vindicated, remorse, or all three?—and how the rumours would echo along Columbia Street . . . And Thérèse Colette Whatsername, would she drink a toast, or shake her head and laugh at star-crossed fools as she tallied her estate from some villa in Nice?

"So," began Maxie in a tremulous voice, "what do you plan to do?"

She was inclined to say that that was none of his business. She thought of informing him that she would devote herself to being a mother. She thought again of returning to Hawai'i. What, after all, were her options in rainy, smoky, back-of-beyond New Westminster? Surely she had family left in Honolulu. Surely she and her son were better off among her own. It had been made abundantly clear that she did not belong in New Westminster, an interloper upon the glory that was the white man's world. She gazed around the room recalling the fragrance of frangipani, jasmine, and hibiscus, the sound of the wind in the palms, the crashing of the waves on the white-sand beaches, the music of familiar voices in her native tongue. Maxie's room, in contrast, smelled of liniment and cigars. The porcelain fireplace tiles were spidery with cracks, the wallpaper with its nymphs and fountains was sooty. "My future? There indeed is a topic. My money would certainly improve my future, whatever it may hold."

"Yes. Of course. It's under way. I promise."

She was about to snort at the word *promise*. Instead she asked, "Do you love her?"

He snarled, "I hate her!"

"*Did* you love her?"

Shrugging pathetically, he downed his whiskey and swung his feet from the ottoman and stood, cinched the robe's belt tight and stepped to the window and stood with his hands clasped behind his back and his shoulders squared as he studied the river, a fallen king surveying the realm he no longer comprehended, much less ruled. "There are thousand-pound sturgeons in the Fraser," he said. "Ten feet long. The Indians say they live to be a hundred years old. That's an old fish." He began to laugh at the absurd sound of the statement. "Here we are talking of fish."

Bringing the bottle of Redbreast, she joined him at the window. It had a deep sill and Chinese pots full of dried flowers. Topping up his glass and then her own, she said, "To the sturgeon."

They drank.

"It has a nice colour," she said.

"I'll get you a bottle."

"I'd have to hide it. Mrs Frame keeps a dry house."

"You can keep it here."

"I think not." She pointed to a slash of blue sky south over the islands. "It always seems brighter down there."

"We could go."

"You'd have to take a boat."

"I don't care. I'll eat ginger."

Ah, she thought, *now you're the seaworthy swain.* Again she wanted to punch him, wanted to grip him around the neck and throttle him, wanted to know how he of all people could have given in to such weakness and left her like that. "Did you think about me?"

He stared down.

"I just need to understand. What did you see me doing once you returned with your white wife? How did you think I'd feel? I need to know what was in your mind. You owe me that much."

"I thought . . . I didn't . . . I don't know. I didn't think."

As much as she loathed Thérèse Colette, she couldn't put the blame on her, nor the English; no, it was Maxie. And perhaps her own naïveté.

––––––

Frisadie saw Maxie twice more. Once at the bank where he paid her seven hundred and fifty dollars. The second and last time at his suite at the Colonial. Thérèse Colette was still abroad and apparently showing no signs of returning any time soon, having added Vientiane and Kyoto to her itinerary. Maxie had changed. He bore about him an otherworldly air, calm and resigned, but strong, as if in his desolation he'd found some form of grace, a man assigned to his place on Charon's craft who was now gazing ahead to the far shore with some measure of dignified curiosity. Frisadie's anger had subsided enough that she was curious about his state. Was he in fact dying? Was he in fact resigned? Had he experienced some epiphany that made it acceptable? She was intrigued and wondered if she wished him to suffer a little more before making his escape into the afterworld.

"I was the Grelleys' parrot," he said suddenly. He was in his chair and dressed in a decent suit, his hair and beard trimmed, his eyes solemn but clear. "I entertained, I was the house raconteur. I believe that is what you liked."

She shrugged noncommittally. "And I was young."

He smiled the smile of one who saw his own absurdity and even managed a not ungraceful twirl of the hand: *Tra la, behold Maxie the fool . . .*

———————

Lying in her room that night, Kai next to her in the bed, the murmurs and snores of the lodgers muted by the walls, Frisadie thought of their future. She now had a bank account with over seven hundred and fifty dollars and could therefore make plans. She considered approaching Mrs Frame about becoming her business partner—certainly she had ideas about how to improve the running of the establishment—but for all that she had grown close to Mrs F she did not honestly relish the thought of being even more closely tied to her, nor of remaining in New Westminster, which would mean that Maxie must inevitably find out about Kai. Something had to be done but she contented herself with the thought that whatever she chose to do, it would be adventuresome.

FANNIN - 1886

New Brighton

THE BRIGHT SUMMER WEATHER DEEPENED HENRY'S GLOOM. He couldn't work and scarcely slept, felt sick when he drank whiskey, and being neither a smoker of hashish nor an eater of opium was therefore condemned to wakefulness. The daylight persisted until late in the evening and was back again to confront him early each morning. During the brief hours of darkness the frogs throbbed and the raccoons fought and owls shrieked and he dreamed that his animals—staring all night from the walls and shelves—jeered him. When he did manage to sleep he dreamed of Leonora's fiancé raising the pistol and fitting the barrel to his temple. He dreamed of Leonora being devoured by Lydia. Less often, though more welcome, he dreamed of Leonora's mother being devoured by Lydia. He woke exhausted and aching.

He'd written and then torn up a dozen notes. Obsessively watched the hotel, desperate not to seem to be spying even as he was doing just that, but he hadn't seen her. A few times he saw George Black in the distance but he appeared busy or evasive and so Henry didn't inflict himself upon him. He listened for sounds from the roller skating hall and never heard anything.

Nonetheless he made regular visits thinking he might find a disconsolate Leonora alone and weeping, but it was always empty. What a cavernous abyss it was without her and the sound of her laughter. There was the trunk with the skates. Henry found the pair he'd been using and put them on. The familiar pinch was welcome. He'd missed it. Standing, he began to skate, slowly at first and then faster, clockwise and then counter-clockwise, tried going backward, fell, got up and tried again, using his legs like springs and pumping his arms like pistons, glancing constantly at the door hoping that she might hear the sound of his skates and join him, that once again they might hold hands and laugh as they flew around and around. By the time he unlaced the skates his thighs were trembling and the blisters on his feet had burst and Leonora had not appeared.

One warm morning a Native woman appeared in the open door of Henry's stump.

"Good day to you," he said.

She did not respond; she was peering in at his animals.

"Come," he said. Then, wondering if she knew English, he waved her in.

She appeared dubious, seemed to sniff the air, and, gauging it bearable, entered. He recognized her from his walks along the shore; she'd seen him collect dead birds even as she was collecting shellfish. Now she scrutinized the many stuffed heads on the walls and various birds on the shelves. Henry couldn't tell whether she liked them or not. She had a wide face and a small nose and her hair hung in two long and complex braids. From her ears dangled abalone shells. She appeared to be about thirty years old and was wearing a geometrically patterned cape that he assumed was cedar bark.

"So this is what you're up to," she said at last. "We thought maybe you were taking them off the beach and eating them."

Her tone and expression were so solemn he couldn't tell whether or not she was taking the piss. "Do you not practise taxidermy, then?"

"Me?" Her eyes narrowed.

"You. I mean . . ." Henry suddenly felt on uncertain ground. "Your people. Natives."

She studied him and he feared he'd insulted her. "Am I all Natives?" she asked. "Are you all Englishmen?"

All Englishmen? Henry had to think about that.

"These are pretty good," she said of the animals.

"Thank you."

"Do you sell them?"

"Do you want one?"

She grimaced as if the idea was absurd. "What's your name?"

"Henry."

She considered this. "What are you most? English or Henry?"

Was she mad? Had a madwoman come wandering out of the forest to inflict herself upon him? "What is *your* name?"

"*My* name," she echoed absently, peering at the owl. "My name . . ."

"You keep your names private?" offered Henry, thinking perhaps it was a Native custom, though how they communicated, or knew each other, he wasn't sure. He had heard once that the Maori of New Zealand knew each other not by their names but by their facial tattoos. She, however, did not have a tattoo, at least not on her face.

She picked up a small cup from his table and as if in demonstration said, "You." Then she placed the cup in a bowl and said,

"English." She then removed the cup from the bowl, put it back in again, removed it again. "See?"

Henry was not so very sure that he did see.

She placed the cup and the bowl side by side on the table, then turned and went out.

New Brighton began to hum with preparations for George Black's annual Summer Solstice Sports Day, which transformed New Brighton from a hamlet to a carnival. Henry watched men erect canopies in the field and lay chalk lines on the grass; bales of straw were stacked, chairs and benches arranged, bunting draped. He watched carts and wagons and vendors' stalls appear. He did not, however, see Leonora. Had she left New Brighton? The thought ached beyond any pain he'd ever known, was of an entirely different order from what he'd endured at losing Eliza and even his father. The night before Sports Day, scores of people camped out on the grass, some so close to his stump that he heard their whispers and laughter and snoring; he'd have fled but for his desperation to speak with Leonora. Twice over the past weeks he'd gone down to the hotel and been told by the char that the young lady was unavailable. And then the morning of the event there she was, as tall and swanlike as ever. Keeping her in sight at all times, Henry attempted, like a master of the dance, to orchestrate a meeting that was seemingly natural and completely unorchestrated, but in the end it was she who came up and tapped him on the shoulder, his view having been blocked by a rugby team gathered for a photograph. They stood face to face, she more beautiful than ever. She announced that she'd behaved shamefully while he said he'd been thoughtless.

She said, "You meant only to help."

He said, "I didn't think." And had to resist giving himself a clout across the side of the skull to demonstrate the depth of his penitence.

"I've missed our skates," she said.

Henry couldn't speak for joy. How clear her eyes were, how radiant her cheeks, and above all she was smiling and apparently as relieved as he was at making amends. "I trust you are as well as you look," he said.

She blushed and he felt somewhat the rake. Furtively, he gave his hand a sniff for fear that it smelled of pelt. It did not; he'd scrubbed it and himself thoroughly with lye to the point that his entire skin stung. Emboldened, he offered his arm and they perambulated, Henry feeling as though he had been recalled from purgatory to paradise due to some clerical error. He asked if the good Lady Mars had recovered, and Leonora laughed and said that the good Lady Mars would never recover and that at the same time she'd never been better, for bile was her best food and she dined at length.

"And your mother?"

"Ah, Mother."

Henry didn't know what to say. Observe that Leonora should be grateful that she at least had a mother? Or was she better off without a mother like hers? He wondered what his own mother had been like, the saint his dad had insisted she was, or, like anyone, given to moods and whims and tempers? They paused to watch the sack race, then moved on to lawn bowling and the long jump. Leonora asked if he would be competing in any events and he said that it had not occurred to him.

"And you?"

She laughed. "Perhaps if there was roller skating."

"You'd win hands down." Then, inspired, he said, "Roller skating and archery."

"What? At the same time?"

"I think you'd make a natural Artemis."

She mulled the idea, smiling and flattered and intrigued. Off to one side pistols popped. Target shooting. Henry and Leonora agreed that archery was far more elegant than all that noise and smoke. They were about to pass on when Black appeared, accompanied by a man whose face troubled Henry. Leonora too was troubled, and she swallowed with difficulty and her face convulsed and she nearly stumbled—Henry held her up—and before Black could complete introductions Henry knew where he'd seen the man: Sanderson's.

The fellow recognized Henry. Chastened, confused, he looked at Henry and then at Leonora. "You . . . you are acquainted . . ."

Now Leonora and her father were looking to Henry for an explanation but he couldn't speak and even if he could he was so undone he wouldn't have known whether to lie or confess.

Sanderson said, "The young man was there." And then, looking, realizing—"Or did you not . . ." Too late he saw that he'd said too much.

Henry didn't think Leonora's eyes could get any wider or her look of shock any deeper; it was as though Satan had been unmasked. Such an expression of betrayal he'd never seen and hoped to never see again, certainly not on the face of one he loved so dearly. Then she was running away through the crowd while the bottom was falling out of Henry's heart and George Black stood there blinking in bewilderment.

Sanderson said, "Fucking hell . . . I've put me foot in it . . ."

Henry started after her, then halted, all strength gone out of him, knowing that there were not enough magnets in the entire earth to bring her back.

The following morning Leonora and her mother left New Brighton. Henry watched from his doorway as Black and one of the hotel boys lugged their bags up to the stagecoach. The only one to look in Henry's direction was Mrs Black, whose glare was a poison-tipped barb that caused him to retreat into his stump.

———————

Perhaps no magnet could draw her back, but Henry was unable to sit idle and so in the weeks that followed he devoted himself to completing four tin hearts—two brooches and two lapel pins—cutting, bending, and shaping them. When he was done he turned and considered his lodestones. He set the lumpy dark rocks with their gleaming flecks, ranging in size from a radish to an apple, in a row upon his worktable, and then leaned close as if he'd hear them whisper. Closing his eyes he rotated his head left and right to bask in their power. Did he feel a cool heat? He'd swear that his thoughts ran more clearly, like a stream quickening through a narrows and yet, and yet, his thoughts were broad as well, the banks of his mind as wide as the horizon. With a deep breath he inhaled the emanations of the lodestones the way Persians were said to inhale the healing perfumes of flowers. Holding the air in his chest, he sat back and after some moments opened his eyes: the tint and angle of the light announced that the afternoon was advancing. He went to work fitting pieces of the magnetic stone into the back of each heart and then packing them with wool so that they were snug and did not rattle, folding the metal into place, and then proceeded to paint each one red. He put two into gift boxes of heavy-grade card, wrapped them in brown paper, and addressed one to Julia Black and one to Leonora Black, care of Poste Restante, GPO, San Francisco, US of A, where, until settled, they were receiving correspondence.

———

"Magnetism keeps the moons in orbit around their planets," said Henry, reassuring himself even as he tried convincing Black. "Why should it not be capable of drawing lovers back together even if they are separated by one thousand miles?" It had been eight weeks since he'd sent the brooches to mother and daughter, and both he and Black had been diligent in wearing their corresponding pins day and night.

This talk of love and lovers caused Black unease. "I don't know much about magnetism—I don't know much about anything, I'm afraid, except horses, I do know horses, and roller skating, and cricket, and field hockey, but that won't help us here, so I do hope you're right."

They sat on the porch, the *terrace* as Julia Black had insisted it be called, their breakfast plates pushed to one side, smeared with the remnants of back bacon and duck eggs, and sipped coffee laced with rum.

"The hotel's been reduced to a way station," lamented Black as he watched arrivals from the morning stage pass by the hotel, skirt wide around Lydia, and proceed on down to the wharf and the boat that would take them to Moodyville on the north shore or west along to Granville. "I think Julia was happy for a brief time after I bought the place. She really was. I think. Or maybe not. No, probably not. She hated it from day one. Gad, what an oaf I am. Of course, after the butcher shop anything was an improvement.

She detested the meat trade. The hotel was a step toward gentility. Apparently not enough of a step. It's the forest and the rain. She blames it for Frederick's . . ." Black fluttered a hand about his head, meaning insanity.

"Your wife approved of him?"

"Freddie was from a good Chicago family. He had plans to return there."

Henry's heart staggered. "With Leonora?"

"Oh yes."

"To Chicago?"

Black nodded.

The fact that Henry felt glad, or if not exactly glad then relieved, that the fellow had shot himself weighed on his conscience. On the other hand, if the fellow hadn't, then perhaps Henry and Leonora would never have met and Henry would know no regret anyway. He'd sent her three letters but received no replies. In the first letter he'd gone on at length, perhaps too great a length, apologizing and explaining. In the second he'd been brief. In the third he'd sent a clipping from the *Chicago Tribune* about Wylie Ferris, the roller skating acrobat, skating across a high-tension wire strung between two buildings. Now Henry's last hope was magnetism. Yet what if the mother had commandeered both brooches and flung them out? Should he send another?

Black stretched his chin and narrowed his eyes as though directing his gaze to regions beyond the mountains. Henry looked as well. The mountains soared straight up from the far side of the inlet and already wore their first topping of snow. "Have you ever skied?" asked Black, knowing that he hadn't, but doing him the courtesy of allowing for the possibility, however slight.

"Not really," admitted Henry.

"It is very popular among the Swiss. Entire families go on skiing vacations. I believe there is potential in such a business right here." He pointed to the mountains. "You build a chalet up top. Customers come from Victoria and New Westminster and of course . . ." He nodded west toward Granville, which, like a blight, was all too swiftly overtaking New Brighton as the centre of commerce and communications on the inlet. "In the morning they arrive, are met by a hostess—a comely young woman—served a complimentary hot beverage, ushered to the ferry, make the crossing, are met by a heated coach in which they proceed up the mountain, take lunch, devote the afternoon to skiing, sledding, hiking, skating, whatever they fancy, and then they repair to the chalet and dine by a roaring fire and, if their knees are not too wobbly, dance to an ensemble. Next day more skiing, and in the afternoon return to the ferry, dine at Black's Hotel, spend the night. No cares, no worries, only gaiety and joy."

Gaiety and joy, thought Henry. Black's initiative and optimism bowled him over. To even think in such a manner impressed him. The logistics, the organization, the planning, the vision, the very scope and reach—what a thing was Man's mind; thus were empires built.

But this vision could not buoy Black's spirits. However mismatched they were, he missed his wife. "We're wounded souls," observed Black, at the risk of laying himself bare.

They faced forward, stalwart in their suffering, while the inlet glittered in the cold, hard, splendid indifference of the October sun. They were diverted by the spectacle of two bald eagles in free fall, locked by their talons, tumbling, spinning, crying, as down and down they plunged to what must surely be their mutual deaths; crashing into the jagged tops of the trees, they emerged seconds later, one to the right and the other to the left, flapping away to rendezvous afterwards and mate for life.

"I thought they only did that in the spring," observed Henry.

"It would seem that love observes no season," said Black.

They considered this profundity until the bell clanged up the hill: the post office signalling that the coach from New Westminster had arrived with the morning mail. Henry did the honours of hiking up the slope. Over the weeks of waiting for a response from Leonora, Henry had tried and abandoned various rituals designed to facilitate a letter. At first he prayed to God. Then he chanted *please*, *please*, *please*. He concentrated on visualizing Blake, the postmaster, sliding an envelope across the counter, an envelope whose source could not be mistaken. Fearing that he was jinxing himself, he changed tack and tried not thinking at all. He tried walking fast up the hill to the post office and then tried walking slow, clasping his hands behind his back, humming, whistling, imitating an owl, jingling the coins in his right pocket, then jingling coins in his left pocket. Nothing had worked. Now he merely walked, his hunch making him appear older than his twenty-two years. The grass had greened up in the autumn rain and some slim-stalked mushrooms had sprouted and the maple leaves begun to turn; if they were to die, then they would die in spectacular colour. Had Leonora said it was her favourite season, or was that Henry being maudlin?

A few passengers lingered, some labourers bound for the mill across the inlet, and a young man in a good black suit with red pinstripes. He had dark skin, wavy black hair beneath a black bowler hat, and large dark eyes. He stood gazing around with such a keen interest in everything he saw that Henry was compelled to look about as well as if there was something he hadn't noticed.

As far as he could see there wasn't. He looked at the newcomer, who looked at him, and Henry nodded and the fellow nodded, and then Henry entered the post office where Blake thrust two packets of letters through the wicket, Henry's decidedly smaller than the one intended for Black. On the way out he again noted the well-dressed young man. Heading back down the slope Henry wondered what could so thoroughly captivate the fellow. Trees, sea, mountains, yes, but these could be had any number of places. He supposed that someone from a desert might be enthralled, a Bedouin, say. But somehow the chap didn't look like a Bedouin, not that Henry had any clear idea of what a Bedouin did look like, though he'd seen a photograph once of a man with a turban and a veil, or not quite a veil, some sort of cloth covering his face to the eyes, sitting on a camel and looking fierce. Tuareg. Yes, that was it. Was the man a Tuareg on a Grand Tour? He glanced back but didn't see him.

Rediscovering his letters, he found service inquiries and a bill from *The British Columbian* newspaper for his taxidermy ad, and, about to thrust the lot into his pocket, saw an envelope whose handwriting he recognized. He halted, felt weak and sick but exhilarated; his pulse quickened and his breath came short. Narrowing his eyes, he raised the letter to the sky as if the sunlight would reveal something the naked eye could not and saw only the flattened pulp of the paper. He weighed it in his hand, glanced around—saw no one—and gave the envelope a sniff. No perfume, but then it had been in a sack in a ship for better than a week. Again he studied the handwriting, wondering what she'd thought while writing his name. Did she curse him? No, she wasn't the cursing type, though certainly she was angry or at the very least disappointed, and saddened, yes, saddened. He felt a weight press down on his heart at the thought of her sadness. He was about to open the envelope but held off, for he couldn't bear the thought of bad news, not right away, not without first preparing himself. He looked around, thinking to creep into the bush or retreat to his stump in order to open the letter in solitude. But as he looked around he saw that George Black was watching him from the porch, meaning he could hardly go dodging off into the bushes.

Holding the letter against the red tin heart of his lapel pin, Henry proceeded down the gravelled path lined by whitewashed stones and up the steps and joined Black, placing his friend's packet before him. As Black leaned forward to take it, a spoon and a knife leapt from the tabletop to his coat and stuck with a clink to his heart-shaped pin. Along with this cutlery some coins jumped and stuck as well. Since they'd begun wearing the lapel pins, nails, screws, bolts, and nuts had proved a hazard, and people were forever pointing to the small clusters of ironmongery attached to Henry's or Black's chest. Were mother and daughter experiencing the same? Had they stopped wearing them? For all Henry knew, Leonora had never even received the brooch and even if she had she might well have disregarded it. Certainly her mother would have rejected it on the grounds that it was simply too crude an object to adorn the noble prow that was her breast. He watched Black sort his mail like bad cards, setting envelopes aside one after another before halting, his glance flicking to Henry, then back to the envelope. "Julia."

Henry showed his letter from Leonora.

"Well," said Black, gravely.

Neither man rushed to open his letter. Instead, they gazed at the chipped blue water and the wall of fir trees on the far shore patched with orange and red maples.

"The almanac predicts an especially cold winter," said Black.

"Perhaps you should go south," said Henry.

"Like the birds," mused Black.

"To San Francisco," said Henry.

Black sank into himself and they meditated upon migratory birds. Henry said that some hummingbirds, so endearingly small and seemingly frail, flew all the way to Central America and then in the spring flew all the way back.

"I'm getting old," said Black. "I wonder if hibernation is not more my speed."

As if recognizing the word, Lydia yawned and groaned below the balcony.

Henry saw the attraction of a long uninterrupted sleep. He looked at the letter lying on the table. He picked it up and felt its texture upon his fingertips, a high-grade stock; even in her envelopes Leonora prized quality. He laid it back down and positioned it just so.

"Was I so wrong to say nothing?" he asked.

Black blew a long exhalation and then admitted that certainly it would have been awkward to speak.

Henry was about to launch into further excuses but halted himself and with a scarcely suppressed groan seized the envelope and peeled up the flap. One sheet, just one single sheet of paper. If his heart had felt weighted before, now it was crushed. Scarcely able to breathe, he tweezed the page out and unfolded it and, simultaneously flushed and chilled, held it in his trembling hands and tried to read, but his hands shook too much so he pressed it flat on the table.

Dear Henry,

Forgive me for having delayed so long in writing. I have no excuse other than that for a while I have resented you. But that has passed, and I know that it was unfair, even if not utterly without cause. I also appreciate how difficult it must have been for you, knowing what you did. Thankfully, time and distance have given me perspective.

As you know, San Francisco is a great city. In time Granville may well be the same. For the moment, however, British Columbia is a little too raw for Mother, though I myself miss it and the immense proximity of Nature. I also miss our roller skating sessions. There are rinks here of course but I've yet to visit one. And you, are you skating much? I encourage it, for it is fortifying, and maybe as you skate you will remember me fondly. I certainly hope so.

Give my regards to my father and assure him that I'll write soon.

PS: Thank you for the clipping about Wylie Ferris. He is due here in San Francisco later next month. Perhaps you might consider coming to town? It is of course a long journey for such a whimsy, though I should welcome seeing you again.

PPS: And thank you for the curious brooch. I wear it often, and often you are in my thoughts.

Yours,
Leonora Black

Henry reread the letter twice more, folded it, and returned it to the envelope. He looked to Black who was reading his own letter.

When Black was done, Henry said, "Leonora gives you her best and will write soon."

"Mrs Black, I'm afraid, has not mentioned you at all. She is not of a forgiving nature."

"Nature itself is not forgiving," said Henry, as though Black's wife was a force as pure and fierce and unstoppable as a hurricane.

Black agreed. "No, it is not."

And considering this, both men raised their rum-laced coffee—now gone cold—and gazed at the startling blue water, their chests encrusted with coins and pins and cutlery that glinted triumphantly in the morning sun, like medals from some distant war.

It was during this moment of contemplation that they noticed the young man in the black suit with the red pinstripes angling toward them up from the beach. Raising his hat in greeting he smiled widely, displaying a gap between his two front teeth, and called out, "Good day to you, sirs."

Henry saw a prudent wariness in the fellow's eyes. His good suit of clothes said that he did not lack for funds; his demeanour radiated dignity, his pronunciation bespoke education.

"Permission to come aboard, cap'n."

Black's letter had put him in a good mood. Julia had asked him to join them. He laughed and said, "Come up!"

The fellow climbed the steps, offered a short bow, admired the view, and then turned his attention to the hotel itself, his eyes seeming to widen as he took it all in.

"Take a seat," said Black.

The young man's glance bounced from Black to Henry and once more to Black; his life had obviously taught him to be cautious. "Thank you." He drew out a chair and sat, his bowler perched on one knee.

Black apologized that the coffee was cold and the fellow thanked him and said he was fine, that he'd already had his morning cup, to which Black responded that there was rum. Would he take a sip of rum? The newcomer said that he was grateful for the offer but that he had yet to acquire the habit of taking spirits, and Black nodded and said that this was most probably wise but that in a cold climate it did heat the vitals, and the visitor agreed and observed that he himself was from a hot place.

"What hot place is that?" asked Henry.

"Hawai'i."

"And what brings you here?" asked Black.

"I've been around the world," he said. "And now I'm on my way home."

Black stated that travel was a fine thing and recalled his own journey as a youth from Aberdeen. Henry too chipped in with a few tidbits from his adventures from London to the West Coast. The young fellow had out-travelled both Henry and Black combined. He'd been to Japan, Hong Kong, Siam, Ceylon, bits of India and Africa, as well as Portugal, France, Haiti, and Mexico.

"What you must have seen," said Black.

"Well," he admitted, "often I didn't see anything because I was seasick." He laughed.

"But not too seasick to miss hearing about my hotel?" asked Black.

The young fellow smiled again though his eyes narrowed, perhaps against the light glinting off the pins and pennies and cutlery sticking to his host's chest, and he admitted that yes, he had indeed heard of his hotel.

MOODY – 1861

NEW BRIGHTON

IN NOVEMBER THE RAIN BEGAN TO FALL more heavily; through December this downpour intensified; in January the temperature plunged and it snowed and the river froze so hard that no ships could reach New Westminster and the city was cut off; by February horse-drawn wagons were crossing the ice to no other purpose than to say that it could be done.

Governor Douglas was unhappy. New Westminster was developing too slowly and costing too much and now it was unviable due to ice. How had this not been factored in? He wrote to Moody: "It seems that I was foolish to allow myself to be swayed by you. New Westminster needs year-round access to shipping otherwise the advantages that you so vehemently touted are rendered useless." He went on to reiterate his suspicion that Victoria—his Hudson's Bay Company stronghold—would be better suited as capital for both the Colony of Vancouver Island and the Colony of British Columbia, which in due course would be united as one.

Douglas was not alone in his criticism of Moody. An editorial in the *New Westminster Times* vilified him.

Colonel Moody's tone on his arrival led us to expect great things of him, consequently the greater is our disappointment at the entire absence of the qualifications necessary for a chief commissioner in a colony such as British Columbia.

It required but little genius to develop the resources of British Columbia. The path was clear. Colonel Moody is found not to possess even that small amount of genius, although the colonists have been unceasing in their endeavours to drive him to a right sense of their requirements. Had he but drifted with the tide he would have achieved for himself a reputation, and done this colony an amount of good which it is impossible to calculate.

Instead, miners leave the country disgusted with the high cost of provisions, and agriculturists are prevented from settling by the want of means of communication with the various towns on the Fraser; in a word, a few more months of such gross mis-management and the colony will be too far gone to recover. The road system, or rather the no-road system, has assumed the form of despotism.

The main body of Sappers and Miners who, under an efficient leader, would have become the sinews of life to the colony, have for months been allowed to remain in comparative idleness, or their energies wasted in beautifying a costly and useless camp.

A costly and useless camp . . . The phrase haunted him. *A costly and useless camp.* Mary tried to heal what felt to him like a stab in the back. She told him to add to Governor Douglas's many good qualities—dignity, strength, prudence—fickleness and impatience and a lack of vision, and urged Richard not to lose confidence. But the wound festered.

"Our life has improved," she reminded him.

They were seated at their kitchen table, for they now occupied a house rather than a tent. It was a modest house, perhaps more accurately termed a shack or a shed, but it did not leak, or not much, and there was but a modest amount of mildew on the walls. More importantly, John, Amanda, and Abigail were well. As was Hilda the dog.

In the spring Moody kept crews on site by offering land allotments and by the fact that the gold in the Fraser Canyon was running out. Many disgruntled miners were dubious about the talk of gold farther inland, in the Cariboo, and so chose to stay in the growing capital city. For despite opinions to the contrary, despite it being *a costly and useless camp*, New Westminster was in fact growing and at long last taking shape. Douglas, however, was not easily mollified, especially when the river became ice again the following winter and once more life all but came to a standstill. Moody was summoned again to Victoria, where he had to point out that the river was more often frozen at Langley than at New Westminster. The governor waved this aside because he had an *idea.*

"Here is what you will do. You will scout and develop a port in the Burrard Inlet, ten miles northwest, and connect it by road to New Westminster. Being salt, the inlet does not freeze, not at this latitude. In this way the city will have a lifeline. It will not be as commercially isolated on the one hand nor as militarily vulnerable on the other. You will begin at once."

––––––––––

Moody consulted charts. He studied the distance and the terrain between New Westminster and Burrard Inlet and then boarded a ship and went to look for himself. Two days later he and his son John stood on the deck of the HMS *Grappler* whose throbbing engine sent gulls screeling while harbour seals—sleek grey skulls poised above the cold grey chop—observed from a safe distance. The sea foamed at the bow and fanned out in a wake that rolled toward the inlet's south shore.

John, newly turned eleven, wore an expression of cautious exhilaration. Moody hadn't intended to bring the boy, but at breakfast he'd looked at his father with a yearning that had made Moody recall watching his own father setting off mornings on horseback to do his rounds of inspection on Barbados. Mary, noting the hopeful expression on John's face, had nodded encouragingly and so Moody had said he could come. Hilda had come as well and enjoyed herself immensely running up and down the deck, yelping and piddling.

"She's an excitable beast," observed Moody.

"Did you have a dog, Father?"

The question had never occurred to him. Had he wanted a dog? The only dogs he recalled on Barbados were the mutts that lurked in the market or lay panting under the stilted shacks, gaunt beasts with open sores haloed in flies. "It was too hot for dogs."

"How hot? Hot, hot?"

"Hot, hot, hot."

"I should like it to be hot," said John, "but not hot, hot, hot."

Moody said that that was very wise, then reached out his right arm and, hesitating at such an unaccustomed act, put it around his son's shoulders and gave John's arm a brisk rub. He felt the boy glance up at him. The boat proceeded and Moody removed his arm and pointed to the longhouse on a bluff to starboard. They had seen other longhouses but this one was truly impressive, for not only was it immense in length, perhaps a hundred feet, but upward of half a thousand people were massed in front, watching the ship as curiously as Moody and son watched them.

"Do they want to kill us?" asked John.

"Why should they want to kill us?" Moody responded, though the question was not at all unreasonable.

"Because we kill them," said John as if it were all too plain. "And we take their land."

Moody reflected upon the world as his son, naive but clear-eyed, must see it. He squinted at the expressions of the people before the longhouse. There were no smiles. He looked away, vaguely disturbed, and watched the grey-black fumes from the ship's stack roll downwind as though an infernal factory spewing lost souls. Grimacing at such an image, he endured the now familiar ache of a deep-seated doubt.

John, seeing the look on his father's face, tugged his sleeve as though to draw him back into the light.

"That village is called Whoi Whoi," said Moody, forcing a heartiness into his voice. "And there, that is Dead Man's Island." He drew John's attention to the cedar coffins perched in the branches of the trees on an islet. Moody watched how this registered. Was the boy horrified? No, he was rapt. Again he put his arm around his son's shoulders, this time with more ease, and gave it a reassuring squeeze happy that John seemed to have forgotten Gosset.

One of the Natives began walking along the bluff, following the ship, tracing strange gestures on the air. Incantations? Curses? Surely not blessings. Moody thought of a priest he and Mary had seen in a church in Valletta—a whimsical excursion into the arcane realm of Roman Catholicism—and could only hope that this Medicine Man, this shaman, was not a very powerful example of his order. The benefits of British administration were as yet unappreciated by the Natives. *Patience*, he wanted to cry out, *give us time to work our own magic, and we shall all benefit!* But did he believe it? He wasn't sure. He had ought to. His father believed. Did Governor Douglas? Did Amelia Douglas? He wondered if belief and wish were related, if one influenced the other, or was that a mark of desperation and superstition? Either way, the momentum of empire could not be slowed: stand in the way and you were ground to gravel like rock under a glacier. He averted his face and was relieved when the ship outpaced the shaman, who was lost to sight in the forest. The engine continued to throb and pump smoke. He imagined a harbour full of ships, their smoke bespeaking industry and commerce and multitudes, a great metropolis spreading out on either shore, with wharves and cranes, buildings of brick and stone, concrete and glass. He risked a last glance back at Dead Man's Island and Whoi Whoi and then faced forward again.

"We will endeavour to achieve harmonious relations with our Native friends," he promised the boy and meant it, or thought that he should mean it—should, ought, must, what trying words. He ordered the helmsman to bring them closer to the starboard shore whose rock and sand were backed by a dense wall of trees.

The *Grappler*'s chugging continued scaring the birds and intriguing the seals. She had four mounted swivel guns, including two howitzers that had impressed John mightily. It occurred to Moody that he was assuming that young John would follow him unquestioningly into the Royal Engineers; was it possible that the lad had other ideas? In a breezy tone he asked, "Where do you see yourself in ten years, John?"

The boy did not hesitate. "I want to fly."

"What? Like Icarus?"

In a solemn tone he reminded his father that Icarus had flown too close to the sun and died. "No. In a balloon."

"And where will you fly to in this balloon?"

"Wherever I am needed," he said without hesitation.

Moody imagined the boy, grown to manhood, descending from out of the sky to do just and glorious battle. His eyes watered at the vision, though it may have been the breeze or the smoke. Eleven years old—it seemed like only last week that he was five.

They proceeded along the shore for some time and then Moody spied a stretch of sandy beach; he pointed and the helmsman brought them in and the skiff was lowered. John rowed, sitting up tall on the thwart and manfully battling the oars while Moody wore an expression of admiration and confidence and restrained himself from critiquing so that the lad might learn by trial and error. Hilda was with them in the skiff and darted from one side to the other, paws upon first the starboard gunwale and then the port. After some zigzagging the keel scored the sand and they splashed ashore—Hilda bounding ahead and barking madly—then kicked the water from their boots and looked around. It was a curve of sand backed by scrub and maple and fir. From atop one of the trees a bald eagle launched itself in a long glide out over the inlet. When it was out of sight Moody turned back to the matter at hand: the appropriateness of this spot as a port and a road connection to

New Westminster. A pair of small streams emptied into the ocean at about a hundred yards' distance from each other. An excellent source of fresh water. The sand itself was clean and there was also a trailhead, meaning the Natives liked it. Also good. He thought of the people before the longhouse at Whoi Whoi, their expressions, what they and that shaman chap must be thinking. What would he think in their shoes? Moody studied the bush near the trailhead and wondered if they were being watched. Was the shaman about to reappear? He looked at the *Grappler*, armed with her guns, rolling in the surf.

John asked, "Are we exploring?" The excitement in his voice was endearing.

"We are indeed," said Moody, regathering his energies. "What shall we name this place?" But before John could respond Moody answered himself: "We will call it New Brighton."

John planted his hands on his hips and adopted what he regarded as the expression appropriate to an explorer, discerning, indomitable, and made a show of turning a full circle.

Hilda began frantically barking at a pair of seals that were watching them not twenty feet from shore with the pert attitudes of young dogs. Hilda plunged in after them and the seals dunked out of sight. The creation of seals struck Moody as inspired, as if the Lord had cogitated and concluded that the sea was a little dull thereabouts and needed something to liven it up, something with a sense of play, and so added seals.

Now John ran into the sea after Hilda, ignoring the water filling his boots and soaking his trousers past his knees right up to his belt. Moody's first reaction was to chastise his son for drenching his clothes but he said nothing. The seals reappeared a few feet farther out. John took a fencer's stance and Hilda barked and the seals barked in response as though inviting them both to play. John turned, grinning with such ebullience that Moody grinned too and laughed loudly and, without thinking, without caring, roared and rushed into the water as well.

ACKNOWLEDGEMENTS

I used to look at New Brighton Park from the grandstand of the racetrack where I lost a lot of money. In the summer I swam in the New Brighton pool. In the winter I often walked along the waterfront past the park and on toward the Alberta Wheat Pool where, just out of Grade 12, I tried signing on to a freighter bound for Yokohama but was prevented by the detail that I didn't have a passport.

I wanted to write a book about New Brighton and the people who'd lived there in the late 1800s. Maxie and Frisadie, George Black, the roller skating Laird of New Brighton, the embalmer Henry Fannin, and the dour Colonel Richard Clement Moody. But the records were scant. How Canadian that we let so much of the past go unrecorded. The project died. Or rather it slept for a couple of years during which those people occupied my dreams. I was forced to resort to my imagination, an inexhaustible if whimsical mine of material, but perhaps all the richer for that.

I'd like to thank the good people at TouchWood for their efforts on behalf of the book, Joy Gugeler for her invaluable editorial advice, and of course my in-house editor and wife, Eden.

ABOUT THE AUTHOR

Grant Buday is the author of the novels *Dragonflies, White Lung, Sack of Teeth, Rootbound, The Delusionist,* and *Atomic Road,* the memoir *Stranger on a Strange Island,* and the travel memoir *Golden Goa.* His novels have twice been nominated for the City of Vancouver book prize. His articles and essays have been published in Canadian magazines, and his short fiction has appeared in *The Journey Prize Anthology* and *Best Canadian Short Stories.* He lives on Mayne Island, British Columbia.